THE WEREWOLVES WHO WEREN'T

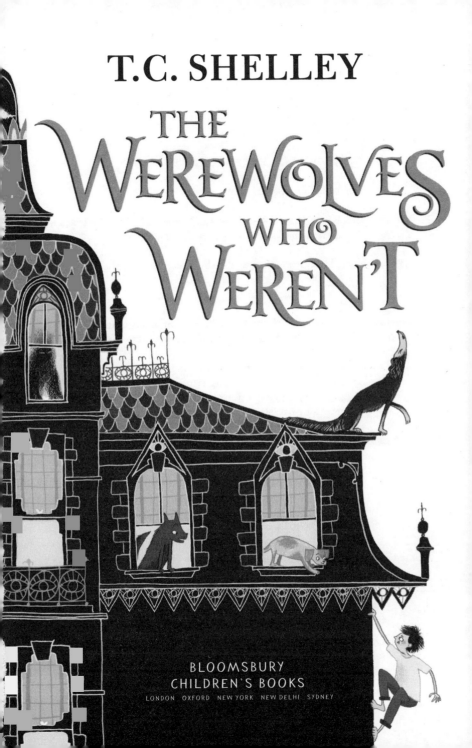

T.C. SHELLEY

THE WEREWOLVES WHO WEREN'T

BLOOMSBURY
CHILDREN'S BOOKS

LONDON OXFORD NEW YORK NEW DELHI SYDNEY

BLOOMSBURY CHILDREN'S BOOKS
Bloomsbury Publishing Plc
50 Bedford Square, London WC1B 3DP, UK

BLOOMSBURY, BLOOMSBURY CHILDREN'S BOOKS and the Diana logo
are trademarks of Bloomsbury Publishing Plc

First published in Great Britain in 2020 by Bloomsbury Publishing Plc

A catalogue record for this book is available from the British Library

ISBN: PB: 978-1-5266-0080-6; eBook: 978-1-5266-0081-3

2 4 6 8 10 9 7 5 3 1

Typeset by RefineCatch Limited, Bungay, Suffolk

Printed and bound in Great Britain by CPI Group (UK) Ltd, Croydon CR0 4YY

To find out more about our authors and books visit www.bloomsbury.com
and sign up for our newsletters

For Wilfred and Amira, kiss kiss,
and Hazel, Beatrice and Boo. Always.

FAIRY DUST

Fairies are creatures of pure mischief. The common myth that they are good is both naive and dangerous. Fairies are amoral, having interest in neither good nor evil, only fun and pleasure. They might save a life because it gives them pleasure, but they would just as easily let someone die. Their interest in humans is powerful, yet short-lived. A fairy may be as enthralled by a human as a human under the influence of dust may be enthralled by a fairy, but their devotion passes and they often leave the once-adored human lost and longing for their fairy lover. These humans will die from a failure to look after themselves, often wandering the places they had walked with their fairy, and refusing food and water until they fade away. This is a result of long-term exposure to fairy dust.

Fairy dust is a by-product of the fairy body, as sweat and dandruff are by-products of the human body, although far more magical and powerful. The greatest source of fairy dust is fairy wings. Like butterflies, fairies have beautiful dust-coloured wings. Unlike butterflies, fairies' wings shed their dust, making it suitable for spells and charms.

Fairy dust can be used for everything: bewitching, manifesting, destroying, travelling, inventing, reinventing, protecting, disarming.

Fairy dust is highly valued in many human occupations. Wizards, magicians, rulers, healers and hunters alike trade great wealth for fairy dust.

From Lowri Fach ferch Cystennin's *The Book of Earth*
(translated by David Evans)

CHAPTER 1

Sam huddled between three gargoyles on top of the courthouse roof and peered down over the court steps. One gargoyle was a winged lion, one a winged bull and one an eagle, but they all had the same serious expression.

Sam pulled at his stiff collar and tie. 'I hear crackling. What is it, Bladder?'

The lion-faced gargoyle cocked his head and screwed up one eye. 'What ... ? Oh, that? That's the arthritis in the judge's neck. It crackles when he nods.'

The stone bull chuckled. 'Even down to the arthritis in the judge's neck. Only a real gargoyle can hear like that.' The bull ran a hoof under one overlarge nostril. 'You'll still be part of our pack, won't you, Sam? When this is all done. You won't be entirely human?' He sniffed. 'There's still a little gargoyle in you, right?'

'Of course there is, Wheedle.' Sam hugged the bull and kissed his friendly face.

The eagle squawked.

'That's right, Spigot,' Wheedle replied.

Sam returned his attention to the courthouse. 'Do you think they'll say it's all right? They won't send me back to Children's Services? They've been talking about my mental health for a long time now. What if ... ?'

'Ooh, look what I have.' Bladder grinned, his stony face turning pink in the reflection of the red roof tiles. 'This is my favourite.'

The other gargoyles pointedly turned their attention to the newspaper clipping. Even Spigot 'oohed'.

'You're trying to distract me,' Sam said.

'Is it working?' Wheedle asked. 'No, look, you've really got to read this, it's very encouraging.' He pushed his bull head between Bladder and Sam.

The article showed a photo of Sam's face, so dirty and mucky it was impossible to recognise him. It was the only photo the Kavanaghs had given the papers. Michelle had wanted one of him clean and neat, but Richard had said this one showed Sam at his best. Sam saw it everywhere: news-agents, bookshops, on those digital boards that rolled through various ads outside shopping centres. At first, Sam had been embarrassed, but he had grown to like the photo because it made him unrecognisable. He'd been near people discussing him and slipped by them unnoticed. The only time he had to deal with people's attention was when reporters showed up, which reminded him of a monster stampede.

Bladder caught him thinking. 'Come on, read it', the stone lion said.

Sam read aloud.

Hero Finds a Home

by Olivia Webb

The adoption claim for the boy who captured the country's imagination when he rescued baby Beatrice Kavanagh has been fast-tracked by legal agencies.

The boy, who answers to 'Sam', the name his future family gave him, has been widely praised for his efforts in relocating the kidnapped infant. Yesterday, in interview, the prime minister said that 'Sam's behaviour is an example of all that is good in British children'. Although Sam has no memory of his own history or how he came to be in Brighton, he returned the baby to her family in a healthy state, while he was malnourished, exhausted and in desperate need of medical treatment. Experts believe his experiences have resulted in trauma. Laura Marcinkus, a psychologist from Worthing, says, 'His stories help him make sense of his experience, which we have managed to unpack to find useful information. Regardless, he is nothing but brave and kind. His imagination may have been essential in helping him.'

By translating Sam's story code, the police believe they have discovered valuable information about a crime ring working in Sussex. D.I. Noah Kong says, 'We've established there is an organisation which goes by the name of "The Ogres". This is led by a male and a female. Sam calls them Thunderguts and the Crone. It is believed that the male is possibly dead, but the Crone, whose real first name is Maggie, is very much alive. We are looking into her whereabouts. She is red-haired and green-eyed. Our young hero refers to her as a "witch" and a "banshee", which, considering her activities, is mild language indeed.'

The police refuse to confirm if this has anything to do with the recent rise in missing person reports from families across Ireland, Scotland and Wales, although one source suggests there seem to be striking similarities between the crimes. They have asked the public for help locating these individuals.

Sam also identified at least two people who helped him, including a tall, fair-haired man known as Daniel, and a wide-faced, big-toothed individual Sam calls Bladder. The latter appears to have risked a lot to help Sam. 'We are hoping these two will come forward and help with our investigations,' D.I. Noah Kong says. 'Sam put himself at great personal risk going up against these criminals and, as heroic as his actions were, the Sussex Police would caution anyone against doing the same.'

No information about Sam's birth family or origins has been established, but the adoption process looks to be finalised this week. Our local hero will finally have a home.

'Well, I know why you like this one best,' Wheedle said. '"... Risked a lot to help Sam".'

Sam stroked Bladder's mane. 'You did, Bladder, and you deserve notice. You all do. If it wasn't for you I wouldn't have survived.' Sam kissed each of the gargoyles in turn. Bladder last. 'You deserve more than one line.'

'It's just nice to know you mentioned me, although I don't know why you described me as "wide-faced" and "big-toothed".'

'I said you looked like a lion. I also mentioned Wheedle and Spigot too. They thought you and Wheedle must be brothers, because he's wide-faced and big-toothed too.'

Wheedle bared his teeth. 'Yeah, but mine are cow's teeth. Not sharp or nothing.'

Sam continued. 'And they kept asking me how big Spigot's nose was, and I said it wasn't a nose, it was a beak. They found that funny. Maybe Wheedle and Spigot will make it into the next article.'

Bladder's voice dropped as if he thought someone might be listening. 'What I can't believe is they think Thunderguts is part of a crime ring. Good thing for them he's dead, or he'd turn up to show them what the king of ogres looks like.'

They went quiet for a second.

'There's not been any mention of you destroying the

Vorpal Sword and letting all those souls go,' Wheedle said. 'I mean, that was seriously important.'

'They didn't seem much interested in that.'

An angel appeared on the courthouse steps. He stood taller than the high doorway. His smiley eyes fixed on Sam and he waved. His face and posture appeared calm and angelic, but the feathers in his startling white wings poked out at odd angles.

'Oh, look, the Plucked Chicken is waving you down,' Bladder said.

'Daniel,' Sam called as he waved back.

Sam clambered down the side of the courthouse and pulled a plastic rectangle from his back pocket. He held it in front of his mouth.

'How long now?' he shouted at the rectangle.

'You don't need to be so loud. Right here next to you,' Daniel said. 'Stop worrying. It's all under control.' He shifted his wings. 'It's hard to get comfortable. My quills keep poking me. What can you hear?'

'Last time I listened all I could hear was paper rustling and lots of nodding.'

'Try again.'

Sam listened to the building behind him, his gargoyle hearing reaching beyond the gaggle of lawyers and their nervous clients, through solid doors right into the wood-panelled room where Richard and Michelle Kavanagh waited for an answer. He heard Michelle's heavy breath as the judge spoke.

The judge had a warm, old voice.

Sam cheered. 'He says I can live with the Kavanaghs if my *real* parents don't show up,' he reported, grinning. 'They *are* my real parents. Woohoo!'

'Hey, Sam. What ya doing?'

Sam turned to see an older, dark-haired boy, his twin in all but age, and pointed at the shiny rectangle. 'Hi, Nick. I'm talking on my mobile phone.'

Nicholas Kavanagh sidled next to Sam, handing him a drink bottle. 'Really? So, who, other than us, do you know?' He took the mobile and placed it against Sam's ear. 'If you want to look normal, you might want to try holding it like this, and –' he pressed the screen, then the large button at the bottom of the phone – 'it would be more convincing if you charged it.'

'Charged it?'

Nick laughed. 'Yeah, the weird pluggy thing they included when Mum bought this for you. You put the pronged end in a wall socket and the other, smaller end in this hole here.' His finger pointed to the bottom of Sam's mobile. 'Do that and you may even be able to use it for what it's for.'

Sam laughed too. He couldn't help it. His happy spilt over everything.

'You're talking to your invisible friend, right?' Nick asked.

Sam blushed. 'Yes.'

Nick laughed. 'It's certainly going to be fun having you around.'

Daniel grinned. 'Just a little job for me to do. See you at the house.'

9

Sam tried to sulk as he watched the angel leave, but he heard the noise of the Kavanagh parents clattering towards the door and all other bother faded. He turned as Richard and Michelle came out of the court, their faces pink and laughing. Richard spread his arms as he descended.

'Samuel Kavanagh?' he called. 'Is there a Samuel Kavanagh out here?'

Sam raised his hand. 'Me?'

'You, my friend ...' Richard stopped and exhaled. 'You, my *son*, are now legally a Kavanagh. The adoption's been approved. You're all ours.'

Nick reached out and grabbed him. Sam giggled.

The lawyers, children's services attendants, the Kavanaghs, even Great-Aunt Colleen kept saying how quickly everything had moved to this point, but Sam had waited more than half his life for this day.

'Can we see Beatrice now?' he asked. With the baby, he would have all the Kavanaghs together. Sam liked the thought.

Michelle kissed him. On the side of the forehead. Above his eye. Sam closed his eyes, he was going to live with that, finally going to be able to live in it day after wonderful day without someone signing another sheet of paper, without another stranger in attendance; and he was ready for all of it.

'Let's go home,' Richard said.

Sam thought he had never heard a more beautiful sentence in his life.

CHAPTER 2

Sam found himself on the front steps of his forever home and couldn't remember getting out of the car. He grinned – maybe he'd floated. The other Kavanaghs had gone in, and he too would be inside soon. He wanted to see Beatrice. The babysitter congratulated him as she passed him on the footpath, and all Sam could do was smile. He looked up and down the street. He studied it. It was *his* street now. On which *his* family lived and *his* house stood. He looked over into the next garden, the garden of *his* neighbour, Mrs Roberts. Her dog, a brown-furred pug, yapped feebly at him. Sam had met a few dogs; they usually barked, swore at him, then ran off, which was a shame. Daniel had said every child should know one good dog. As Mrs Roberts's dog was now the dog next door to *his* home, Sam hoped he could make friends with it.

The pug normally ran away, but today it stood its ground on short, shaking legs.

'Go away, go away', it yapped, one eye staring at Sam, one at its house. Was the dog even barking at him?

Sam headed to the short concrete wall and knelt. He was still twice the pug's height.

'How are you?' he asked. 'I'm moving in permanently now.'

The dog stopped yapping, as if shocked Sam had spoken to it. 'What are you? You're not going to hurt me, are you?' the pug asked.

'No, of course not.'

The dog cocked its head and lifted its tiny, flappy ears a little higher. 'You smell funny', it said. 'Like a monster.'

'Wow, good nose. To be honest, I do have a little monster in me, but that's not all I am. Sniff deeper.' Sam breathed in, showing the dog how to take a full whiff of him.

The dog did so, its back fur shivering. It cocked its head the other way. 'Well, that's odd. Now you smell like chicken necks and Yummo Treats. I like those.'

'I'm half fairy. It makes me smell of things you like. I'm not all monster, see? Just a little bit.'

'My mistress says all boys are monsters.'

Sam reached towards the pug. It trembled but leaned forward, sniffing his hand. 'I won't hurt you', Sam said.

'What a relief. I've been all nerves and tingles since I heard you were moving in.'

'Really? I'm sorry about that. I'm Sam, by the way.'

'My name is One-Who-Bites-At-Heels, but my mistress calls me Hoy Poy. You're –' the dog breathed in again – 'smelling more human by the second, how odd. You may call me Hoy Poy too.'

'Thanks, Hoy Poy.'

Hoy Poy's curly little tail wagged back and forth. Sam had made friends with the neighbour's dog, and he wanted to be friends with everyone on the street. He reached out, patted Hoy Poy's head and the dog licked his hand.

Nick called from the door. 'Do you want some lunch?' Sam peered back, Hoy Poy still licking his hand. 'What are you doing?' Nick asked.

'Hoy Poy and I are making friends. He says he's not scared of me any more.'

'And why would he be?' Nick laughed and stepped back inside. His voice carried to Sam. 'It's going to be a lot of fun having you around.'

Hoy Poy yapped at Sam and trotted cheerfully to the side path of Mrs Roberts's house. Before the dog turned down it, he wiggled his bottom again, his sturdy tail waving at Sam, and said, 'Tell your friend to be careful not to fall.'

'My friend?'

Sam looked up. Daniel hung from the roof, upside down, his celestial garment miraculously staying in place. He had painted symbols down the front wall.

Daniel waved. 'My homecoming gift. Wardings. Angelic sigils,' he called out in answer to Sam's unasked question. 'This round one here stops the Kavanagh smell floating about, and this one makes the house invisible to earth-based supernatural creatures. We don't want Maggie sniffing around.'

Sam sighed. Maggie was a banshee. She had stolen him from his family, tried to start a monster revolution and looked at humans as nothing more than tasty ogre treats, yet they had formed a bond and he thought of her fondly. Still, Maggie was dangerous, and she wasn't the only monster he didn't want finding him.

Daniel continued. 'This is a general blessing. It'll cover most of the street ... when ... the last bit ... is ... drawn.'

As soon as the sigil was complete, Richard stepped out on to the front stoop and a voice called out from the park opposite. 'Good day.'

Richard flushed pink and glowed at the speaker. The other man's grin grew and he glowed a little too.

'It is a fabulous day, isn't it?' Richard replied.

'See. Working already,' Daniel said. 'Although it's probably you being home that's making everyone so happy. You made friends with the dog, then?'

'Hoy Poy. Yeah.'

'A dog is a great friend to have.' The angel sat down on the footpath to admire his artwork and gave a deep sigh. 'You'll need some protection now. They're recalling me.'

'Who?'

'Upper management. The Power That Is. They say they have to retrain me.'

'Why do you need retraining?'

'My wings are giving me grief. Everything's solid to

me. Again. Walls, doors, even windows. Going into water gets my wings wet and –' Daniel grimaced – 'they sink. My wings never used to sink!' The huge archangel slumped. 'It's the promotion.' He said the word bitterly. 'Becoming an archangel is hard work. They're probably disappointed with me.'

'It can't be that bad.'

Daniel's voice went up a strained note. 'Angels are creatures of pure spirit. We should pass through and around things. There's no reason for pure spirit to be contained by anything physical, but getting in, getting out, it's not happening for me. Even in humans the physical part can be contained, but if the soul chooses not to be bound, nothing can hold it.'

Sam frowned. 'But maybe it's some sort of magic? The souls in the Vorpal Sword were bound.'

'Because they believed they were. That's why the mage used the souls of slaves. They lived all their lives bound, they didn't realise their thoughts and ideas were their own. Any one of those souls could have flown away without you breaking the sword. A soul is a free thing wherever it is. Even magic can't hold it.'

'Oh,' Sam said. He didn't know what else to say.

'No, it's me. Just me.' Daniel slapped a frustrated hand on the wall. 'For some reason, my body just doesn't want to do it. It's the difference between having a concept and knowing it ... so Taki is recalling me.'

'Taki?' Sam said.

'Taxiarchus, the Lieutenant of Angels. We call him Taki.'

Daniel leaned forward. 'Taki says the message came from the Highest Office. He says *He* wants me to stay at home for a bit.' Daniel's wings drooped. 'What's wrong with me?'

'Maybe you haven't done anything wrong,' Sam said. 'Do you have to go straight away?'

'They've given me a few things to tie up down here, but then ...' Daniel sighed again. 'Have you got time to talk tonight? Do you think you can stay up that late?'

Sam smiled. He thought he could.

Lunch was chicken pie followed by raspberry tart. Daniel loved raspberry tart, so Sam asked if he could have one for later. This was followed by board games in the living room. Nick tried to show him how to play a video game, which was fun, but it was going to take him a long time to get as good as Nick. Everyone was tired. Each day at court had been stressful, and Sam had had to go back to a foster home while he waited. The Langwades were lovely, but they weren't his family. This was his real home.

Then it was night, and they all got ready for bed. Sam was tired too, but it was glad-sleepy, nothing awful. He put the tart on a plate, hoping it cheered Daniel, and went up to his room.

My room, he said to himself as he opened the door. *His own* bed had been tucked against one wall, its blue quilt spattered with stars; *his own* walls plastered with pictures of churches, gargoyles and angels. He had a desk and a lamp and a bag for school. Sam had absolutely everything he'd ever wanted.

Outside, Daniel struggled to lift the window. Sam opened it and let in the angel. Daniel's wings jammed in the frame before he pulled them free and tripped into the room.

'How are you feeling?' Sam asked.

Daniel gestured over his shoulder. Behind him, four faces peered into the room. Bladder, Wheedle, Spigot and the tiny white dove perched on Spigot's back. They all wore shiny party hats. Even the dove wore a small gold one.

'Yonah, you're here too,' Sam said. The dove landed on his shoulder and pecked his face.

'Thought we'd come and crack open a box of champagne truffles with you,' Bladder said. He shoved an already opened box into the boy's hand.

'Thanks so much for coming,' Sam said.

'Coming?' Wheedle replied. 'We're moving in. You've got a nice patch of roof up there.'

'Really? Really? That's wonderful. But how did you get here from the courthouse?'

'Not the courthouse,' Wheedle said. 'We've been at The Lanes all afternoon. Shopping for chocolates.'

Spigot squawked.

'All right, maybe "shopping" isn't the right word.'

'Didn't anyone see you?' Sam asked.

Spigot squawked again.

'Like Spigot says, "It's Brighton",' Wheedle replied. 'People expect to see things that are out of the ordinary, so no one looks twice at us. The Lanes are fantastic!'

'We've spent most of the day pretending to be ornaments outside one shop or another,' Bladder said. 'Someone took a photo of me holding a milkshake. I'll be on Twitter soon.'

'We just move and then freeze,' Wheedle said.

Sam laughed and popped a chocolate in his mouth.

'I'm a supermodel.' Bladder waved his head side to side. 'Vogue, ladies.' And the three gargoyles struck ugly poses and stood stony still. 'If they're passing we pose outside a shop door. Now vogue.'

The gargoyles changed position.

'I did hear one girl note we'd been shifted,' Bladder added. 'One more time!'

The gargoyles did a final glamour pose, glancing coyly over their shoulders at Sam. He laughed and choked on his chocolate, and Wheedle had to thump him on the back. The chocolate flung itself from his lungs and, regardless of his sturdy imp frame, Sam knew his back would be purple and yellow soon.

They all settled down to scoff the rest of the chocolates.

'So, this is it then?' Wheedle said. 'Pack together. We can go out on night adventures. Sam can sleep during the day, and the Kavanaghs will keep him safe. And it's just fun, fun, fun, gargoyle style.'

'He has to go to school,' Daniel said.

Bladder spat a chocolate at the wall. 'He what?'

'I have to go to school on Monday,' Sam said. 'It's all part of becoming human.'

Spigot shrieked.

'That's right, Spigot, four days away.' Wheedle pushed

his cow face into Daniel's ruffled wing. 'You haven't told him, then?'

'Told me what?' Sam asked.

''Bout the dangers of school life. There *are* movies,' Wheedle said.

Bladder stalked back and forth on Sam's carpet. 'All the movies we've seen, all of them. Terrible things happen at schools, and with teenagers.'

'You do tend to watch horror movies,' Daniel said.

'Documentaries, you mean. We watch musicals too,' Bladder said.

Spigot carked.

'You're right, Spigot, *West Side Story*. You have to watch that one, Sam. It's horrible, there's singing and dancing.'

Sam studied all three gargoyle faces. They shook their shaggy heads. Yonah rolled her eyes but carried on pecking her chocolate.

'Oh, good grief.' Daniel shook his head. 'Really, it's a place full of kids like Sam. Or at least Nick. You gargoyles shouldn't start worrying him about school.'

'I know about schools.' Bladder turned to face Sam. 'I know a lot about schools. You need to do stuff to protect yourself.'

'Schools are quite ...' Daniel started.

Bladder shook his mane. 'Don't you send him defenceless to one of them institutions. They're called institutions for a reason, Sammy. They're like prisons, and other dodgy places. You need to go in armed.'

'Armed?' Daniel asked.

19

'Take a stick,' Wheedle suggested. 'Take a big stick.'

'And what do you think is going to happen to Sam at school?' Daniel asked.

'It's worse than an ogre wrestling match. Horrible. It's a dog-eat-dog world out there, Sam,' Bladder said. 'You gotta look after yourself against humans.'

'Really? Dogs *eat* dogs?' Sam thought of Hoy Poy. Dogs ran from him but they didn't seem ready to eat each other.

'It's just a figure of speech,' Daniel explained.

'Yeah,' Bladder agreed. 'It's not dogs you gotta watch, it's humans.'

Sam felt sick. He thought he'd rather face an army of ogres than humans who wanted to eat him.

Daniel put his head in his hands. His wings ruffled, every feather sticking out at a bad angle. He grumbled. 'Humans don't eat each other.'

'That's not what I read,' Bladder said.

'Yeah, but the angel's right, ain't he?' Wheedle asked. '*Most* humans aren't cannibals, are they?'

'There's still a word for it,' Bladder said. 'What's that tell you?'

Daniel stood up then, banging his head on the ceiling and making the light swing. 'OK, you lot, on the roof. No one at school is going to eat Sam!' He spread his wings angrily, but his lack of coordination and the wings' dishevelled appearance made him look odd.

'Yeah, but they could try,' Bladder said.

'Go!' Daniel pointed to the top of the house. 'Get back up there.'

Wheedle scarpered away; Spigot followed. Yonah fluttered off the eagle's back and landed on the desk.

Bladder stepped towards the window, but he turned and said to Sam, 'Just watch for groups of people in leather jackets. Run if they start singing at you.' He rolled his eyes as Daniel pointed again, then climbed outside.

'They will look after you fabulously, even when training takes me away, but don't listen to a thing they say, all right?' Daniel said.

'I'll try not to,' Sam said.

Daniel grimaced.

CHAPTER 3

Sam lay tucked up under his covers, thinking. School tomorrow. He reminded himself, as Daniel had told him to, of the awful things Bladder had said about all humans, but the Kavanaghs had turned out to be lovely. He lived with them because they loved him. These humans were great, so maybe the others were too. Maybe school wouldn't be as bad as all that.

Someone tapped at the window. Sam opened it to see Wheedle's grinning face.

'We're gonna go explore the town tonight. Wanna come?' Wheedle said. 'Don't worry about what Daniel said, we're gonna paint the town red now the pack's back together.'

Sam shook his head. 'No, Daniel's right. It's a school night, and Children's Services say Michelle and Richard must know of my whereabouts at all times. At least to start off. Maybe some time during the day?' he asked.

'I'll discuss it with His Grumpiness.' Wheedle scampered to the footpath where Spigot and Bladder waited in the lamplight. Bladder harrumphed, and the trio faded into the dark.

Sam had almost floated into a dream when he heard Michelle and Richard, on the floor below, discussing him.

Michelle yawned. 'I worry about sending him to school. What happens if memories of his old life come back to him while he's in class?'

'He'll be fine. Besides, as much as I'd like to, we can't have him to ourselves forever. Kids need kids. He'll love school.'

Michelle's sleep-faded voice agreed. 'Yeah. You're right.'

Sam exhaled. OK, it couldn't be too scary if Richard and Michelle didn't think it'd be so bad. Maybe school might help. He hadn't had enough time to learn how to fit in, but he had to start somewhere. Although he'd had no practice being *normal* – maybe the kids would pick him out in seconds. Even Beatrice, who was seven months old, had had more practice than he and she hadn't stopped blowing bubbles or pooing her nappy.

But it was either Nick's school or back to the tutors at the Children's Services, and for that he'd have to live without the Kavanaghs, which was too dreadful to consider. He'd face a hundred schools to stay with them.

Two dozen square glass eyes stared at Sam. Despite the sunshine lighting the building, something about those windows reminded him of holes in a cavern wall. Sam searched the strange construction's face, and was pleased when a little glow caught his eye. More sigils. Daniel had protected the school too.

A crowd of taller kids Nick's age moved towards them with grins and chatting. Nick shifted Sam in front of him and put his hands on Sam's shoulders.

'Hey,' a girl in a blue jumper said. 'How you doing, Nick?'

'Yeah, good.'

'This the infamous Sam?'

Sam heard Nick inhale.

Another boy, a head taller than Nick, patted Sam on the head. 'Hey.'

'Hey?' repeated Sam.

'Check out your hair. Nick was right when he said you're a wild child.'

'Did he?' Sam looked up and Nick smiled.

'It's a compliment,' the tall boy said. 'You have the dubious honour of being liked by this loser.'

'You were in the news, that's pretty cool,' the girl in the blue jumper said.

'Yeah,' the boy added. 'Couldn't make you out behind that grime though, but you really look like Nick. Like a lot. To the point it's bizarre. But you're adopted, right?'

'That'll do for the questions, Isaac. First day's stressful enough without you lot poking at him,' Nick said.

Isaac groaned. 'Come on, you twerp, we've been waiting months to meet him. Call yourself our friend?'

'You can interrogate him more some other time.' Nick

steered Sam towards the monstrous concrete building. The double doors of the school hung open like an ogre's maw.

'Why were they so rude to you?' Sam asked.

'We've known each other a long time. Isaac and me always talk like that. Guys talk to each other like that when they're friends. Come to think of it, it is pretty stupid.' Nick laughed. 'Oh, but don't try it till you've known someone forever, or you're close.'

'OK, I won't insult anyone anyway. I don't think I want to.'

Nick smiled, then patted Sam on the back.

'Give me your mobile.' Nick held out his palm. 'Come on.' Sam pulled the phone from his pocket. Nick looked it over. 'Fully charged? Good. Remember, hold it to your ear, none of this yelling, all right? Too many people will be looking at you. If you need to talk to your friend, get the phone out first.'

Sam put the phone back in his pocket and nodded.

Nick gave him a side hug. 'I know you've had it tough, but it will make your life more difficult if other people think you're weird.'

Sam didn't like the word 'weird'. It was important to not be 'weird'. If the services didn't think he was adjusting to living with the Kavanaghs, they would find him somewhere more 'appropriate'. He didn't like the word 'appropriate' either.

The reception office buzzed with people moving and people talking. So many people all in one place who seemed to have no unified purpose.

Violence could break out any moment, Sam thought.

The receptionist huffed at Nick and raised one pencilled eyebrow at Sam. She didn't even attempt a smile, just hurried through what she called 'the paperwork' then asked him questions. Did he have lunch? Did he have all his books? Could he sit and wait? His 'buddy' would be along soon.

'I have a buddy?' Sam asked Nick.

'It's just someone who will help you around the school. You have to make your own friends.'

Sam took a deep breath as Nick left. He tapped on the notebook hidden in his pocket.

A scruffy boy with dark hair and dark eyes appeared at the reception desk.

'Sam,' the receptionist called. 'Come and meet Wilfred.'

Sam picked up his school bag and looked up to see Wilfred's wild and wide eyes, like terrified pixies Sam had seen in the middle of the stampede. Even the most nervous of humans had never looked at him like that, and it was such a pure expression, Sam understood it fully.

The boy gave him a sniff.

Sam sniffed back. It was a nice smell. A mixture of warm fires, and runs through a meadow, mixed with a happy pet scent. There was hair on his coat. Sam liked him straight away.

'Sam, give Wilfred your timetable. He's in most of your classes, so should be able to show you where to go.' The receptionist peered at Wilfred. 'Are you OK?'

'Do I have to do this?' Wilfred asked.

The receptionist looked Sam up and down. She turned to Wilfred. 'Yes', she said.

Wilfred rubbed his nose and whimpered. 'OK', he said.

'I'm Sam', Sam said, putting his hand out like Richard had taught him.

Wilfred looked at it. 'OK', he said again.

'Wilfred, this isn't like you', the receptionist said.

The messy boy scurried away.

'He's normally friendly', the receptionist said to Sam.

Sam raced after Wilfred. The boy had his timetable.

Wilfred moved quickly, almost as if he wanted to lose Sam, but even when he nipped around a corner, Sam could smell that warm, friendly aroma. He followed at a run.

Wilfred was waiting outside a door. He turned and winced to see Sam behind him.

'Uh', Wilfred said. 'This is ... this is ...' he snivelled. 'This is our form room.'

'Can I have my timetable back?' Sam asked.

Wilfred handed it to him, holding the corner of it between a thumb and forefinger, and stepping back as Sam reached for it.

Sam entered the room straight after Wilfred, who slid on to a chair. Sam chose the one next to him as Wilfred put his head on the table. Sam wasn't sure that a 'buddy' would behave like that.

A woman sat up at a big desk at the front of the room. She peered up at them both and went back to reading her books.

Sam looked at the timetable: History, English, Science, Mathematics. The psychologists had talked about 'History', Sam's history, trying to get him to tell them everything that had happened to him. Was that what that class was for? Talking about the bad things that had happened in the past? He recognised 'English'. He spoke English. The Kavanaghs were English. Most of the humans he'd met so far were English, except Mr Speirs, who was Scottish, and Lila Chandran from the services who described herself as Anglo-Indian. Maybe it was a subject that helped him become more English. He had no idea what Science and Mathematics were. The knowledge Thunderguts had breathed into Sam when he first hatched was useful to monsters, but he had been human for only ... he closed his eyes and counted ... twelve weeks. All he'd learned at the Children's Services was how to work with numbers, and they'd left him alone to read a lot and answer questions out of books. He didn't know if any of those skills would be useful.

Sam pulled out a notepad with a bored gargoyle on the cover and wrote 'subjects', 'lunch' and 'books' on the page titled 'School Behaviour'. He was glad that the Kavanaghs made sure he had food for lunch: He liked food.

More students came in. A boy with black hair peered at Sam as he sat down to Sam's right. A girl with blonde hair eased herself into the chair in front of Sam. Two girls, both as messy as Wilfred and wrapped in similar jackets, slid in around him. Wilfred pointed at Sam, and both girls inhaled. No, not inhaled. They were sniffing him. Sam looked at the door, and although it was no more than a metre away, the corridor between the other students and their desks seemed dangerous and distant.

Another twenty or so people entered, sat down, chatted and became quiet when the lady behind the desk stood and shushed them. Sam guessed she was Mrs Grisham, the form teacher; that's what it said on his timetable.

'Everyone, we have a new student. Would you like to come up and introduce yourself, Sam?'

'No', Sam replied.

'Pardon?' said the teacher.

'Sorry, Mrs Grisham.' Sam gulped. 'I meant, no, thank you.'

The students grinned at Sam, some sniggered, and then they turned to watch the teacher's face. The three messy students in woollen jackets glared at him.

'Sam, please come out the front', Mrs Grisham said.

'Yes, Mrs Grisham.' Sam got up and went forward, his notebook and pencil still in hand.

'Class, this is Samuel Kavanagh. I want you to make him feel welcome. I know you can. Sam, why don't you ... ?' She stopped and stared at one of Wilfred's friends. 'Amira! Why are you making that ridiculous sound?'

The messy girl with the pale face and dark hair sat growling at him.

Mrs Grisham added, 'Amira, it's not like you to be unfriendly to people.'

'No, miss', she said, but Sam heard a rumble in the undertone.

Amira and the other messy kids glanced at each other and then back at Sam.

Mrs Grisham looked at them all. Her face looked like Michelle's when she said she was 'bemused'. 'Go on, sit down, Sam', she said.

Sam did. He studied the messy kids.

Amira lifted her nose and sniffed the air. Sam sniffed back. The trio smelt like wet dogs. They all glared at him.

Relief came when the teacher let them out, although Sam had learned nothing except that the cricket team would be meeting in the gym, and all year sevens needed to remember their devices for Drama class. He dashed out of the door, the first one out. Unfortunately, the messy kids followed him too.

He had History next, and wondered if it would run like the group sessions in the Children's Services building, but it turned out to be sad stories, which made sense. It wasn't personal history; it was what had happened to England and the rest of the world.

'We'll be focusing on World War One, the Great War', Mr Heasley said. Sam listened, writing in his notepad anything odd the teacher said or did. Sometimes, when the teacher mentioned someone dying, he had a triumphant look on his face, as if it were a good thing. It was a strange subject, the stories of how humans hurt each other. They discussed things like courage, but overall, it was a bit depressing. Still, Sam listened and read with open eyes and open mouth. The best way to learn to be human was to learn about them and why they did things. He decided the Great War didn't sound that great at all.

The end of the lesson came with a she-goblin's shriek. No one but Sam jumped, like they expected it, and Sam remained seated after the others rushed out. Sam walked slowly to the classroom door. He put his head outside and peered into the corridor, reminding himself Daniel said humans rarely ate each other.

Outside, in the corridor, the musty-smelling, messy-haired trio waited.

The girl called Amira glared at him again. 'Wilfred, Hazel and me all agree you smell odd. Not human,' she said.

Sam gulped. Not being human was worse than 'weird'. If these kids told the services he was off somehow, he might have to leave his home.

Sam decided he didn't need a buddy any more and ran down the corridor. He'd find English by himself.

CHAPTER 4

Already, day one, and someone knew he wasn't human. He felt like crying.

At least he only saw them during class time when there was a teacher present. He'd not seen so much undiluted anger and fear since he'd left the Ogres' Cavern. In Study Skills, he sat hunched so they wouldn't pay attention to him, but he felt Amira, Hazel and Wilfred glaring at him from behind. The other kids in class were mostly nice to him, and even they seemed surprised by the behaviour of the trio. Someone said it wasn't like them.

Sam avoided the Sniffers all day, but they seemed determined to corner him. He made sure he moved with the bulk of students so he was never alone, and tagged along behind Nick and his friends at the breaks. The Sniffers waited for him after every shared class and a couple of times he'd had to run for it, slipping past them to get to the canteen. They smelt of threats and battle, although Hazel would shake when she saw him.

Maybe Bladder had been right. People didn't like him. Sam didn't think he'd ever fit in, and he hoped they weren't planning on eating him.

They all wore jackets, just like Bladder said. Maybe not leather jackets. Sam thought he'd ask Bladder what happened if they danced.

After school, Nick met him at the school gate and Sam sighed as he saw the Sniffers glaring at him from the benches.

'What's the matter?' Nick asked, following his gaze.

'They don't like me,' Sam said.

'Who?'

'Those three. The Sniffers.'

'Yeah, I know them. They're normally quite easy-going. Don't worry, you'll be safe at home. What makes you think they dislike you?'

'I have no idea. They keep sniffing at me.'

Nick put a hand on his shoulder. 'New schools are hard for everyone. Don't worry, you'll make friends and those kids will calm down.' Sam looked at Nick's face. The words sounded comforting, but the line between the older boy's eyes deepened.

When Richard and Michelle asked him how his first day went, he didn't want them to worry, so he said 'fine'. They needed to tell the Children's Services everything, and Sam would much rather the service people not hear about this.

Michelle kissed him. 'Don't worry, you'll make friends soon.'

She'd known. How had she known?

The Sniffers were at the gate when he arrived at school the next day. They stood back from the gathering students, but Sam watched as Amira took a deep whiff of him and gave such a low growl only Sam could hear. He was sure, had he been alone, she would have attacked him. Ogres gave those types of grumbly pre-battle growls.

In class, Amira glowered under her dark fringe, her face pale and her eyes too bright. Sam wondered whether she was sick. Hazel and Wilfred peeked at him and looked away.

When the bell went for break, he fled out of the class and straight to Nick's table in the canteen. It was nice to have a place to hide.

Nick frowned. He had encouraged Sam to make friends in his own year group, and here he was, heading towards Nick for the second day. Sam hoped Nick wasn't annoyed with him being with his friends.

All Nick asked was, 'Hey, Sammy, you OK?' He shoved over so Sam could squeeze in between him and Isaac. Nick didn't seem angry.

Sam looked up. The Sniffers had followed him into the canteen. They saw him stuck between the bigger kids and glared.

'What's wrong with them?' one of Nick's friends asked. 'They're normally quite sweet.'

'The Sniffers don't like me.'

One of the girls laughed. 'Sniffers? What an interesting name. Normally, everyone likes the –' she giggled – '*Sniffers* and they like everyone. Always doing favours for people. They're very helpful. If you ask them to go get something they will.'

'Did you say something to them?' Nick whispered. 'Or do something a bit ... odd?'

Sam cringed. 'Odd' meant the same as 'weird'.

'No,' Sam replied. He hadn't done anything to upset them. It was his smell. He didn't smell right. He could hear a low rumble in the backs of their throats which no one else would have heard.

Then Daniel flew through the door, hitting his wing on the way in and landing against the far wall with an *oof*. Sam groaned. Sam was always happy to see Daniel, but it was awful timing. He was at school, in the canteen, surrounded by hundreds of people. He pulled out his mobile phone, and Nick stared at him too, shaking his head. 'Sam, no, you don't want to make that call now, do you?'

'Sorry, Nick, I have to.'

Sam marched towards Daniel and stabbed randomly at the face of the phone. He put the phone to his ear. Nick nodded. That meant he looked normal.

Daniel slid down the wall so he was head height with Sam. As his legs stuck out, a girl carrying a full plate picked her feet up and stepped over Daniel's ankles. She stared at the ground as if wondering why she felt the need to do it.

'I'm having a hard time right now,' Sam said.

'Me too. My wings are all over the place and it's time for me to go. Just thought you should know. It's my last day down here until retraining is over.'

'I'm sorry,' Sam said.

A trio of kids passed Sam and Daniel, unconsciously ducking and weaving to avoid the angel's wings.

'Did you feel that?' one asked. The group stared hard at Sam as if he'd done something.

Daniel half-smiled at Sam, then pointed behind him. 'Why does she look so angry at you?'

Sam turned. Hazel, Amira and Wilfred were at the food counter. Amira stared at him, a snarl forming on her face, but Wilfred and Hazel looked beyond him, staring up and to his left. Right into Daniel's face. Both their mouths opened a click, and their eyes glowed, reflecting Daniel's light. Then Wilfred did something Sam had never seen a human do in public. He'd seen Richard do it to music as he wandered the house, and then there was Mrs Roberts next door who wore headphones and did it while gardening in her backyard, but never out the front. So maybe Wilfred could hear music too. Sam listened but couldn't hear anything.

Daniel lifted one eyebrow and looked at Wilfred and Hazel. 'They can see me. That's very odd, you know.'

Wilfred wiggled his bottom. It seemed unrhythmic and unmusical. Sam had seen someone else do it exactly the same way. It wasn't Richard or Mrs Roberts though.

Amira put her mouth to Wilfred's ear. Sam's gargoyle ears heard her whisper, 'Wilfred, stop that!'

Wilfred pointed directly at Daniel. 'But the angel ... it's so beautiful.'

'Angel? What are you talking about?' Amira forced the boy's arm down. 'You're so untrained. You're not in the least bit ready for upright school. Hazel, help me.'

'I can see something too. A light,' Hazel said. 'Can't you?'

'The wall is glowing, but ...' Amira looked around the room. Sam guessed she was trying to find the source of the light.

Wilfred grinned and wiggled again.

'Wilfred, we've got more important things to deal with,' Amira said.

Sam realised he might have been the only one to over-hear the conversation, but he wasn't the only one watching Wilfred. A few other kids stared; some were giggling.

Wilfred watched Daniel's face, looked at Sam, then back at Daniel. The angel put a hand on Sam's shoulder and smiled. Wilfred smiled in return at both Daniel and Sam.

'Wilfred!' Amira dragged the scruffy boy out of the canteen door, glaring at Sam every step of the way. Hazel smiled in the angel's direction, Daniel waved his hand at her, and she stopped, peered at Sam and sniffed again. Her eyes smiled as if she were remembering something pleasant. Amira growled, pulling at Wilfred, who continued grinning, his tongue sticking out between his teeth.

Hazel turned from the sight of the angel with slow reluctance and followed the other two through the door. They disappeared outside.

'That doesn't happen too often,' Daniel said. 'They must have very sweet souls.'

Sam frowned. The Amira, Wilfred and Hazel who had spent the last two days snarling at him weren't people he'd describe as sweet souls. Not with all the growling, the whimpering and ... Wilfred's wiggling bottom? Who had he seen doing that before? He tried to remember.

'It's time for me to leave,' Daniel said, disrupting the thought.

'When will you be back?'

'Maybe not for a long, long time. They haven't really said.' He hung his head and put a hand on Sam's shoulder.

'I'll miss you, Daniel.'

Daniel didn't reply. A tear glittered on his lashes, which burned Sam's eyes, and the angel swallowed a sob. Daniel hugged Sam, then kissed him on the top of his head, taking some time before letting him go. Then he flew from the canteen, hitting his wings on the door on the way out, making unhappy noises and using words Sam was more used to hearing from Bladder.

Sam returned to the table. 'That was weird,' one of Nick's friends said.

Sam felt his stomach turn. He hoped he hadn't embarrassed Nick. It would have looked weird being hugged by an angel.

'Well, Wilfred is a bit odd,' the girl opposite said. 'He's kind though. He was at my little brother's school last year. He always stuck up for the smaller kids. And Dougy says

Hazel's adorable, and he doesn't say that about any other girl. I think it's puppy love.'

'What about Amira?' Sam asked. She was the one who always growled at him.

'She's on the Student Care Committee. Mrs Kelava says she's the best listener they've got. A real good soul.'

Sam sank. If they were so nice, why didn't they like him? What was wrong with him? Even Daniel had liked them.

Nick looked at him and winked. 'Try not to worry about it, Sam. They'll come around. Even the neighbour's dog has stopped barking at you all the time.'

Sam stared at the door, and then it came to him in a rush. Maybe he was wrong, but he thought of wiggling bottoms and knew exactly where he'd seen the same thing. Then there was that lovely homey smell they all gave off, even though they didn't like Sam's scent. And Wilfred could see Daniel. Other than Beatrice, he didn't know any humans who could see angels.

Even if he was wrong, he had to risk it. He'd never make other friends wandering around worrying about Amira growling at him and them following him everywhere. Besides, it'd be nice to know someone who saw Daniel as well as he did.

If he was right, then they were good souls. The best. For the first time, it was Sam who rushed after the Sniffers.

CHAPTER 5

By the time Sam caught up with them, the Sniffers had turned the corner of the building towards the basketball court. Amira shook her head at Wilfred, and Wilfred hung his like he had been scolded.

'But I did see it,' Sam heard Wilfred say. 'Just because you can't, doesn't mean it's not there.'

Amira growled. Deep in her throat. Sam smiled. He recognised the sound now.

'You saw the light too, Amira,' Hazel added. 'And if an angel's with him, then surely ... he can't be a monster.'

Sam raced towards them. 'Hey!' he yelled.

The trio swivelled to face him.

'What do you want?' Amira snarled.

Wilfred wiggled his bottom again and grinned at Sam.

Sam took a dangerous step forward. 'You know, you've made coming to school almost as hard as being in the monster world.' Sam took another pace closer. 'And you're right, I'm not human, not totally, but I don't think you are either,' he said. 'You said I didn't smell human, but ...' He counted one finger. 'Your ability to smell is better than human.' Second finger and third fingers. 'You can sense angels, and you, Wilfred, wiggle your bottom when you see them.' He inhaled their musky aroma. 'At first I thought you smelt like Hoy Poy because you had pets, but it's not that at all, is it? It's cos you're like Hoy Poy.'

'Who's Hoy Poy?' Hazel asked.

'That's my neighbour's dog.'

Amira rammed him, making him stagger. She grabbed his collar and pushed him to the wall, hissing low, so no one else could see or hear them. 'It's our job to protect humans, so you shut your mouth, you monster.' She looked around to see how close the other kids were. She was angry all right, but from under the anger came the strong, dank whiff of fear.

Wilfred grabbed her wrist. 'No, Amira, he must be good. He talks to angels.'

Hazel's dark-golden eyes glowed. 'Yeah, I'm pretty sure too. That light felt nice. No, not nice. Good. It makes sense he's good too.' Beige-blonde hair bounced around her shoulders, catching the sunshine, and she smiled warmly at Sam.

Sam stared straight at Amira. 'You smell like dogs, because somehow you're like me. You're a mix of something. Like you are dogs.' Even as Sam said it, it sounded ridiculous. They were obviously human.

Amira pushed him again.

'Amira!' Hazel yelled.

Sam fell to the asphalt with a heavy *oof*. If he'd been a normal boy, it would have hurt.

'I didn't mean to; I didn't mean to.' Amira's heart-shaped face paled. Fear and anger. Sam saw them again, both flaring in her dark eyes. The irises grew, covering the whites in a shiny black. Human eyes didn't do that.

Sam kept talking. 'Dogs don't like me at first. Hoy Poy didn't, because I smelt wrong to him.'

Amira burst into tears.

'He won't hurt anyone.' Wilfred pulled at Amira's blazer. 'He's a mixture of something odd, but he won't hurt anyone.'

Sam sat on the ground, waiting for Amira to thump him. Her dog smell got stronger. 'You smell funny too. All musty. I thought you'd been rolling around with dogs, but it's more than that.'

Amira whimpered. 'He's a monster. We're supposed to protect humans from monsters.'

'I'm not going to hurt you,' Sam said. 'Or anyone else.'

'I believe him,' Hazel said.

A teacher bellowed across the yard. 'Amira Saluki, I cannot believe I just saw you push someone? Lunchtime detention.'

Wilfred helped Sam up and dusted him off. Wilfred's bottom still wiggled.

The bell rang for the end of break. Amira gave a low, throaty growl at Sam.

* * *

They were already seated by the time he got to Maths, their three heads huddled together. Wilfred smiled, Amira scowled, and Sam couldn't read Hazel's face. It was somewhere in between.

After the fifteen-minute point, Sam was called to the teacher's desk. As he passed Wilfred, the boy sniffed him deeply. Wilfred sat up straight, his eyes twinkling. 'Chicken nuggets,' he said. No one else looked; only Sam heard.

Wilfred leaned towards the Sniffer girls. 'Sniff deeper,' he said.

'I got a hint of something earlier,' Hazel said.

Wilfred grinned in Sam's direction. 'Yeah, it's different when you take a deep whiff.'

Hazel peered at Sam and inhaled deeply. Her expression brightened too. 'Go on, Amira.'

Amira peered at Sam. He knew she didn't know about his super-hearing, so she wouldn't have realised she'd hurt his feelings, but when she shook her head, he did feel wounded.

Hazel poked Amira until she huffed, 'All right. All right.'

Amira sniffed.

Hazel poked her again. 'Deeper.'

Amira frowned.

When the lunch bell rang, all the other kids dashed out, but Sam took a few more seconds to pack up his book. He felt heavy; his attempt to make friends hadn't worked.

When he stepped into the corridor, Wilfred stood

43

waiting for him and took Sam's arm. 'Come on. Amira's in detention, but she doesn't have to do it alone. Let's go.'

He led Sam up the stairs to a corridor on the top floor that lay empty, as if students did their best to avoid it. Amira and Hazel sat inside. A teacher Sam didn't recognise was poring over his marking.

Amira scowled. 'Oh, is everyone coming for detention?' She finished a mouthful of sandwich and then glared at him.

Wilfred and Sam took extra seats.

'Who are you?' the teacher asked.

'I'm Samuel Kavanagh.'

'The boy Amira pushed?' The teacher's eyebrows lifted.

'It was an accident, sir,' said Sam.

The teacher beamed at Amira. 'You know, I thought so. It's not like you at all, but Mrs Henderson said the boy looked hurt.'

Sam shook his head. 'No, I was fine.'

'Well, Amira, as you are my only detainee, I might just head back to the staffroom for lunch. I'll talk to Mrs Henderson. Thank you for clearing that up, Sam. You lock the door after you, I'm trusting you all to not touch anything.'

'No, Mr Lincoln,' Wilfred, Hazel and Amira said.

As soon as he was gone, Amira leaned forward and sniffed Sam again. She pursed her mouth. 'So tell us, then, what are you? When you first arrived, I got a strong scent. You're something, you're a bit monster? But lots of other things too.'

'He's a good boy,' Wilfred said. 'I don't think we need to be scared of him.'

'Hush, Wilfred,' Amira said.

'Shhh, let him talk, Amira. I think Wilfred's right. You've been human so long it's harder for you to tell, but Sam's nice, I'm sure of it.' Hazel looked at Sam. 'You are nice, aren't you?'

'Yes, I think so.' Sam nodded.

'Why do you smell so off?' Hazel asked.

'I am half monster ...'

Amira growled.

'... but I'm half fairy too. Half fairy, half monster, but also human,' Sam said.

'Wow,' Wilfred said. 'Sounds cool. What's that like?'

Amira elbowed him.

'Ouch! Well, some people could question our humanity too. We know what being a mix is like, don't we?' Wilfred asked.

Sam relaxed a little. 'So, what are you? You can see angels, and your noses are really sensitive, which is not like most humans. You're not entirely human, are you?'

'I don't know what you mean,' Amira said.

'He's not a normal human either, remember? I think it's safe to tell him,' Wilfred said. 'And he's surrounded by a glow. It's really strong.'

'Right, smart guy, shall we tell anyone else?'

'Amira, you're just being stubborn. You said yourself he smells nice when you sniff him more. Not just nice – there's deep goodness there, isn't there?' Hazel asked.

Amira snarled. 'I don't care what he is. All I know is he isn't one of us.'

Hazel hugged Amira until she groaned, then said, 'Amira's really sweet, but she's very overprotective of us and all the humans about. It's an instinct in dogs, you know. It's hard to turn off, and we often need it. Some of us bring a little too much attention to ourselves.' Hazel raised her eyebrows at Wilfred and patted his head.

'So, what are you?' Sam asked.

Wilfred took a deep breath. 'We're twin-souled.'

Amira studied Sam's face, but she didn't say anything.

'Twin-souled?' Sam asked. 'What's that?'

'Both dog and human at once. Shifters.'

'Like werewolves?' Sam asked. He'd watched a few werewolf films with Nick.

'Yuck! No!' Amira said. 'Not like werewolves. Shifters are completely different to 'thropes.'

'Sorry, what's a 'thrope?' Sam asked.

'Someone born human that gets infected by another 'thrope. A werewolf bites you, you turn into a werewolf yourself. Lycanthrope is the proper name for a werewolf.'

Wilfred continued, 'And a were-bear is called a callisto-thrope, a were-bird is an ornithrope.'

'Wow,' Sam said. 'So there's more than werewolves?'

'Uh-huh,' Hazel said. 'Were-otters, were-badgers, were-cats ...'

'Are they dangerous?'

Wilfred shrugged. 'It depends on the animal they become or the person they were before. There's a lodge of were-otters out in Hove. They just go swimming all night on a full moon. Those otters aren't really dangerous, and they're nice humans too.'

Amira jumped in. 'Although there was that case where a were-beaver kept chewing up people's houses. Beavers are normally nice, so this guy must've had a nasty streak when he was human. Most people are nice, so usually people who turn into bears and wolves and could hurt people on a full moon, they self-isolate. They have their own police system called the 'Thrope Control who help them sort all that out, and if they're new 'thropes, the Control tracks them down and helps them adjust.'

'Wow! And regular humans don't know any of this?'

All three of them shook their heads.

'So how are you different to 'thropes?'

Amira rolled her eyes as if she thought Sam was a bit thick. 'Weres can't control when they change, but shifters can, and we don't forget ourselves when we're in our animal form. We're always the same person. When we look human, we call it being "upright".' Amira continued, 'We smell like dogs because that's what we are. Shifter dogs. Just like there are different kinds of weres, there are different kinds of shifters. There are even shifter wolves, but most of them live in Canada.'

Wilfred pushed his hand at Sam. As Sam watched, the hand shrank to a fuzzy black paw.

'Shall we start again?' Hazel asked. Both she and Wilfred gazed at Amira, waiting for her to approve.

Amira half-smiled.

'Hazel Kokoni', Hazel said. She lifted her hair and showed Sam a furry beige ear. He chuckled.

'I'm Wilfred Kintamani.' The end of Wilfred's nose grew black and shiny. He waved a hand over it and it was a human nose again.

'Amira Saluki.' Amira offered her hand. She gave him another half-smile.

'Go on, Amira. Show him,' Hazel said.

Amira grinned and Sam saw all her teeth sharpen into canines. She grinned again, and they were human teeth.

'Samuel Kavanagh, but I can't change anything.' He listened. The corridor sounded empty. 'Although I can do this.' He jumped at the whiteboard, and his hands and feet stuck for a few seconds. He dropped again.

'A human fly,' Wilfred said. 'How cool is that?'

The three shifters cheered. Even Amira.

Hazel leaned in to shake his hand. 'It's always hard to make friends when you join the human world. Shifters struggle to make friends with humans when we're upright. The rules are so different. Humans don't make sense, and they think *we're* weird. They're so inconsistent.'

Sam laughed at the relief of someone saying exactly what he thought. 'I know. I'm really struggling to make sense of them.'

'No one gets being this different, but I guess a fairy-monster might,' Wilfred said. 'When you're a dog it's easy. They say, *Can I scratch your belly? What lovely ears you have. You're so cute.*'

'So, are we friends?' Sam asked, looking at each of the three in turn.

'When I first met you your smell seemed wrong, but now I understand why, I like you,' Amira said.

'When I first met you, you growled at me and I was scared, but now I understand why, I like you too,' Sam said.

Sam and Amira grinned at each other.

'I like you too,' Hazel added.

CHAPTER 6

'We just got off on the mistaken toe,' Sam said.

Michelle studied him. 'Do you mean the "wrong foot"?'

Sam opened his pad and scribbled out a line on the page marked 'Idiom'. Beatrice bounced stars at him. He batted them back with his pen.

'So, can they come over?'

Michelle teared up, looking at him. 'So, what do you think of them, Nick?'

'Weirdest, nicest kids at school. Seems appropriate they'd like Sam.'

Wilfred, Hazel and Amira showed up at his door on Saturday morning. They were in casual gear and their hair looked scruffier than ever, as if they all needed a good brushing.

'Your street smells like Heaven and your house glows,' Amira said. 'It's unbelievable.'

'Wanna go for a walk? Huh?' Wilfred asked. 'I brought a ball.' He held an orange tennis ball in one hand.

'Sure,' Sam said, and yelled back into the house. 'Michelle! My friends are here!'

Richard and Michelle arrived at the door, Richard holding Beatrice, and grinned at the shifters. 'Nice to meet you.'

'Can we take the baby to the park?' Hazel asked.

'Really?' Michelle said.

'Oh, yes, the little ones are the best fun. So cuddly,' Wilfred added.

Michelle looked at Richard. The line between her eyes deepened.

'I will let nothing happen to her,' Sam said.

Michelle's face relaxed and her eyes shone. 'No, you never would, would you?'

Richard nodded.

As Hazel strapped Beatrice into the stroller, Sam thought of something, and dashed up Mrs Roberts's path.

Mrs Roberts answered the door, her mouth pulled down in a deep curve. 'Can I help you?'

'Hi, Mrs Roberts, I was wondering if I could take Hoy Poy for a walk.'

'That's very nice of you, but ...' she started. Hoy Poy ran out with his leash in his mouth, then dropped it at Sam's feet so he could lick Sam's hand. 'It seems Hoy Poy would love to.'

After she closed the door, Sam heard her say, 'Well, I never.'

In the park, between the hedgerows, as Beatrice sat in her pram while Wilfred smelt her head and smiled dreamily at the lovely baby scent (Sam loved that smell too), Hazel said, 'Your mum was nervous about us taking Beatrice.'

Sam sighed. He liked that Hazel had called Michelle his mum. 'Beatrice was taken by ogres, and it took a while for ...' Sam's face felt warm. 'For them to get her back.'

'Beatrice?' Amira stopped on the footpath. 'Oh my goodness. You're that Sam. From the newspapers.'

Sam's face got hotter.

'See. He's definitely a good one.' Wilfred grinned and started shrinking. Sam had seen the boy's hand turn into a paw and his nose go black, but the sight of him fading away was unusual. Wilfred grew a black beard and moustache as he shrank, which spread across the rest of his face. His nose grew longer, and there amongst the boy's clothes sat a black pup.

Hoy Poy screamed.

'Really, Wilfred?' Amira said.

'Oh, come on,' Wilfred said. 'There's no one about. I want to play.'

Hoy Poy sat down. 'I may throw up.'

'I want to play too,' Hazel said. She peered up and down the lane, her hair changing to light fur as she did, her skin springing with beige fur, and her cute nose darkened to a deep brown while her pupils grew larger and larger until her whole eye was golden. In Hazel's clothes sat an adorable beige pup.

Hoy Poy screamed again.

'You did bring the ball, Sam?' Hazel asked.

Amira flustered and shooed the pups away from their clothes, pushing the bundles into the undercarriage of Beatrice's pram. Wilfred shoved his nose into Beatrice's hand, and she fireworked sparkles at him. She liked puppies, that was obvious.

'Go on, Amira', Hazel said.

The girl looked at Sam. 'Wouldn't you prefer I remain in my human form?'

'He doesn't mind', Wilfred said.

'I really don't', Sam agreed.

'OK. This is so embarrassing doing it outside of home.'

'We won't tell', Wilfred said.

Sam picked up Hoy Poy. 'It's all right, I'm not going to change.'

Amira shrank too, but her long limbs turned into long furry legs, and she had to pull them out of her shirt fast before she got stuck inside. Sam could see it was harder for her; she didn't become a small pup like Wilfred and Hazel. She became long and lanky, her heart-shaped face turning to a muzzle with heart-shaped beige markings, and her black hair to black fur. Finally changed, she stepped regally out of her pile of clothes and opened her mouth in a doggy grin. 'I think somebody mentioned a ball?'

Even Hoy Poy liked that idea.

An hour or so later, the three shifters lay panting on the grass, while Hoy Poy curled up on Sam's lap. Beatrice had laughed at the dogs, and they had made sure to give her doggy kisses and let her suck their ears, and now she slept in her pram.

'So, what are you, that you can change like that?' Hoy Poy asked.

'Twin-souled,' Wilfred said. 'Two souls in one body.'

'How'd that happen?' the pug asked.

'Go on, Amira. She tells it best.' Wilfred rolled over so his four paws pointed at the sky.

'She really is good,' Hazel agreed.

The saluki pup sat up, regal and calm.

'When the earth was young and time was fresh,' Amira Saluki started, 'humans and dogs were separate. They stayed with their own kind, but as is the way with the very young, children and pups would wander. Weaving, walking about in the wide spaces where we go when we look for something lost.

'Dogs and humans are meant for each other. They did not know this in the first days and would avoid each other and yell and yelp when they crossed each other's paths.

'But one day a human child became lost wandering. It had been searching for something its heart yearned for, but it could no longer find its way back to its parents. A wild pup came across the child and recognised it as human, but felt no fear as it might have with a spear-carrying adult. It saw the child was vulnerable, and in the cold night, after the child fell asleep, the dog leaned its warm, furry body against the child's back and kept it warm, and it kept itself warm too. If a predator came close the dog would growl. When morning arrived, the child awoke to find itself warmly wrapped in the paws of a good dog.

'At first the child was afraid. Humans told their young of children disappearing in the woods, leaving blood and torn clothes for memories, but the dog sniffed the child's hand and the child patted the dog's head, kissed it between its eyes, and they were friends.

'The dog and child stayed together for many days in the wild, away from their camps. They played and hunted, picked berries which the dog tasted with one eye closed and its nose wrinkled. The child laughed. They swam in a pool and, at night, slept under a starry canopy, a mix of child skin and dog fur. They dreamed of playing forever.

'One day the sun rose and the pup missed its parents and knew the child's mother and father would miss it too.

'It was time to go home.

'The child was frightened; it did not know how to find its way home and it did not want to leave the dog. The dog laughed. It could easily find the child's scent and its own path. It would show the child the way back to its kind.

'The path was hard, not because of thorns or rocks or dangerous ground, but because neither dog nor child wanted to lose the other, and they knew the humans would not let the dog stay, nor would the dogs feel comfortable with the human among them.

'One day the child saw its camp. Even in the distance, it could hear its mother's wail and the anger of the people as they yelled at the fire.

'The pair knew the child must go to its people alone, for fear of risking the dog's life, and yet the child knew it would never be happy without the dog, and the dog whined for the same reason. But they could not go off into the wilderness and die together, which is what it would mean if they did not return to their homes. A dog and child are not always enough against all nature.

'*One more night*, the child begged.

'*One more night*, the dog agreed.

'So, they hunted and played, although sadly, and when the sun set they curled into their fur-skin ball and each wept for loss of the other.

'In the morning when the sun rose, the child leaned in to hug the dog and the dog moved its head to lick the child's face and found they were one creature. Two souls in one body. They did not know what to do: neither could go home now.

'The child wept for its mother and father, for it would never see them again, and the dog wept for the brothers and sisters of its litter, for it would never see them again.

'The dog-child did not know what to do and returned to the pool, to look at its new face in the water. It conversed with itself, trying to decide. As it did this it noticed that when the dog led the conversation the creature's new body became the dog, but when the child wailed and sighed for its parents, the creature's body resumed a human form.

'It learned that it could decide its form, even as two voices ran in its head.

'It went home looking like the child and told its story to the humans.

'At first the people did not believe, but the child let the dog take form and the people understood.

'At first, people were suspicious of this union. The hard of heart talked of killing the twin-souled creature, but the children of the tribe loved the dog and could see only play in its eyes. At night, the adults watched the child for signs of deception and each one saw only peace as it slept, a quietness none of them had ever felt after dark.

'One day, the child told the people that the dog wanted to go home and the people agreed. They had learned the good of dogs and some of the children harboured in their hearts a desire for their own pup.

'When that first shifter returned to the den of its kind, it did not arrive alone. It took its other soul, and the children of the human tribe.

'One by one, the children of dogs and the children of humans entwined and became shifters.

'The twin-souled sleep peaceful at night, their dreams full of play, they walk confident in the day, knowing a friend is always close. Blended by a generous hand, there are none more at peace in this world than the twin-souled.'

'Well, I'll be ...' Hoy Poy said. 'So just a boy and a dog smooshed together? Does it happen a lot? I don't know if I want to be smooshed with someone.' He got off Sam's lap. 'No offence, Sam. Although I realise the dogs in the park told the truth – there is such a thing as a good boy.'

'It's fine, I'm just getting used to being monster, fairy and human. I'm not sure I'd cope with anything extra.'

Amira laughed. 'I don't think so, but who knows?'

Just before lunch, four human-looking children and one human baby returned a happy pug to his surprised and grateful mistress, then went into Sam's house.

Richard sat in the living room, the volume down on the TV. He put a finger to his lips. 'Michelle's been asleep three hours. She only meant to lie down for thirty minutes. What good kids you are. I suspect that's the deepest sleep she's had in ages.'

'Let's go for another walk tomorrow,' Wilfred said as they left. 'Please.' He held up the ball and all three shifters nodded.

'Well, I hope you're not going to neglect us next weekend. I thought we were going to have a day out finally,' Bladder said as the stars arrived over the roof of the Kavanagh house. 'Can't go out at night, and now you're too busy for us during the day.'

Sam apologised.

'Don't worry about him, Sam. It's important you make friends more like yourself, and closer to your age,' Wheedle said.

Bladder harrumphed. 'Beatrice is older than Sam.'

'But Sam is closer to twelve than four hundred,' Wheedle said, poking Bladder with a hoof. 'Give it a rest, you grump, you're making him feel bad.'

Spigot leaned into Sam. The bird stared up at the stars, ignoring the conversation. He put his beak on Sam's shoulder.

Bladder peered at Sam. 'Oh, well, I didn't mean to do that. I just missed you. I thought we could show you The Lanes and the sweet shops.'

'Next Saturday, hey?' Wheedle asked.

Sam agreed.

School got better very quickly.

The shifters were in most of his classes. At break and lunch, he walked with them to their bench outside and they all smelt the air. He'd sometimes go through the canteen and wave at Nick, who was happy he'd made friends as bizarre as him. He didn't have to watch what he said with the shifters, and when he told them things they didn't nod and ask what he thought it meant. When he described ogres and pixies, they knew he meant ogres and pixies. Words meant what he meant them to mean.

He'd even been able to swap bits of his lunch, although he drew the line at Wilfred's Puppy Treats. He didn't like the smell of those.

CHAPTER 7

On Friday night, Wheedle tapped on the window. He was not alone; Bladder was on the other side of the ledge and Spigot stared sadly into the night sky.

'Misses the little birdy,' Bladder said. 'What's 'er face? Yonah.'

'I'm sorry, Spigot. I'm sure she'll be back when Daniel returns,' Sam said.

The eagle sighed.

Wheedle shuffled against the bricking. 'You did say we got you tomorrow. You did, didn't you?'

'Definitely,' Sam said.

The gargoyles grinned.

Wheedle continued. 'So, anyway, we're off now to get to The Lanes. Don't wanna get caught on our way there, but you'll meet us at in Brighton Square in the morning? D'you know where it is?'

'I can google it,' Sam said.

'Ooh, could ya? Can we see what that is?' Wheedle asked.

Sam let the gargoyles into the bedroom and he showed them the phone Michelle had given him. They were very impressed when he found the map.

The gargoyles left a little later. They climbed down the wall to the footpath.

Sam watched them disappear down his street, chatting and carefree. Each one happy.

Sam was excited to be free to see his pack in Brighton Town. He even used a bus by himself and thanked the driver profusely, showing his bus pass until the man said, 'Just get on, will ya?'

The traffic dragged along the packed street. He remembered those first few days living on the cathedral; the world had grown so big since then. He knew how to use public transport, he could dress himself, even when it involved buttons and shoelaces, he'd gained family and friends without losing his pack. Could life be any better? The sun shone, the sky was the colour of Michelle's eyes, and he wandered around without having to explain anything to Children's Services. He could see the gargoyles every day, without them having to break and enter (the gargoyles had set off the alarm twice at the children's centre. Bladder had broken a CCTV to stop from being videoed).

That world was three weeks ago, and already it was fading into a distant past. He'd never been allowed out to have an outing with the gargoyles while in the service, and this was another new and wonderful freedom that came with being with the Kavanaghs.

His stomach lifted when he saw his stop.

Sam got off along North Street near the first narrow corridor of The Lanes, a 'twitten', Michelle called it. His phone showed the way to the square and peering at the map on the screen he almost missed the sweet shop. Its smell caught him and he had a wonderful thought and felt for the pocket money Michelle had given him.

Inside the shop, the shelves displayed all sorts of sugary wonder. He didn't have to beg, wasn't expected to steal, and he enjoyed the experience of choosing something he thought his pack would want. He smiled at the girl behind the counter, who repaid him with a sweet grin reminding him of May, the girl from his first sweet shop. She put a dozen sugar mice inside a paper bag, and he bulged it into his pocket. He hoped it might make up for not spending the previous weekend with the gargoyles, then he stepped out into the captured heat of The Lanes.

Old shops tight-lined the corridors. Small squares of dark-framed glass peered at him, some clear but many with the misshapen blur of melting glass. They barely allowed light in, and did not welcome the prying gaze of an imp child wondering what secret human business went on inside.

He trotted until he came to where the sea breeze from Brighton Beach cleared out the warm stifle. It was a good day, sunny but cool.

He wondered if moods controlled the weather. Everyone seemed happy.

Gaggles of chatting teenagers pushed by him in the direction of Churchill Square and he found himself in a small quadrangle which was the central hub of The Lanes. In the bright morning light, people wandered in couples and triples, throwing pennies into a fountain overlooked by a statue of a boy and a girl riding two dolphins. People dived into the coffee shops and restaurants and used the square as a thoroughfare to other places. Sam looked in the windows; there was no specific pattern to the things you could buy, except small, everything had to be small. There were ice creams and jackets, bed linen and toys.

Two benched pigeons with grey feathers and greyer faces gaped in his direction; seeing just another boy, their gazes slid over him as they flew away.

Outside the cafe, Bladder, Wheedle and Spigot posed with silly faces. Stony still.

'I love these,' a girl said to her friend. 'I see them all over The Lanes. Someone must move them and reposition them. They can't be stone. What do you think they're made of?'

'Sighs,' Sam said.

She studied Sam. 'Why would it have anything to do with their size?'

'Not a lot of regret in them,' Sam replied.

'Sounds artistic. Do you know who made them?'

'No, sorry, I don't, but whoever it was must have been very kind.'

The girl nodded. 'I think you're right. They do make everyone happy. Anyway, really clever, whoever made them.' She and her friend walked on, and for a minute the square was clear.

'Told you, if anyone looks at us in The Lanes, it's just to admire our handsome faces', Bladder said.

'Yeah, though trying it in the park didn't work out so well', Wheedle added.

Spigot gave a gleeful shriek.

'Let's get up there. You should see the view', Bladder said.

The four of them slid around the corner, checked no one was looking and scaled the wall, pulling themselves up on to the top of a flat overlooking a pretty rooftop restaurant and the cafe they'd just been sitting near. A brisk Channel wind tickled Sam's face. It felt so nice to be in an open breeze; the warm square had nothing on clean sea air.

'I brought you something. Three each.' Sam pulled out the deformed paper bag and shook open the top, showing the sugar mice to his rocky family.

Spigot pecked at one and held it in his beak. 'Kark!' he said.

'An attempt at bribery?' Bladder asked, and laughed.

Wheedle seized a mouse, popped it straight in his mouth. 'That'll make Spigot feel like a real eagle', he said as he sucked. (It came out 'rike a rear igor', but Sam understood.)

'Next time I'll get green liquorice grass so you can feel cowish.'

'I'm fine,' Wheedle replied through sugary sucks. 'Besides, I don't want to have to think about what you'd have to bring to make him feel more ...' Wheedle nodded at Bladder, who opened his mouth and hissed like a strangled pussycat.

'Cherry liqueurs for me,' the lion-faced monstrosity said as bits of sugar flaked between his fangs.

Sam stood up to see the pier. He liked the sweets but his imp nose could make out the tangy aroma of vinegar and oil on hot chips. The sign for his favourite chippy was easily readable. Another sharp wind hit him. He shivered. He had noticed the nights getting colder lately; he hoped it didn't last long.

'So, you got here?' Bladder asked.

'Yes, by bus. I'm learning all the ways humans do things. I'm learning so much. Even at school.'

'They teach stuff at school?' Wheedle said.

Sam chuckled. With all the talk of new friendships, they'd never had a conversation about why he went to school in the first place.

Bladder leaned forward, taking nips of his sugar mouse. 'Yeah, go on.'

'I've learned about war.'

'Good grief,' Bladder said. 'Do they teach anything useful?'

'They teach us about numbers in Mathematics. Also, we read a lot of stories in English. Who knew stories could be so wonderful? I learned about force in Science, velocity and mass – it's about how if you throw something heavy it has more power behind it.'

'I could have told you that,' Bladder said.

'Tell us everything,' Wheedle said.

Sam explained his lessons in detail and described the teachers and their methods to a giggling audience; he drew diagrams in the air. He promised to let them have a look at his books when they got home.

They all sun-baked on the roof and enjoyed the daylight. When they got bored with that, Wheedle asked, 'Wanna do a tour of The Lanes, then?'

Before Sam could answer, Bladder sat up. 'What's that?' His voice had dropped and the good humour had gone.

Spigot sneezed, then Sam smelt it too. He sneezed as well.

'That's fairy dust,' Bladder said. 'Back up, Sam.'

'Can you see her?' Wheedle asked.

Sam knew who *her* meant. If they could smell fairy dust, it only meant one *her*: Maggie.

He squinted and looked between the words on the shop window – *Collars and Crufts* – and saw a dazed-seeming man behind the counter talking to a big man whose back was to Sam. 'No, just two men in the shop.'

'That ain't her,' Wheedle said.

They all peered down. The big man stepped out of the shop wearing an impossibly heavy coat. He carried two cages out of the door and put them on the pavement in front of the window. He had a wide face and mouth and a flat nose. His eyes were quick and dark, scanning everyone and everything in the square. He stank. The scent of the man was wild and potent, it made Sam want to scream, it made him want to run down there and tear at him. Bladder's mane fluttered and the stone lion snarled.

'I want to kill him,' Bladder said.

Even gentle Wheedle's face twisted into a scowl, his nostrils flared and a front hoof scraped the tiles.

The man dropped the cages and then turned back to the store. As the door opened, Sam's attention was caught again. The scent of fairy dust blew out. It didn't intoxicate him the way it would a normal human, but it did distract him. It was more powerful than before. The humans in the square talked louder and giggled, breathing in the heady powder.

'Wow, it's really pongy,' Wheedle said. 'How's he got so much dust?'

'Don't know, but I'm pretty sure I should bite him,' Bladder replied.

'What's he doing, do you think?' Wheedle squinted through the shop window. 'I can see the man behind the counter, he looks as dust-dazed as they come. There's a woman in there now. Where'd she come from?'

'There's a woman?' Sam peered too, but the glaze caught so much sunlight he had to move about to see the three shapes. The man behind the counter had a sickly pale face and looked like he wanted to vomit, but the big man who'd been outside and the new woman both had their backs to Sam.

'It's Maggie, isn't it?' Wheedle asked.

Spigot twittered.

The cages rattled, and Sam's attention turned to them. Each one held a dog. A larger dog in one, and a lanky pup in the other. Their fur was mostly black, but a beige love heart shape encircled each dog's eyes and nose.

Sam gasped. 'Amira?'

The larger dog paced the two steps inside the cage. 'Help!' it barked. 'Someone, please, let us out.'

'All right, you save the dogs and I'll bite the man,' Bladder said, but Wheedle and Spigot pulled the stone lion back from the edge. 'Let me go. That man wants biting.'

'Don't be stupid, Bladder,' Wheedle said. 'That's Maggie down there.'

'Me? What about him?' Bladder said as Sam tore down the wall.

Sam slipped to the pavement as Wheedle bellowed, and Bladder's *oofs* followed as he tried to climb down too, but Wheedle and Spigot held back the stone lion. Sam darted around the fountain to get closer to the cages, and the smell of panicked dog hit him. He studied the cages. Each had a slide lock. Up close to the dogs he could smell fairy magic again, deep and strong. Someone had sprinkled a lot of dust on them.

'Back away, monster!' the adult dog said.

The pup darted to the front of her cage. 'Sam?'

'Amira!'

'Is this the boy from school?' The mother dog took a deeper sniff. 'I see what you mean,' she said to Amira. 'My apologies, Sam. Your top tones are very ... um ...'

'Don't worry about that now,' Amira yapped. 'Let us out, Sam, before that creep comes back. Before she sprays more of that stuff on us.'

'Shush, then,' Sam said. 'Don't make them hear you.'

Both dogs stared at him. Quiet.

Sam heard the chipping of gargoyles sneaking down the side of the building.

'If I get you some clothes, can you go upright?' Sam had no idea where he'd get clothes from, but he had to do something. 'No one's going to let them cage humans. How'd you get in here anyway?'

'We were at home, and they rang the bell. When Mum opened the door, I saw the man throw something at her. I raced up the stairs, but *she* came in too and then the smell filled the house,' Amira said.

'Fairy dust,' Sam said.

'At first, it made me dreamy. She told us both to shift into our dog form and we followed her right into their car. It was awful. I wanted to go. It seemed fun for some reason. Then the man drove us here. The woman said something about setting a trap. They threw that stuff over the man in the pet shop too, and he just gave them these cages.'

'A trap?' Sam asked.

Amira's mother said, 'I can't change at all. She threw that fairy-dust stuff over me and I couldn't focus. My head's clearer now, but I still can't shift back. Let us out, Sam. There's a safe house only a street away. We can get there before they've even realised we're gone.'

Sam looked through the window, the strange man and the black-hooded woman faced away from him. Neither seemed interested in the dogs.

The mother dog barked, 'Please', and brought Sam back to his immediate problem.

'OK', he said.

'Baby, listen', the mother dog said to her pup. 'When I give the word, you run!'

'Yes, Mum', Amira replied.

'No yapping, very quiet.'

Amira's cage was closest to the shop door. The big man looked out of the window. Sam squatted. As soon as he turned, Sam moved forward.

Shuck. Sam undid the lock on Amira's cage. Sam looked up to see the man staring out of the window, his eyes glowing yellow. Sam didn't know if he was seeing right; maybe the fairy dust had befuddled his thoughts too.

Shuck. He undid the mother's cage, and stepped back towards the gargoyle pack.

From the safer distance, Sam turned his ears to the trio inside, eavesdropping on their conversation. The woman didn't speak, but waved her hand, and a pounding began in Sam's ears. The big man was the only one talking, his voice low. A couple came out and sat at the cafe table right next to the door and began talking loudly. Sam missed words from the ones inside, but he still heard snippets: 'safe house', 'promised gold', 'doing the dangerous work' and a word that made Sam shudder: 'souls'. Sam flinched when he realised the man had taken a step towards the door, opening it so the dazzling fairy smell escaped and burned Sam's smell and sight, until his thoughts thickened with memories: Maggie cradling him in her arms, Maggie's singing, soft and gentle.

The cage doors swung open and Amira and her mum padded on to the pavement. Sam bent over, pretending to tie his shoe, and pointed at the door. The dogs turned as the big man stepped out and stared at the free dogs.

'Hey!' the big man yelled.

The woman slid out of the shop too. It seemed leisurely, but she was a moment behind the man. A lock of red hair escaped her hood. She picked up the hair between pale, lazy fingers and nursed it back under her cape.

Her movements were graceful and languid, like a banshee's.

It was from this figure the overpowering stink of fairy dust came. Sam sneezed – the stuff always irritated his nose – and the figure turned, just slightly, as if it recognised the sound. Sam leaned closer to see her, to hear her.

'Maggie?' Sam whispered.

Hearing him, the big man turned his head from the dogs and frowned at Sam.

The hooded woman studied Sam too. A vagrant gust of wind gathered her bright red hair as she pushed back her cowl, and Sam could see fine features and the sparkle of bright green eyes. Her face was masked by glistening fairy dust hanging in the air. She pointed directly at Sam and her hands glowed.

The dogs barked and raced by Sam out of the square.

The big man went to chase the dogs, but the woman stopped him with her hand on his shoulder and stared at Sam, until both of them seemed to see nothing but the boy, and they stalked towards him. The big man knocked against the table of the cafe customers. 'What are you ...' one asked. The red-haired woman turned to look at them, the dust around her face falling like tears. The tea-drinking woman looked at her, and gave a dust-befuddled smile.

'Come here, boy.' The big man threw dust at Sam. Sam sneezed again.

'Run, Sam,' Bladder screamed at the same time Wheedle yelled, 'Maggie!'

The pair looked straight at Wheedle and the gargoyle took a step backwards.

Sam remembered his legs and hustled down the lane, passing the three gargoyles.

Sam took his first corner. As he turned the man called to him, 'Come back, boy!'

'Run,' Bladder said. 'We're right behind you.'

A crowd made noise up ahead, and Sam and the pack dived to their left, trying to avoid being seen by people.

As they veered, Sam looked over his shoulder to see the big man following along. Maggie was not with him.

Construction signs appeared ahead. Danger, Way Closed. The whole footpath had been dug open, leaving a nice hole in front of them.

Spigot shrilled.

'I don't want to go down either, Spigs,' Wheedle said.

'She's in there, waiting,' Bladder said. 'It's a trap. Stop.'

Sam felt sick. Part of him wanted to talk to Maggie, but the gargoyles were terrified. They all did as Bladder said, and stopped.

The big man followed a few paces behind, but the

gargoyles swung around and formed a stone barrier across the small lane separating him from Sam. The great brute looked at the line of gargoyles, pushed off the ground to start an impressive leap over Sam's stone guard. Bladder popped up and gave him a rock-solid punch to the upper leg, and the man fell with a hard yelp to the paving.

'What the ... ?' the big man roared and tried to push himself up, but Wheedle cracked him on the head with a solid wing. The man dropped again, his skull smacking on the footpath with such force it made them all wince. If he'd had a gargoyle's head, it would have broken off.

'Get up on the roof,' Wheedle said to Sam, 'before he wakes up.'

Sam ran for the wall and climbed. He pulled himself up the side of the building.

On the roof, they all took one last look at the big man lying below, then backed away from the edge. A minute later they heard him sit up and go screaming back the way he'd come, still yelling, 'Boy! Boy!'

Sam heard happy barks coming from far away. At least Amira and her mum were safe.

Wheedle puffed. 'Are we sure it's Maggie?'

'Who else smells like that?' Bladder answered.

'Let's have a look around,' Wheedle said. 'See where she is. She must know you're about somewhere.'

Bladder pulled Sam into his stony paws. 'Nobody's searching for her. We get Sam on the next bus home to where Big Bird's paint job can protect him.'

CHAPTER 8

Sam stayed home all Sunday, and found himself nervous on the walk to school Monday morning, but when he came in sight of Daniel's protective sigils high up on the school building, he relaxed. He waited at the gate for his new friends, especially wanting to see Amira to check she and her mum were OK.

He saw Wilfred wandering down the path, and waved at him. Wilfred waved back and ran at Sam.

'Hey, Sam.' Wilfred grinned and grinned. 'So happy to see you.'

'Me too. If you were in your Kintamani form, I'd pat your head.'

'You saying it makes me feel good.'

'Where are the others?'

'Aren't they here yet? I'm normally the last one.'

'Did you see them yesterday?' Sam asked.

'I saw Hazel yesterday afternoon, and we left a message for Amira. She didn't call back, but this is her weekend to go to her dad's.'

Sam told him about Saturday.

'A big man in a heavy coat caught Amira and her mum in cages? Then he chased you?'

'Yes.'

Wilfred's face paled more than usual. He pulled out his mobile phone and stabbed a few buttons. It rang and rang and rang until Amira's voice reported she couldn't take a message, so leave a phone number. Wilfred hung up. He stabbed a few more keys. That number rang too long as well. 'Hazel's not answering either.'

Without explaining, Wilfred ran out the school gates. Sam took off after the shifter boy and ran next to him.

Wilfred gave him a strained smile. 'You helped Amira escape, so she should be at school. I haven't heard from either of them at all. I got to get home to tell my dad. Hazel's place is on the way home.'

'Tell your dad?'

'He's a policeman. Not the human kind – he's with the Shifter Authorities,' Wilfred panted as he ran.

Sam trotted with Wilfred as he headed home. He knew he wasn't supposed to leave school, and Nick would make all sorts of horrified noises if he found out, so Sam hoped to get back before breaktime. Although a missing Amira and Hazel did seem more important. Sam had been sure Amira would come to school and now Hazel hadn't appeared either.

'Sixteen people in Ireland.' Wilfred's voice was breathy. 'Two whole families in Dublin. Twenty people in Scotland. Thirty-seven in Wales. Most Welsh shifters are corgis. There's a lot of corgis up there. Were. Were a lot of corgis.' He looked at Sam as if this was supposed to make sense. 'Whole families have gone missing.'

Sam remembered the newspaper clipping Bladder had given him at the courthouse had said something about missing families. 'In Ireland, Scotland and Wales? Were they all shifters?'

'Yep, I overheard my dad telling Mum. He had to go to Anglesey because some of the authorities went missing too.' He looked at Sam. 'The authorities!' The creases around Wilfred's mouth deepened. 'Dad told her they'd tracked most of the shifters down; they'd been sold as pets and didn't seem themselves any more, weren't able to shift, or didn't want to. No one knows what's wrong with them. Dad said when they talked they didn't make sense.'

'He told you all this?'

'No, but if I shift into a pup at bedtime I can hear everything downstairs. Dogs have way better ears than humans. Not as good as yours though.' Wilfred stopped, bending over to catch his breath. 'When he came back from Anglesey, he was pale and didn't talk much to me.'

Sam felt sick to his stomach. 'Are there a lot of shifters around here?'

Wilfred, still huffing, shook his head.

'Don't talk any more, let's get to Hazel's house,' Sam said.

The boys raced along the footpath.

Sam had no idea where they had run to, but Wilfred halted sharply and Sam studied the house they'd stopped near. Its door stood wide open. Wilfred yelped and dashed up the steps. Sam noticed him struggling with his trousers, as if his legs were too short. He was shrinking right in front of Sam. His shirt hung off him and the glossy black hair on his head stuck up in two points.

The shifter staggered across the threshold. Sam chased him inside and found himself in a house like his own. It smelt of cooking and laundry powder and shampoo. All the odd scents that filled a home. It also smelt distinctly doggy.

Wilfred shrank smaller and smaller, still wrapped in his clothes, until all Sam could see was the head of the black and fluffy dog struggling to get out of his school uniform. Wilfred yelped. 'I've shifted. I've shifted.' He put out a paw and stared at it. 'Sam, why can't I shift back?' he yapped, struggling inside the shirt.

Sam smelt the overwhelming odour of stale fairy dust and reached down to undo Wilfred's buttons.

As soon as he was free, Wilfred dashed up the stairs, his yap high and shaky. 'Hazel, Mr Kokoni, Dr Kokoni!'

No one answered.

'If we find Dr Kokoni, she might be able to tell me why I can't change,' the pup called from the top floor. 'She specialises in shifter medicine.'

77

'It's not medicine you need, Wilfred. It's fresh air. This place is filled with fairy dust. It's the dust that stopped Amira and her mum changing back on Saturday.'

Wilfred sprinted down the stairs and followed Sam to the kitchen door. Sam put his hand out, wanting to ward off what they might see in the next room. The pungent scent of dust was coming from there.

Wilfred laughed as if Sam had told him a fabulous joke.

'It's magic,' Sam said. 'Don't breathe too deeply.'

'What? No, it's …'

Sam clamped a hand over Wilfred's muzzle and opened the door. Even without a good nose, he'd have known that something was wrong.

Chairs at the dining table had been overturned, a pot on the stove had fallen to the tiles, spilling red sauce across the floor. It looked like blood against the blue-and-white pattern.

Wilfred, who had obediently held his breath, opened his mouth and gasped. Then he giggled. He couldn't help it, he wagged his tail and sniffed more of the stale fairy dust. The pup was giggly and excited. He rolled on the floor and when Sam reached for him, he darted to one side, wagging his tail.

'Throw me a ball, Sam. Throw me a ball.'

'We're here to find Hazel …' Sam started, but the puppy's bottom wriggled so wildly. 'Outside,' Sam said.

'Yeah, yeah,' Wilfred hustled.

At the threshold of the back door, Sam smelt the source of the dust. It was strong and pungent, and that was with the door wide open and the wind clearing as much as it could.

As soon as Sam had him away from the kitchen, in the middle of the back lawn in the sweet, fresh, magic-free air, Wilfred sat fluffy-bottomed on the grass and howled.

A cat in a tree a few gardens over swore loudly.

'What was all that? What was I doing?' Wilfred asked.

'Fairy dust,' Sam said. 'You just needed to be outside.'

'Fairy dust? Did you say that before?'

'It's magic. It'll muddy your thinking. It's what made you giggle. It's stale though, from last night.'

'Wow, if that's stale, what can the fresh stuff do?'

'An awful lot of damage,' Sam replied.

'It made me feel good, like I just wanted to float away.'

'You wait here, I need to look at the kitchen again. You shouldn't go in there though. It affects you more than it affects me.'

'Lift me to the window,' Wilfred said. 'I can help. I'm good at understanding what I see.'

Sam picked up the pup. It was an odd feeling, holding your new and (Sam had to admit) adorable friend in your arms. Wilfred licked his face.

Wilfred leaned his forepaws on the ledge and they both looked through the window.

Sam studied the scene. Two toppled chairs and a pot of spilt sauce. 'The Kokonis were frightened at some point, weren't they? The chairs – I guess if someone jumped up

79

they would have knocked over the chairs, right? And they would have jumped up if they were startled.'

'You might drop a pot of sauce if you were surprised too,' Wilfred agreed. 'That doesn't make sense because they must have let them in.'

Sam studied the houses on either side and the height of the fences. 'I don't think they did. The smell of fairy dust is strongest at the back door. I think someone showed up there.'

'That would alarm anyone, and whoever it was threw dust into the room. They wouldn't have time to respond. It's ... it's ...'

'Bewitching,' Sam suggested.

'Yeah, even now I feel a bit happy. Excited. I know I shouldn't. This is awful. It makes you feel good and you don't think much about anything.' Wilfred's ears pricked. 'It didn't affect you the same?'

'No, maybe because I'm part fairy.'

Wilfred sniffed at Sam's shoulder. 'Oh, yeah. It's stronger on you right now.'

'Maggie's been here. That's what that smell means. She's ... taken them, using magic. They would have just followed her wherever she wanted them to go.'

The dog tilted his head and lifted his ears. 'Who's Maggie?'

Sam told about his first meeting with Maggie, who'd attempted to use fairy dust to lure Nick away, which would have worked if Sam hadn't been there. He described her tiny tin of dust, and the hooded figure in The Lanes when he'd seen Amira in dog form.

'You've mentioned the ogres before, but never Maggie,' Wilfred said.

Sam pressed his lips together. He didn't know what to say about Maggie. He had no idea how he felt about her. He shook his head.

'That's OK. Is she behind all the kidnappings, do you think?'

Sam had a tumbling feeling. *Is she? What does she want with shifters?* And the worst thought of all. 'Is she taking them to get at me?'

'Sam, no. These disappearances are all over the place, and they've been going on for months.'

'How many months?'

'At least two, maybe three.' Wilfred licked Sam's face again. 'It's not you.'

Sam didn't say anything, but he'd brought Beatrice back three months earlier, not long after Thunderguts had been destroyed. Three months meant it was exactly the right time.

Wilfred howled. The cat in the tree a couple of back gardens over directed another swear word at Wilfred. 'I need to get out of here and tell Dad,' the pup said.

Sam carried Wilfred through the kitchen. Sam clamped the doggy mouth shut and didn't let go until he'd closed the kitchen door on the other side. Even then the pong of dust hung in the air and Wilfred's tail wagged of its own accord. Sam grabbed Wilfred's clothes, bustled the dog into the living room and opened the window to let air into the room. The smell of dust was weak in there, but it still needed airing. Sam waited in the hall, listening as Wilfred's series of yaps changed to *mmphs* and *akks*. Wilfred appeared, his hair falling smoothly and darkly around his ears.

'Well, come on, let's get to my house,' he said jauntily.

Sam was not looking forward to how bad Wilfred would feel about the situation when the dust totally left his system. Wilfred picked up his shoes and sat on the doorstep to put them on. Sam pulled the front door closed and sat down next to his friend.

A woman with an old-looking Labrador crossed from the other side of the street and held up a hand to wave at them. Wilfred waved back.

'Is she ... ?' Sam looked at the Labrador.

'Just a normal dog,' Wilfred replied. 'So don't mention the shifter thing. Remember Hoy Poy.'

The Labrador barked. She sounded old and cantankerous. 'Wilfred, get away from that ... boy.' She growled at Sam. 'And you get away from Wilfred. We don't want your type around here. This is a respectable neighbourhood.'

'Dora, Dora, calm down,' the woman said, rubbing a hanky under her nose. Her voice sounded throaty and sore. 'I'm so sorry, Wilfred, she's not normally like this.'

'Hi, Mrs Kelly,' Wilfred said, then bent down as if to pet the dog. 'Hey, Dora, he's OK. Sniff deeper.'

'Master Wilfred, he's not human,' Dora replied.

'Sniff deeper,' Wilfred repeated.

The dog stopped barking at Sam and sat down, her nose in the open air. 'Oh, I see what you mean. The wrong thing hits you first, but there's a lot of lovely things too.'

'I don't know how you do that,' the woman said to Wilfred. 'You and Hazel both have an uncanny ability to understand what's bothering Dora, and she seems to understand you too. Thank you for walking her yesterday afternoon. She does love it when Hazel and her friends take her out.'

'Have you seen Hazel or her family since yesterday, Mrs Kelly?'

'They still aren't back? Oh dear, that's why I came across. I saw you and thought they must be home. I've been knocking on their door since last night. Their dogs got into a car as I was walking by. A man was shoving them into his Mercedes. I told him, "Just because you're rich doesn't mean you can treat animals like that," and what did he think he was doing with the Kokonis' dogs? He said he'd bought them. Well, I didn't think Andreas and Chryssi would want such a rough man taking those sweet little dogs. I've visited three times to tell them, so maybe they could get them back, but no one's answering. I got worried, because the door's been unlocked all this time. I even went inside.' Mrs Kelly blushed to admit such rudeness.

Wilfred leaned on Sam. He shivered like a pug.

'What did he look like, Mrs Kelly?' Sam asked.

'Big, bulky. His coat was too heavy for the weather, I thought. And I swear he had yellow eyes.'

'Was there a woman in the car, Mrs Kelly?' Sam asked.

'Yes, lovely-looking she was too, and very smiley, quite different from that awful man. Big beast! I hope she's the one looking after the dogs. Do you know them?'

Wilfred shook his head. 'Did you see where were they going?'

'I'm sorry, Wilfred, no. Now I'm more worried about the Kokonis.'

Dora the dog trotted up the steps. 'Pat me,' she said. Wilfred did. Sam too. She looked at him. 'Does he understand me like you do?' Both boys nodded. 'I only remember seeing a beautiful lady. She smelt odd, really odd, a bit like him.' She pointed her nose at Sam. 'The smell that makes you feel good, but there was so much of it, and I couldn't stop wagging my tail. Mr Marks and his poodle, Zack, were there too, they live three houses down that way, and both of them seemed as dazed as me. When I saw Zack this morning, he said his tail was going ten to the dozen when that woman looked at him, but as soon as they walked around the corner Mr Marks had to sit down. Mr Marks told Zack he didn't know what had come over him, and the poodle had to guide his master home. My Joy has a cold, you see. I think whatever the smell was, it didn't work on her because her nose is blocked. She keeps telling people about a rough man, but I don't remember him. I would have bitten any man's leg if I'd seen him treat a dog the way Joy says he treated them.' The dog sighed, and the boys kept petting. 'I hope they're OK.'

'It's that man and your Maggie from The Lanes?' Wilfred asked Sam.

'I think so.' Sam looked at Dora. 'So you don't remember the man? He might have smelt odd.'

'I couldn't tell you a thing about him,' Dora replied. 'I

84

don't remember him, just the beautiful lady and the lovely smell. I'd have to trust Joy's description more than my own, and that's not usual.'

Mrs Kelly was still talking. '... and I hoped they'd be home again. I have a very bad feeling. So bad, I feel I need to call the police ...'

'You do that, Mrs Kelly,' Wilfred said.

'Do you think it will help?'

'I don't know.'

'I should get my Joy home,' the Labrador said. 'I think she's very upset now. She thought they'd be back all safe and sound. Hazel and her friends are the only children I ever let touch me, even before I knew you spoke Dog. Hazel's such a good girl and always makes sure she doesn't have sticky fingers. Just like you, Wilfred.'

'It's not nice having gunk in your fur,' Wilfred replied.

'You have such a lovely understanding of dogs, you children. Just lovely,' Dora said, and licked both boys' hands.

'Will you let me know if you find out anything, Wilfred?' Mrs Kelly said.

'Yes, Mrs Kelly, I promise.'

'Oh, good.' Mrs Kelly blew her nose again. Sam noticed the dark circles under her eyes and the wanness of her skin. She looked quite sick. She must have thought it was very important to come and check even though she felt so poorly. Sam thought her a very nice person indeed.

Dora led Mrs Kelly away.

Wilfred stood and when Sam copied him, the shifter

boy gave Sam a hug. 'I'm going home,' he said. Already the pleased flush of the fairy dust had faded and he looked tired. 'I have to tell Dad. He'll know what to do. He's with the authorities.' He studied Sam's face. 'I told you that already, didn't I?'

'Do you want me to come with you?' Sam asked.

'No, you go back to school. At least both of us don't need to be in trouble for bunking off.'

As soon as Wilfred was out of sight, Sam regretted it. That cold place in his stomach grew. Hazel and Amira were missing and Wilfred was alone. And Sam didn't have any of their phone numbers.

Not one shifter came to school the following day. None. And Sam had lots of classes scheduled with them. The receptionist wouldn't give Sam anyone's address or phone number. She insisted that if they were friends, he should have got their details from them. She wouldn't even tell him if they had called in sick. 'None of your business,' she said.

The other kids gave him pitying looks.

Sam tried to explain the problem to Nick without giving away too much. It didn't work. Explaining that a neighbour saw someone's dogs get into a stranger's car is not a problem to humans, unless someone reports them stolen, and there was no one left to report them.

Michelle said she was sad Sam's three new friends had all missed school so soon after he met them. 'There is a cold going around,' she added.

CHAPTER 9

At the end of Tuesday, Sam waited for Nick at the school entrance alone. He was in a rush to get home. The gargoyles had promised to do some detective work while he was at school. He'd managed to sign in late with a weak excuse the previous day, but he couldn't risk it another day. Children's Services would want to know why the Kavanaghs couldn't keep him at school. Other kids avoided looking at him, except for the few who asked about Wilfred. Was he sick too?

Sam wished Nick would hurry. Where was he?

'Sam.' It was Michelle's voice. She sat parked along the road, waving at him. The passenger door swung open and he climbed in, lobbing his bag on to the back seat.

She didn't ask him anything, and they drove home in silence.

He arrived home to find Nick stomping around the

kitchen, while Richard, who should have been at work, held him too long then sat at the table clutching the newspaper and watching Sam over the top. He stared and he sighed and his eyes dropped, but he didn't turn any pages or make frustrated grunts at articles he didn't like.

Sam's own eyes felt hot and prickly and his stomach knew something was wrong. 'Is everything OK?' Even though he couldn't read faces well, the weight of the air was enough. He had fallen into another well. On the outside nothing had changed, but somehow all the goodness had been sucked away into darkness. The shifters were gone, and something important had disappeared from his own home. He just didn't know what it was.

Richard smiled, but it didn't reach his eyes and he had that hard line above his nose. 'We're all here,' he said. 'Shall we talk somewhere more comfortable?'

'I've just got to ...' Michelle said, left the table and went into the bathroom. She was gone ten minutes. When she joined them in the front room, her eyes glowed too pink. Richard reached out and pulled Sam to him, touched him on the shoulder, while Nick studied his feet, glared at his toes and kicked the coffee-table leg. Only Beatrice sent her normal tangle of stars at Sam and threw sparkles in his direction.

Sam felt like he was back at the court again.

'Well, go on. Tell him,' Nick said into the aching silence.

Richard coughed, and Michelle blurted out, 'They've found your real dad, Sam. He wants to meet you.'

Then Michelle checked Beatrice's nappy as if it had gold inside it.

'No!' Sam said. 'I don't have any other family besides you.'

Nick smiled for the first time since Sam had got home and gave an abrupt nod. 'Right.'

'There's been a mistake,' Sam said.

'No mistake, Sam. He described you perfectly,' Richard said.

'No, no, no! Just no!' Sam said. He couldn't think of anything else to say. Then it hit him. 'It must just be some man who *thinks* I'm his son. It'll be so sad for him when he realises I'm not.'

'Well, Mrs Petersen is coming tomorrow to talk to you about it,' Richard said.

'Do we really have to do this? I've got so much ...' Sam needed to see the gargoyles. He didn't have time for this, so he rushed up to his room. It was too light; the gargoyles still weren't home.

Downstairs, he heard Nick say, 'See, I told you. He's not happy either.'

'He may meet him and remember,' Michelle said. 'And then ...' She wept.

When Michelle came to him later, he pretended to be asleep and she tucked him in the way she tucked in Beatrice, pushing the blankets under him so he was safe and snug. She kissed him, her warm lips lingering on the ticklish place above his eyebrow.

After Michelle left, Sam got up and went to the window. He waited two hours before the trio of grey faces appeared. They remained quiet as they clambered inside.

'Anything?' he asked.

'The smells seem to come from the east, that's all we can establish, but they're distant. We would need a vehicle to get there. Otherwise it'll take us weeks,' Bladder said.

'We can only travel at night. If we go hunting them, we'll get seen,' Wheedle added.

Spigot squawked.

He told them about his 'father'.

The grey faces paled.

Bladder scratched his chin. 'D'you think Maggie's behind this too?'

'Nope, nope, nope,' Wheedle said. 'Why use a human system to get at him? It don't make sense. She'd just steal him. I think you're right, Sam, it's just a mix-up.'

Still, the healthier grey of their gravelly complexions did not return.

They didn't leave. The gargoyles peered about, sat on the floor and formed a guard around Sam. His eyes closing, Sam watched them solidify into statues as Bladder's head rested on the foot of Sam's bed.

Sam didn't sleep straight away. He wondered if Maggie had bewitched some poor man into finding him, maybe the poor man in the pet shop. It was something she would do. As he thought, he became more sure it was her. They were safe from her in the house, but she was behind the shifters' disappearance and the sudden misery that had fallen on his home.

Sam got up early the next morning. He kissed each of the gargoyles and headed downstairs. The house was so quiet, so very still, that he was astonished to find Richard sitting at the kitchen table. Sam grabbed a piece of dry bread and moved for the door. His stomach seemed intent on the idea that it would feel much, much better if it got outside and took the rest of him with it.

'Why don't you stay in and have breakfast with us?' Richard asked. 'Come on. Pancakes. You like pancakes.'

'In the middle of the week?'

Sam smelt fear on Richard. The house smelt of it, like the Great Cavern smelt of ogre paddies and brownie tears.

Sam's insides chilled. *What if they* wanted *to give him up? What if it was that they ... ?*

But pancakes. Daniel said pancakes were a sign of love.

Sam sat. Michelle came in and cooked the pancakes, a special treat, although darkness ringed her eyes as if she peered at him from a dim burrow. When Sam had returned home from The Hole a few months before, carrying Beatrice in his arms, her eyes had looked like that, like she was close to dropping into The Hole herself and never returning, like she hadn't slept in a long, long time.

'Mrs Petersen is coming today,' Michelle said.

'I'm staying home too,' said Nick.

Richard shook his head, and Nick scowled. He got up and clattered his bowl into the sink. Sam heard something crack. 'Better get ready to leave then. Obviously, nobody here can do anything but get ready to leave.'

'I'd rather go to school,' Sam said.

Michelle shook her head. 'Not today, Sam.'

'I'll get dressed, shall I?' Nick stamped to the stairs.

Sam followed Nick to the bottom of the stairs and the older boy pulled him into a bear hug. He kissed Sam's head, the way Michelle or Richard kissed him. Sam hadn't thought Nick would ever do that, not even in private. Nick clambered up the stairs as if wounded. 'It is all a mistake, right?' Nick asked.

'Yes,' Sam replied.

Nick's tread was a little lighter as he walked to his room.

Sam sat at the bottom of the stairs, Nick came down again and Richard appeared from the kitchen. They arrived at the same time. Nick moped red-eyed and glaring; Richard clapped a hand on his shoulder. 'This is not goodbye, you know. Even if it does turn out to be his dad, we'll do whatever we can to see Sam as often as possible. Right?'

Nick grunted. 'I've got a test today,' he said.

'Nick!'

'Sorry.' Nick scowled.

'It'll be all right,' Michelle said, appearing behind Richard.

Nick hugged Sam and pecked his mum on the cheek. Sam took out his pad and wrote 'significance of excessive hugging?' He would ask Daniel about it if the angel came back soon. Blow! Daniel wouldn't be back for ages, not until he could move through walls again.

Sam followed Nick out of the house and looked up at the softly glowing warding on the walls. Three sigils stood side by side: 'unsmellability to unwanted monsters', a general warding against 'supernaturals', so Maggie and her lot couldn't find him, and the third one, waxing and waning like a beating heart, a simple 'blessing', which Daniel had put up to cover them all. All three shone.

It'll be all right. It will be all right!

Nick peered over his shoulder several times before he turned up the street towards school.

Sam went back to his room; he didn't feel so good.

Michelle snuffled and clicked away downstairs. Sam recognised the system of taps and tones as the sound of messaging on a phone. She would be texting a friend, or Great-Aunt Colleen. Someone. The phone bipped out its replies.

He looked at the digital clock and sighed. Nick would have arrived at school.

Sam rushed down when he heard the feet coming up the outdoor steps.

Michelle and Richard moved with him to the door as the bell rang. It was 9:30 a.m. They exhaled in unison and Michelle unclicked the lock.

'Hello, Mrs Petersen', Michelle said to the woman outside.

'Mr and Mrs Kavanagh', Mrs Petersen replied. 'Sam.'

Sam smiled at her as well as he could. He tried to remember that Mrs Petersen had always been nice to him.

* * *

Sam did not like meeting in the front room. For a start, Mrs Petersen sat in his favourite place in the middle of the couch. The place where he sat between Richard and Nick. His spot. His belly tightened, he didn't want her there. This was the 'Relaxing Family-time Room', not the 'Terrified Kavanaghs' Space'.

Mrs Petersen had dark skin, and deep-brown eyes and hair. She wasn't frowning. In fact, she smiled, as if she had good news for him.

'Come and sit down, Samuel,' she said. 'You've been told, I suppose?'

Sam turned and saw Michelle's face pale underneath her pink blush. Richard rubbed his hands like he was scrubbing grime.

'How did he react?' Mrs Petersen asked Michelle and Richard.

'He thinks the gentleman who says he's Sam's father is wrong,' Richard said.

'Is that right, Sam?' Mrs Petersen asked.

'I'm positive.'

Mrs Petersen opened her folder. 'Your father's name is Edward Samuel Woermann.' She studied Sam's face, waiting for some reaction. 'Your name is Samuel Woermann.'

'No, it's not,' Sam replied. 'I'm really sure it's not.'

'I have all his paperwork. I've seen photos of you when you were much younger.'

Sam smiled. It was definitely a mistake. 'There aren't any photos of me when I was younger.'

'Is that right, Sam?' Mrs Petersen asked. 'Because you're only a few months old? Because you're half monster?'

Sam knew Mrs Petersen hadn't believed a word of what he'd said, but he wasn't a liar. 'That's right.'

'We expected you might feel that way, but he seems to know you intimately. When we talked about your... memories, he described what you might say perfectly. He said it was a book he had read to you, when you were very little. You loved it. It was your "safe" book, he said. He told us things we only know between us, Sam. About the pixies and leprechauns. The ... what did you call it? ... the Vorpal Sword. Things that haven't made the papers. Your memories are...' Mrs Petersen paused and looked at her page. She didn't finish. He'd heard the counsellors use the phrase 'false memories'.

Mrs Petersen smelt of fairy dust and this man had built a whole rat king of lies. Who was he? If it was Maggie who wanted him, surely they'd be talking about his real *mother*?

'Nope. He's lying.'

She didn't argue. She looked at Richard and Michelle. Neither of them spoke. Michelle stared at her hands while Richard continued to dry-scrub his.

Mrs Petersen continued, 'I know this is hard for you. The service advised your father against seeing you today, he was desperate to come. If he'd known where you lived he'd have been here days ago. He really wants to see you.'

Samuel shrugged.

'Maybe if you met him, it'd bring some memories back,' Richard said.

Sam looked at Richard's face. He looked twenty years older. Sam breathed in. Richard wasn't any happier about it than Sam was himself. At least there was that.

Sam thought hard. 'The memories you want me to have. What if they never come back? The Kavanaghs are the only family I remember. Will you make me go and live with this man? Even the court said I had a say in staying here.'

'We will always take your wishes into consideration.'

Sam exhaled. It didn't matter what this man said – he could convince everyone else that he was Sam's dad, but that didn't mean anything if Sam didn't want to live with him.

'Even if he were my father, I still don't have to go with him if I don't want to, right?' Sam asked. 'I'm not saying he is, I just want to know what I'm allowed to do.'

'You are likely to change your mind, Sam.'

Michelle and Richard looked grey as gargoyles.

'The service recommended that your father give you time to adapt to the news, or maybe remember ...' Again, the sentence ended with a questioning note.

Michelle and Richard stared at the coffee table, waiting for it to contribute something to the conversation. The light outside on the street got dark as the talking stuttered and stalled. No one got up to turn on the light. Sam looked outside to see the sky had grown heavy and grey.

Richard said, 'They can't just take him away from us?'

Michelle turned her head back and forth. 'No. She said Sam has a say, and we have adopted him.'

'That's right, we do only what Sam wants and at Sam's pace. His father promises to take it gently, meet with Sam in your company. Maybe see if anything jogs his memory. We've explained the sensitive nature of Sam's condition.' Mrs Petersen turned to Sam. 'Your dad asked lots of questions about what you said about yourself.'

'I bet he did,' Sam said.

Mrs Petersen turned to Richard and Michelle. 'You might be able to argue for shared custody. The court would take Sam's wishes into account,' Mrs Petersen said.

Beatrice writhed in Michelle's grip and reached for Sam. Michelle handed the baby to him. She settled against his chest, all her sparkles covering him, wrapping around him in a shiny blanket. She knew something was wrong with Sam.

'You have no memory of your life before, do you, Sam?' Mrs Petersen asked.

Sam opened his mouth and no words would come. When he told them the truth, that he was monster born, that he was about four months old, not one of them believed him. Even the Kavanaghs saw it as his coping mechanism. Mrs Petersen knew what he would say already; it was in a notebook somewhere in one of the offices, probably entitled 'Why Sam Won't Ever Fit In'.

He decided on: 'I don't want to go.'

Mrs Petersen didn't leave without fixing an appointment with Woermann. At Sam's leisure, she had said, although, when Sam stated 'Never', she had answered, 'Tomorrow, then?' Michelle had suggested a place, and all Sam could think was that it was a cafe he liked and he didn't want this strange man knowing where he went with his family.

Around three thirty, he heard Nick's shuffling feet stagger up the steps. Sam raced down the stairs to meet him. Nick dumped his bag and, with a high cry, grabbed Sam and shook him back and forth.

At bedtime, each one of them came in kissed him and hugged him, kissed him and hugged him again. Nick rocked him in his arms as if Sam were Beatrice and needed extra soothing after a fit of crying. Sam did not cry; he was sure it would be OK. He had the final say.

The paper church angels covered his walls. He was watched over. Daniel would be back sometime.

Sam hoped it would all be OK.

CHAPTER 10

When the phone rang, it was Mrs Petersen setting up details about how to ruin their lives, so though everyone was trying to be nice and loving, every action felt soured. Every moment they had together was sucked of pleasure and conversation and energy.

Sam felt doubly lousy. He was so distracted by the impending, implacable arrival of 'Dad' that he found it hard to focus on the other problem: how to find Wilfred, Amira and Hazel. He didn't even know how to start doing anything. 'East' was vague information, and he couldn't ask Michelle to drive him and three gargoyles in some random direction looking for bewitched dogs.

Sam sat on the rooftop watching his street. He had rubbed Daniel's sigils for luck before he hit the tiles, reminding himself that it would work out. He kept coming back to Maggie, her red hair, her pale skin, wishing he could see her, wishing he never had to see her again. The light dust smell on Mrs Petersen might have meant Maggie was behind it all, but he had smelt a lot of fairy dust lately.

Wheedle put his head on Sam's lap. 'It'll be OK, kid, it will.'

'I just don't have time for this. I should be at school. I should be figuring out where Wilfred, Amira and Hazel have been taken.'

'Enough time for that later,' Bladder said, swishing his grey lion tail and making a nasty noise on the tiles.

Someone was having a barbecue, despite the overcast day, a brave soul taking an opportunity to enjoy the last rain-free weather.

'I like it when they eat outside, it smells nice,' Wheedle said.

'You know they're eating cow, don't you?' Bladder asked. 'Steak, rump, diced, a nice bit of roast.' He prodded Wheedle's shoulder. 'From about here.'

'I like the smell of the pudding too.'

'Come on, Sam, give us a happy face,' Bladder said. 'Whoever he is, he can't take you, you know. I will pummel anyone, then I'll bite them, then I'll ...' Bladder stopped. 'It can't be Maggie – she can be a crone, she can be beautiful, but she can't be a man. And she wouldn't send anyone else. It's not like her.'

Wheedle winced. 'You don't think it's that man she was with the other day?'

'Nope. Nope. Definitely not. It don't make sense, her doing that. He's human, for goodness sake,' Bladder said.

'But even if it is, what can he do against Wing-Nut's sigils, hey? She's panicking, I say. It's a last-ditch effort.'

Wheedle nodded his head with enthusiasm as Sam hung his. 'It'll blow over and you'll be back to normal,' Wheedle added. 'I think you're right, it's definitely that big man and Maggie up to something, but don't you worry, everyone's got you covered.'

'We will always be here for you, you know?' Bladder said.

Sam gave his best smile, but it felt crooked. Then he climbed down the building face first.

He flipped off the wall; one twist over and his feet landed on the floor of his bedroom.

'Sam?' a voice called. Sam looked out of his window. Nick stood on the footpath, his mouth so open Sam could throw a ball into it.

'How ... ?' Nick said. 'I was looking for you.' He screwed up his eyes, rubbed them and stared again. 'You were climbing. On the wall. Upside down.'

Sam nodded.

'Are you some kind of circus performer?'

'No.'

Nick had gone an awful colour.

'Please, don't tell Michelle and Richard.'

Nick's expression cleared. 'You know, it wouldn't matter to them, Sam. Mum and Dad are always gonna want you with us, no matter what. I know you're really different, but you're really great too.' Nick stuck out his chin. 'And I want you to stay too. Me too.'

* * *

A trollish wind bit deeper as the Kavanaghs trudged to the cafe door. Sam normally loved the seaside, but not today. The wind moaned and whipped past them, circling Nick, who gazed out to the broken remnants of the rusted West Pier. Sam looked up to encouraging grey gargoyle faces peering over the balustrade above the shopfront.

Nick struggled behind Sam; he hadn't spoken for hours. He looked like someone had pinched his nose, making his eyes water and his face pale. Sam smiled at him and Nick strained out a smile in return. *Thin-lipped*, Sam thought, *watch those thin lips*. They meant the smile wasn't a happy one. Nick kept opening his mouth, as if to ask a question. It never came out. Michelle and Richard stared at both quiet boys, patting and grabbing their shoulders to comfort them.

'I'm going crazy,' Nick said outside the cafe.

'Aren't we all?' Richard agreed. He opened the cafe door.

'Two more minutes,' Sam said to them.

'Don't go anywhere,' Michelle replied.

Sam moved to the corner of the building, his back to the window so that they could all see him through the glass front. His three grey friends scurried down the side of the building and huddled in the tight alley. Spigot moved to a post on the fence next door, guarding them, upright and motionless. Bladder and Wheedle grinned at him.

'I'm glad you made it,' Sam said.

'Wouldn't miss it, lovely boy,' Wheedle said. 'Like I've said before, "pack looks after pack".'

Spigot shrieked from his post.

'So true,' Bladder said. 'I can smell your family's misery for miles. Tell 'em, don't worry, we're here.'

Spigot shrieked again.

'Yeah, agreed. Maybe not.'

'Incoming,' hissed Wheedle. Sam leaned on the wall and they solidified as a couple with a slick metallic pram walked by talking in low, angry voices. They turned on to the next street.

Richard tapped on the window. Sam looked over his shoulder. All four Kavanaghs watched him. Nick pointed to a blue mug and a plate with something brown on it. 'I better go in,' Sam said to the gargoyles.

'We'll be watching,' Bladder said.

Wheedle winked at him and the gargoyles clambered back to the roof.

Sam turned to the cafe door and sighed again.

The Kavanaghs huddled over the table and waited behind a window laced with salt residue.

Sam sat down and watched the marshmallows in his hot chocolate rock back and forth. They made him seasick and the hot chocolate wasn't as good as Richard's.

The Kavanaghs had a stilted conversation about biscuits and coffee, about school and holidays, about everything except why they were in the cafe. Richard watched the street more than his family's faces, and often gave the wrong answers to questions.

Michelle patted Richard's arm.

Sam smelt a familiar stink of animal overconfidence even the sea breeze couldn't smother. Another smell floated in with it, a sour, frightened scent. Then something that tickled his nose, just under the smell of perfume. He recognised the first and last scents and narrowed his eyes as Mrs Petersen and a man entered the cafe.

Sam felt a burning in his throat as the hot chocolate and the muffin clogged his mouth. Every part of his body wanted to run, wanted to flee the cafe. He could not believe it, but here was Maggie's henchman sent to get him.

As if she read his mind, Michelle reached for his hand under the table.

The big man was still wearing the bulky coat. This time it looked right, with the bitter wind trying to freeze everyone. He had a plaster over a lump on his head. Wheedle had certainly given him a nasty bump, but his lumbering arrogance had not diminished. His gaze darted around the room, probably looking for gargoyles.

'Edward Woermann,' Mrs Petersen said. 'These are the Kavanaghs. You know Samuel.'

Woermann slumped his shoulders. He studied the mottled brown carpet beneath the cafe tables, and his glance darted to Sam and then went back to his concerted analysis of the pattern under his feet. Sam wanted to be sick. Woermann was pretending to be shy and nervous. He rubbed one dry eye with hairy knuckles. Mrs Petersen patted his arm and Sam smelt more stinking arrogance come off him.

The big man licked his flubbery lips and put a hand

on his chest under his furry chin. 'There you are, my son. You've got no idea how I missed you,' he said, then dabbed again at his left eye. He reached his dirty hand towards Sam.

Sam shook his head. 'I'm not your son.'

'Hush, hush,' Mrs Petersen said as she pulled a chair up at the table, forcing the Kavanaghs to form an even tighter knot. Sam peered at Mrs Petersen. Her eyes focused beyond them and she smelt of fairy dust. 'Edward knows an awful lot about you, Sam,' she said cheerfully. 'Even down to your active imagination. He said you've been like it all your life. It's so wonderful that you're finally back together. You know, he even described the stories you two used to make up. They're all in your folder. He discussed Maggie and Thunderguts too. It was a book he read to you when you were little.'

Sam felt cold. Who could have told him about Thunderguts except Maggie?

'He's not my father.'

Mrs Petersen nodded and sighed. 'Oh, Sam, you must admit this is a good thing.'

Michelle's hand tightened, squeezing Sam's.

'I have been looking for you for ages, Sam,' Woermann said. 'Please.' He reached out his huge arms. Sam recoiled and noticed hair pushing out from the cuffs of Woermann's coat. 'I won't make you come and live with me, if you don't want to.' He smiled warmly at Richard. 'But maybe you would visit my house. I rented nearby, so if it is too difficult for you right now, I'll be close by. We'll do everything the way you want.' His voice was soft and purring. Greasy. Sam remembered his brutish yells in The Lanes.

What did Woermann think he could get Sam to do?

Michelle nodded. She seemed to believe Woermann. 'We just want to be able to see him. If you don't take him too far away ...'

'Of course, dear lady.' He grabbed her hand in both of his, dwarfing her delicate fingers in his filthy paws. He smiled at Sam, arrogance stinking off him. Sam stared at their hands together and hated that the brute was touching her.

'What happened?' Richard asked. Sam turned to look at Richard; his voice had taken on a nasally quality and sounded deeper than normal. He didn't normally speak like that. Nick sneezed.

'His mother took him to see his grandparents for a couple of weeks. A surprise visit.' Woermann stared out at the wind blowing a paper past the window and wiped at his eyes. *Was no one else seeing how dry they were?* 'She just packed Sam and herself into the Mini Minor and disappeared. I was out fishing. I got no phone calls for a couple of days, I thought she was busy. No answer, I called my in-laws, but it was a surprise visit so they weren't expecting her and ... I'd heard nothing from her. I hired private detectives.' Woermann looked at his hands, his knuckles cracking as he rubbed them. He pulled his mouth down into a frown, but Sam saw a smirk. He was a moment from laughing at them all. 'We found Grace a week later, she had been signed in to the hospital, but there had been no sign of Sam when paramedics got to the car. She'd lasted thirty-six hours all alone, none of us to hold her hand as she slipped away. I'm lost without her, and I'm half a man without my son.'

Woermann faked a sob and reached across the table. Sam managed to move his hand out of the way, knocking over the remnants of his hot chocolate and painting the front of Michelle's coat and sweater. She jumped up and patted herself with a disintegrating napkin.

'Please.' Woermann caught Sam's arm. Sam looked down to see the hairy arm and the long, scraggly nails holding him in a rocky grip. He remembered the ogre's arm reaching through the church door with the same look of Stone Age strength. 'Look, please, just give me five minutes of your time. I can see you still don't remember me, but if we talk I think you'll recall something. Maybe not me. Maybe your mother?' Woermann put his head into his hairy hands and fake-sobbed again. Mrs Petersen patted his back. Even Richard and Michelle looked teary. Sam rolled his eyes and realised Nick was watching him. Nick gave a questioning frown. Sam shook his head.

'Just listen to the man, Sam,' Mrs Petersen said. 'Maybe spending time with your father will bring back those memories.'

Sam shook his head. 'Nope. You said I don't have to do anything I don't want to.'

'That's right, Sam,' Mrs Petersen said. 'But talking shouldn't hurt ...'

'Maybe seeing me ... maybe I remind you of your

mother too much, what happened to her. The doctors said that's why you might refuse to remember me, but what about your dogs? You loved your dogs. And they love you. I don't know how much longer they can live without you.'

'My dogs?' Sam asked.

'I didn't know you liked dogs,' Richard said. Michelle stared at him. Richard's sob did not sound faked. Nick glared at Woermann across the table.

'Here.' Woermann pulled out a photograph and handed it to Sam.

Sam didn't want to take it, the edges might be poisonous, but he looked at the picture anyway. In the photo, Woermann had one burly arm around three dogs. Two miserable soft-furred pups lying prone on a rug, one beige, one black. They were listless and close mouthed. The lankier dog sat up, misery all over the love-heart face.

'It's them! You've got them all!' Sam said. He realised his mistake too late.

'Yes! Yes!' Woermann said. 'Purebred pups. I brought them with me. They're just waiting at the house. For you.'

'You recognise your dogs, then?' Mrs Petersen said.

Nick yelled something incomprehensible.

'I need time with you by myself. Just five minutes,' Woermann said.

Sam folded his arms. 'No.'

'Just give me five minutes to explain, please. Michelle and Richard will understand. A father will do anything to be with his son.'

Richard nodded. 'You don't have to be so loyal to us;

you need to spend some time with your ... Mr Woermann.'
He grimaced.

'Go on,' Michelle said. She must have splashed coffee on her face; she dabbed at her cheeks with her napkin. As they got up, she grabbed Sam's arm. 'It doesn't matter what you choose, I love you. But if he is your real family ...' She dabbed her eyes again.

Woermann opened the door and wrapped his own scarf around Sam's neck. It smelt vile. He steered Sam back out into the grey day.

Woermann's stifling breath swirled over his shoulder. Sam turned and looked back inside. Each Kavanagh face peered through the window at him. Muscles in their faces pulled at their eyes and mouths. His heart felt as cold as the wind off the Channel. His own face had looked similar in the mirror that morning. Then Michelle smiled, a thin toothless smile. Woermann smiled back at them all and Nick flinched.

Sam looked up. The gargoyles glared at Woermann from the roof. Wheedle mimed a karate chop. Sam shook his head.

Woermann steered Sam on to the footpath. A low lion's growl carried down. Woermann stopped and shuddered, but his heavy hairy hand rested on Sam's arm. 'We'll stay where everyone can see us.'

Sam stared across to the beach, the unsettled water throwing itself on the pebbled shore. The wind left the seashore crowd free; the only people Sam could see had wrapped themselves in their coats and jackets, hunching as if it would keep the cold away. They rushed past, not paying any attention to the man and boy standing on the footpath under a sky bleached to a bland shade of grey-green.

'All right, boy, just play along.' Woermann smiled sadly at the cafe window. 'Nice little catch-up we're having here.'

'What do you want with me?'

Woermann frowned. 'Not me that wants you. It's my queen'd do anything to have you. I'm just curious what makes you so valuable? In the end, it doesn't matter to me, as long as I get paid. You know, I've been selling on those shifters to raise a bit extra, but nabbing you will make me a man of means. I'm rich.'

'Queen Maggie? Is that what she's calling herself these days?'

'She's got a hundred names. I call her whatever she tells me to. She's paying the bills.'

Sam looked up to the gargoyles. Bladder was biting the air and nodding at Sam. Then he looked at his Kavanaghs and their innocent sad faces. 'What does Maggie want me for? What does she want the others for?'

'She's says you're necessary to win the coming war.'

'War?' Sam remembered Thunderguts wanting to be free of The Hole, to take over the human world again. 'Do you understand what that means? How bad it could get? Even for you.'

'Dunno. Not my problem, I just gotta make sure you come with me, then I get paid.'

'I'm not going with you.'

'I think you are. I saw your face when you looked at those pups. What will happen to them if you don't protect them, do you think?'

Woermann opened his coat and pulled out a plastic bag with a thin grey blanket inside it. Even before he opened it, Sam could smell the heavy scent of shifter dog urine pumped with the biting smell of fear. The overpowering stink of helplessness poured out and stung his nose as Woermann popped the seal. It was fresh and it was Amira's; Sam could see in his head the story the smell told. She'd been chased in her puppy form, cornered, huddled on this piece of cloth, panicking. As someone with large hands reached for her, she peed.

'You'll go. That's if you want your shifter friends to survive the night. You'll be nice and friendly now, won't you?' Woermann put a hand on Sam's shoulder and pushed sharp nails through his jacket into the skin. 'Now, just nod, because you're coming home with me, lad. Those pups are waiting desperately for you. As is the queen. You're worth your weight in gold.'

'Is that what you were doing in The Lanes?' Sam asked. 'Setting a trap for me?'

Woermann chuckled. 'Not you. We set the trap to locate the shifters' safe house. Those dogs did exactly what I wanted and I caught about three different kinds of shifters in one haul. You were just a bonus; you should have seen my customer when she spotted you. You are the greatest prize of all. I smell out the shifters, she sets up the stings, gets the dust working, so to speak, but I do all the grunt work. I sniffed a few all the way to Brighton, and she shows up and says she's noticed something special about the air here. I guess that was you. She talks about you like you're a little prince,' Woermann said. 'I lost you on the first round, but I managed to catch the others at the safe house. They always pick houses at crosswinds, carries the scent away, but we just followed the dust and your little friend gave herself up by asking if you were OK. If she was worried about you, we figured out you would be worried about her. And, wham! The trap snaps. I used her scent to track down your other friends too. After you get one, it's like fishing in a barrel. They all stick together, and Her Maj chucks one handful of dust and they come willingly.'

Sam sniffed deeper. Up close, he realised that wretched scent Woermann gave off wasn't human. Woermann smelt like a wild animal. 'What are you? Are you a shifter?' Sam asked. 'Are you catching your own kind?'

'Not me. I am very human. I just had a little accident a few years back and it's caused me a few changes. Nothing I can't handle.'

'You're a 'thrope?'

'Oh, you *are* informed, aren't you! So we know what your friends are, and we know what I am. What are you? You're not a shifter, not a fairy? I sniffed that on you at The Lanes, but you've some kind of magic on you. Are you a magic 'thrope? That's my guess. You were with those animal statues. You're on the nose, as it were. I'm thinking you all escaped from Faeryland an' she wants you back. You her special pet?'

Woermann tapped a gnarly-nailed finger on the side of his nostril. Sam realised he could see thick, fair hairs growing from the bridge of the big man's nose. His eyebrows were one broad line, without even thinning at the middle. Bladder had walked down the wall towards them. 'Oh, you brought them. If I get another lump, I'll give ten times to your little chums, remember that.' Woermann stood up straight and saluted Bladder, who started down the wall at him. Sam shook his head and saw the confusion on Bladder's face. 'Shame the dust doesn't work on you. Got Rashmi on a string with fairy dust.' Woermann smiled at Mrs Petersen through the window and gave her a little wave. 'I love that stuff, although if I smell too much it does strange things to me too. But not you. Not you.'

Sam knew if he spoke it would be to tell the gargoyles to pummel the man, but Amira's fear sat thickly in his nose. He couldn't risk her getting hurt, so he said nothing.

Woermann chuckled. 'Well, this has been nice; shall we go back to the cafe? Now, you're going to agree to come home with me. You'll be safe enough. You're precious.' Woermann resealed the bag, the wind stole Amira's smell and it faded to nothing again as Woermann tucked the bag into his coat. 'I think you're smart enough to understand what I can do if I don't get your agreement. Normally, I sell the dogs afterwards, gives me a little bit of cash, you got no idea what you can ask for a purebred pup, but if you don't do as I tell you, I'll dispose of them one by one, drown them in a hessian sack like days of yore. It happens every day. Maybe you'll choose to stay where you are, but that's a lot of lives on you.'

'I'll tell.'

Woermann chuckled again. 'And who would believe you?'

Sam felt the colour leave his face. The wind nipped at his nose. His ears hurt.

Finally, he nodded.

'Good lad.' Woermann took him in a bear hug. 'My boy. I missed you so much. It's so good to know you remember me.'

From behind the dull glass of the cafe, Nick's white face peered out.

CHAPTER 11

Michelle said nothing as she packed Sam's bag. She folded clothes with slow-moving wrists and lethargic hands and put them into an old black case.

'Will you want your posters too?' she asked.

'It's just for two weeks. I'll be back,' Sam said. 'Just to see whether ...' Sam didn't know what to say; any excuse would be a lie. He couldn't look at her when he spoke. He wanted to stay, he never wanted to leave Michelle, Richard, Nick or Beatrice. He didn't want to be away from the house for one moment, unless he was where one of them was. He couldn't say that.

If Daniel were here, he would put a hand on each of them and let them know it was all right; but Daniel wasn't there, only Sam.

I'm pathetic. What good am I to them?

Sam thought of Woermann's triumphant stink. Even

without the puppy wee wrapped under his coat, the man was stale and dusty. His coat smelt of other creatures' dread. Sam had no idea where Woermann would take him, but he was sure there'd be no nice room of his own with sweet-smelling sheets, the lingering scent of Michelle's perfume in the air, or Richard's musky underarm deodorant and Nick's even muskier underarms.

Sam stared at his posters, at the angel brooding over a gravesite, the one that most reminded him of Daniel.

'Do you want to take your posters?' Michelle's voice cracked a little at the end. Did she realise she'd already asked that?

Sam shook his head. Vigorously. If he took his posters it would no longer be his room. Maybe they would turn it into an office or a storage room for their other things. It had been something like that before he'd arrived. They'd had an attic conversion so they could store all the bumf and clutter away and give Sam his own space. He would find some way to come back. He would! And he wanted his room to be here waiting for him, complete with angels and gargoyles.

'No, I'd like them to stay.'

He put his hands on Michelle's as they fussed at folding pairs of socks. She looked up and smiled. 'I'm happy you found your real dad. He's ... he's your family. We only wanted you to be happy, you know. We would never keep you where you didn't belong.'

I *belong with you*, Sam could have said, but he needed to do something else too. He needed to make sure Hazel,

Wilfred and Amira were safe. They were friends, and friends were a type of family. He pondered how his family continued to grow: Daniel, Bladder, Wheedle, Spigot, Hazel, Wilfred, Amira. Kavanaghs.

The three gargoyles crowded Sam's window.

'You can't go,' Bladder said. 'We'll wait for Daniel to get back and he can fetch your shifters.'

Sam wished it were that easy. 'I don't know how long he'll be. He could be back in months, maybe years.'

'How long did he say last time you saw him?' Wheedle asked.

'He didn't. But what if I don't go and Woermann hurts the shifters? What in the world does Maggie want them for? And what if Daniel comes back today and still can't get through walls? I can't rely on him.'

Wheedle thrust his nose to Sam's. 'You don't need Daniel. Let us get this Woermann. We can do something about all this. You can't go with him – if you do, you're just delivering yourself into Maggie's hands. I know you love your new pack ...' He trailed off and sighed. He shook his head. 'You have to, don't you? Pack looks after pack.'

Sam stroked Wheedle's head.

Bladder muttered something.

'Say again,' Wheedle said.

'I said, we could kill him for you, if you like,' Bladder snarled. It made all of them jump. Bladder's eyes darkened to onyx black. 'I will track you both down, I will, and I will never be far behind you. Never, Sam. I will stick to you like mortar to bricks.'

Spigot shrilled.

'We all will,' Wheedle said.

'Sam?' Michelle said from the door. 'Are you all right?'

Sam shooed the gargoyles out of the window. 'Come in,' he said.

Michelle put her head around the door. 'I just wondered ... you're in here by yourself and ...' She peered at him, then closed her eyes as if to shut out a painful thought.

'Shall I come downstairs for a snack?' Sam offered.

Michelle studied Sam's face across the table. 'If you aren't happy there, if you want to come home ... you know we would fight for you. And the service says you have a say.'

'You just have to tell them what you want,' Richard said.

'You don't look any happier about this than we are,' Nick said.

'Nick!' Michelle said as Sam muffled his misery in her jumper.

Then Richard pulled him to his neck and held him as tightly as he could.

After too short a time in the hug, Sam pulled back. 'I have to go.'

'Even if he is your real father, you can stay with us. The court ...' Michelle started.

'Michelle, he's got to do what's right for him.' Richard spoke a little higher than usual.

Sam shook his head. For Hazel, Wilfred and Amira and the other shifters Woermann had locked away, Sam had to go. Michelle must have seen the resolve in his face. She stopped talking.

Although Nick was in Sam's room, he stayed back, leaning against the wall, clenching and unclenching his fists. *He's angry with me*, Sam thought. He was fascinated by how easy it was getting to read them.

'Two weeks. I'll call you as often as I can.' Sam held up the mobile.

'You know how to use it, right?' Nick asked. 'You got the charger?'

The boys laughed a little and both studied each other in the quiet room. When the knocker on the front door rapped it made them jump.

'Mrs Petersen's here,' Sam said.

Sam, Richard and Michelle descended the steps with slow, heavy tread. Nick waited at the foot of the stairs, swaying and kicking at invisible footballs on the carpet.

Beatrice slept in her cot above them. Sam wished she'd been awake for him to say goodbye. She was the opposite of everything he was going to: light, sweet, miraculous.

Richard opened the door. Mrs Petersen stood on the doorstep.

Sam lugged his black case down the steps past her.

'We'd like visitation rights, please?' Michelle said.

'I'm sure that will all be sorted out. Just give Sam two weeks with Edward, and we'll revise this in two weeks according to Sam's wishes,' Mrs Petersen said.

'His school?' Michelle asked. 'No one said anything about school.'

'I will liaise with them for work. Edward may want to discuss his schooling with Sam too.'

Sam looked up. The gargoyles sat up on the wall of his home, encircling the blessing. He was leaving all that protection behind. Bladder picked up one forepaw, claws extended, and leaned down. Sam understood the move – the stone lion was ready to drop and attack Mrs Petersen even if the whole world saw him, but it wasn't her fault Sam was leaving, so he shook his head. He didn't want her hurt.

Richard threw Sam's case into the back of the car. Sam waved at the Kavanaghs from the back window. Behind them, a little higher on the wall than before, Bladder gave a pained and silent roar, then he watched as the trio raced back to the top of the house.

The gargoyles bounded from roof to roof, leaving the Kavanagh house far behind them and making sure they could see the direction Mrs Petersen's car headed.

'She'll be taking him to the services,' Wheedle said as she turned right.

'We can cut her off,' Bladder said.

The car raced away. Wheedle shook his head. 'Too fast, but if we get there, we can pick up his scent.'

Bladder peered at the streets, figuring out the best way to get across the road without being seen. 'No one else smells like Sam, so I think we can follow pretty easily.'

Wheedle sighed. 'We were wrong, you know. There are

good humans. The Kavanaghs love him so much.'

'More importantly, he loves them, and they make him happy,' Bladder said. 'An' it's our job to get him back to them, back to us. Come on, you lot. Let's go. Hopefully, Mrs Petersen's crew will make the process as slow as possible. Hey, look, there's a bus coming.'

'You're kidding?'

Bladder grinned so every fang could be seen. 'You never wanted to ride a bus before?'

Spigot hooted like an owl as they headed for the street.

Mrs Petersen drove to the city centre, towards the Children's Services. When they arrived, she parked next to a slick black Mercedes. Woermann leaned against the driver's side. He opened the back of Mrs Petersen's car, grabbed Sam's case, then threw it into the back of the Mercedes.

'Get in, son,' Woermann said.

'Paperwork? We've got a few things you need to sign.' Mrs Petersen smiled. 'Mrs Spiers noticed we didn't have an address, couldn't you ... ?'

Woermann waved his hand, a daze of pink wash coloured Mrs Petersen's eyes. She giggled.

Sam sneezed at the fairy dust, and Mrs Petersen gazed out across the street, her eyes unable to focus.

Sam climbed into the passenger seat; he hadn't forgotten the pathetic rag of blanket Woermann had shown him and the car, as clean as it looked, reeked of puppy. He smelt Hazel along with the Kokonis and a few Labradors, and Amira. The strong fearful smell of Wilfred stood out from the passenger seat. There were other strange animal scents too; so rich with confusion and sleepiness.

The car hummed along the road out of town. They passed the marina complex where Michelle shopped, zoomed by a girls' school with its stately Victorian architecture snubbing the sea road. They went through a little town with pretty period houses (one built in Shakespeare's time, Richard had said, although, at the time, Sam had had no idea who Shakespeare was), drove by a few modern suburbs full of white houses over which seagulls wheeled. Sam read all the signs; he hadn't been with the Kavanaghs long enough to visit all these places. They'd said they'd take him. They sped along the part of the coast where a ferry waited to take people to another country. Michelle said when they sorted his passport he'd go on that ferry; he'd visit that country. When she told him this, Sam had got so excited he'd told Daniel, who'd laughed at the information. The angel had marvelled that Sam knew the tunnels through The Hole could lead to different places – China, Australia, Bolivia – but that Sam somehow thought they were on this one small island. Wheedle had spoken a bit of French for him.

'Toured Notre Dame once, had to fill in for a broken chimera,' Wheedle had told him.

Sam sighed. He missed Wheedle and Spigot and wondered if he would see them again.

Or Bladder. He wanted Bladder with him so much he imagined the hard edge of the gargoyle's mane under his hand.

Moving beside the coastline, the grey break of water hiding other islands beyond the horizon, made Sam feel further away from the Kavanaghs than he'd ever felt. The hastening wheels, the too-smooth motion of the vehicle rushed him from them.

Woermann drove until they lost sight of the beach.

'You know, I realise I can talk to you. Can't I?'

Sam frowned. 'What do you mean?'

'Well, the queen, she's all business, isn't she? She'll come and help when we start a new area. We need a few insiders to get the programme up and running, but even fixers and knockers don't want to deal with anything they don't understand. The average human really doesn't want to know about supernatural things and all that. She sets that up. Finds the right locals, befuddles them with dust so much they forget their names, then I have my go-to people.'

'Don't you do that yourself? I saw you dust Mrs Petersen.'

'Her Majesty showed me how to get someone to do what I want on the spot, maybe to see what I want to see, but only she can do the long-term charms. We need each other to go the long game. She's enchanted the pet shop man. He's one of my drivers, and he's great for selling the animals on afterwards. Nothing suspicious about a pet shop man selling dogs. He likes them too, so they'll end up in nice homes. I'm not as awful as you think.'

'You kidnap innocent people for money?'

Woermann tilted his shaggy head and stared at Sam with his golden eyes. 'Money's just part of it. I used to be a private investigator, you know. I liked the hunt. I liked finding out about people. All their nasty business. Then one day, it all changed. I had a client who was a bit suspicious of his business partner. Where he was going to? What he was spending his money on? It turned out to be beyond what I expected, and I saw him ... Well, suffice to say, he attacked me. Wasn't human when he did, and I thought that was the end of my life, but it turned out it was the beginning. I changed. For the better. My hunting instincts are stronger. My sense of smell, my eyesight.' Woermann flexed his hands on the steering wheel. 'My strength. But I need a challenge, something other than chasing up people who haven't paid bills. She must have known. She found me wandering around miserable near Norfolk.'

'Maggie?'

'She calls herself something different every time. Mabh, Mab. Maggie? Yeah, I think so.'

Woermann turned down a small side street.

'She found me up north, working a boring contract for a small secretarial company. Dropped it like a hot cake. It was sending me nuts working those jobs. I could have ripped someone's throat out.'

Sam inhaled.

Woermann smirked. 'Oh, yeah, quite literally. I needed something to distract me. And this is perfect. You must have supernatural skills to hunt shifters, really sniff them out. Even she can't do that, which is why I'm precious to her.' The big man looked over at Sam. 'Shifters mix so well with humans, it's hard to tell them apart, and hard to find them. It took me a month to get all the ones outside Glasgow. They were my first catch. You got no idea how the hunt gets my blood racing.'

They hurried towards a grizzled green country. The cold air leached the colour from the fields, and bushes died in the cold winds. Trees clung to their few leaves, half naked and vulnerable, beaten and sad. Sam wondered where the sunshine had gone.

'Are we going straight to her?' he asked.

'No, you've got two or three days to settle in.' Woermann turned to Sam and grinned, showing pointy yellow teeth. 'I've got a lovely room set up for you. All the trimmings. You're special. Got you a PS4, games, your own TV. And a mini fridge. You're a little prince, she says, and I've got to treat you like one. And as they say, the customer is always right.'

Sam exhaled. He had a bit of time before Maggie showed up. Then he thought about it. 'Why isn't she coming straight away? What's she doing?'

'Busy lady. Not my job to ask. Although she did say something about Italy. Maybe we're going there next. You too. We may all get a nice holiday to the Continent. Hunt for a few shifters. Wouldn't you like that? I can't do anything until after the next moon, though.'

'Why not?'

Woermann rolled his eyes.

'Oh, yeah,' Sam said.

Sam thought about it. Two days minimum. Forty-eight hours to help the puppies then get home. He looked out of the window and saw no sign of Daniel. He was on his own.

They turned from the solid asphalt two-way road into a single lane, lined with hedges cramming against both sides of the car.

Then Woermann rolled his Mercedes into a gravelly driveway between two bitter brown fields. More evergreen hedges separated an area further in, shielding a building from the road, although Sam doubted many people would even bother looking in. The gate, which Woermann beeped open with a remote, looked like every other gate they'd passed.

It was an expensive area.

They drove through a break in the hedge towards a three-storey mansion. Its wide Victorian front might have been beautiful on another day. It had soft golden-coloured bricking with large windows gaping down at him. Naked vines climbed the walls, although the odd dead rose poked out here or there. They looked uncared for. On a day when storm hung in the air and the sea wind cut like claws, the large windows peered at Sam in misery as if the house too had had its dreams stolen. It was a beautiful mansion haunted by Woermann.

Woermann beamed as Sam studied the building. 'Gorgeous, isn't it? Come on, son. Let me show you your room. You're gonna love it.'

Sam stared at the grey sky, calling silently for Daniel to appear. Any angel would've done.

From the door, Woermann looked back at Sam. 'What are you doing? Come on.'

Sam saw a blur of white in the sky, but it was just a small, rushing cloud. He watched it go, then turned and entered Woermann Manor.

Wheedle gasped and wheezed.

'You can't be short of breath,' Bladder said. 'You don't breathe.'

'I'm having a heart attack.'

'Paperwork,' Mrs Petersen said.

'What she said, panic attack. Gargoyles don't have heart attacks neither.'

'Are you sure?'

'Nearly five hundred years sure.'

They'd missed Sam by twenty minutes. The smell of him and that beastly Woermann filled the air. Mrs Petersen leaned against a car, repeating 'paperwork, paperwork' to herself.

'She can see us,' Wheedle puffed.

'She can't see no one,' Bladder replied. 'She'll be in this state for another hour. Poor soul.'

'Paperwork,' Mrs Petersen agreed.

Spigot's beak rose in the air and pointed east.

'Yep, we gotta keep moving,' Bladder said.

Wheedle struggled to speak. 'But. We've. Lost. Him.'

Spigot walked over to a metal grate on the road and squawked long and high. Wheedle collapsed on the bitumen and Bladder went marble white.

It was a few seconds before Wheedle could say anything. Bladder stared at the drain.

'You're right, Spigot,' said Wheedle. 'There's plenty of drain exits to the east and it would be quicker. Much quicker. We might get ahead of them. Or Sam might even be down there already.'

'Nope, Woermann's not going to take her straight to Maggie. He may be awful, but he's not a monster. He won't be able to get through the drains.' Bladder shook his stony locks. 'We've still got a little time. You're both very brave, but you ain't never been completely smashed. If you go down there, into The Hole, there'll be ogres and goblins everywhere, an' they all know Sam is part of a gargoyle pack. No gargoyle's been back since Sam broke that sword. Any one of us goes down there gets massacred themselves. We are Enemy First Class. It's not good Sam is gone off with that man, but we won't do him no good if we all get demolished.'

'So we follow along the street? Let's get moving, then. Come on, come on.' Wheedle still panted, but he rushed away, leading them between a parked Ford Escort and a VW bug. Spigot followed. Bladder sat for a few seconds at Mrs Petersen's feet. 'Paperwork,' she said to him. He nodded in agreement, and studied the leaf-covered drain. He sniffed. The smell of monsters floated up, stale and manky.

It wasn't a good idea, was it?

CHAPTER 12

Woermann led Sam through the foyer. The deep warmth of mahogany shone from the floor, and the walls were painted in muted gold. A huge mirror frame, reflecting Sam's misery, appeared to be tarnished bronze (although Sam thought it was paint), and the carpet ran up the stairs in deep olive. Sam saw a living area to the right where more deep green rugs lay under leather chesterfields. The smell of furniture polish filled the space, and a huge fire burned at the end of the room.

'I got my own place further north, but this is glorious. If all goes well, I might move here permanently. The weather's nicer. I thought the money she was paying me to kidnap shifters was nice enough, but for you? Phew! You're literally worth a king's ransom. I don't have to just rent a castle; I can own one!' He threw his arms out to show Sam the grandeur of the place. The stench of fairy dust filled the hall; Woermann's strut became longer, and his eyes grew large. Woermann was drunk on it. 'This way.'

In a room at the top of the stairs, the man chucked Sam's bag on the bed. 'Here you are. It's the second-best bedroom, but I'm led to believe that your presence in the house will be wanted sometime. I'm to tend to all your needs and keep you happy. Might as well get comfortable.' Between his fingers he rolled a big brass key with a red ribbon through its eye. 'I'm to treat you like a prince for the next few days, but that doesn't mean you get to run around.'

Sam stared at the room. It was as opulent as the room below and contained a four-poster bed, its old, blackened posts carved with pictures of hunting. Over it, a navy velvet canopy fell and draped the sides. The bedcover, also navy, was threaded with gold, silver and soft grey. It showed a pack of large cats sleeping under a sky littered with tiny stars.

Sam pulled back the cover. The bed did have sweet-smelling sheets, but it wasn't Michelle's perfume.

'The decor's great,' Woermann said. 'But this is what I think will keep you happy.'

The biggest TV Sam had ever seen covered the opposite wall and black cords ran to a series of boxes with blinking blue and red lights. Woermann pointed at the glossy box next to it. A small fridge gleamed whitely at them.

Sam was more interested in the room's window. It was large enough, and broken up into a series of little panes, what Michelle called a 'divided-light window'. Sam went to it and touched the frame. It *was* paint. It had a hospital-style extendable arm, which meant it opened an inch and no more. Sam forced it again and it creaked but stuck.

'It'll hold well enough,' Woermann said. 'If you could break out, it's still a solid three-storey drop. Don't think I could fall all that way without breaking a bone. Maybe. And even if you somehow managed it, you have a strong smell and scrawny legs. Even with a day's head start I'd hunt you down and bring you back. Don't make me do that. I think I'm going to like to have you around. Someone to talk to. You do this goody-goody business, but there's something nasty about you that I like.'

'Can I see my friends?'

'Later. I have things to do.' Woermann gave a bone-freezing grin before he walked out into the corridor.

The lock clicked into place, and Sam was imprisoned.

'But you promised,' Sam yelled through the door. He hit the door.

Sam sneezed.

The room smelt of dust – not house dust, but magic dust tickling his nose, its power potent even in the leftovers settling on window sills and tables. Some of it smelt like the dust Woermann had waved at Mrs Petersen, but there was something raw and basic about it too.

Sam didn't know if he could hate Woermann more.

He lay down on the bed on his belly and looked over the cover, the embroidery turning its surface into a landscape, the rising grey of feline backs and jaws. Small hillocks of white and yellow formed an array of stars. He ran his hand over it. It smelt of fresh air with the undercurrent of another dust on it as if someone had hung it outside to get the mausoleum smell out of it.

He cried for a bit, not out loud. If Woermann's ears were good enough to hear around his own house, Sam didn't want the monster to overhear him; he suspected it would please him too much. The patch of bedding under his eye became wetter and wetter, spreading until he felt his forehead and his cheek dampen. The strongest feeling, though, was the huge hurting in his torso. Breathing hurt. His back ached. His chest ached. His head felt hot and his heart had climbed, beating at the top of his chest as if it were working its way to the nearest exit. He wanted Michelle and Beatrice, Richard and Nick. He wanted Bladder and Wheedle and Spigot. He wanted his own bed and he wondered where Daniel was.

He awoke and saw the outside world had got a little darker. The house was also quiet and he wished he could hear one friendly voice.

Sam sat up and rummaged through his bag. His phone clicked on. Nick had made sure he charged it, and Sam stroked its shiny face. *Click, click, click.*

Michelle answered immediately. 'Sam, darling?'

'Hi, I'm here.'

'Where's here?'

'Not far. We didn't drive long.'

Michelle sighed. Happy. Disappointed. Sam didn't

know. He wished he could see her face. 'Send some photos of where you are.'

'OK.'

'You're just settling in, of course.'

Nick's voice called in the background. 'Is that Sam? Is it nice? He got you locked in a dungeon?'

'Hi, Nick,' Sam called back. 'No, it's a lovely room.' He couldn't lie. 'I've got a TV, my own fridge.'

Nick groaned. 'You won't want to come back.'

'Trust me, it'll take more than a fridge to keep me away.'

'How're your dogs?' Nick asked.

'I haven't seen them yet.'

'What? I thought that's why you went.'

'Yeah, me too.'

'Is everything OK? Just give us the address and Dad'll come and get you.'

'I'd really love to, but I ...'

Sam stared at the gap in the window, too small to slip through, and even if he could, he was here because Wilfred, Hazel and Amira needed him.

'Next time we FaceTime,' Nick said. 'OK?'

Sam wanted so much to see their faces, but if he saw theirs, they would see his was murky with tears.

'I want to see what's in your fridge,' Nick said. 'I want my own fridge.'

Woermann was at the door. He had entered as softly as a cat and Sam, with a phone against his ear straining to hear his family, had not heard the big man arrive.

'Bye,' Sam said. 'Speak soon.'

'Where are you … ?'

Woermann grabbed the phone and clicked the red symbol that closed the call. The Kavanagh voices were gone. Sam would have cried there and then, something to let out the sick feeling in his throat, but he remained determined not to let Woermann see him cry.

Woermann grinned. 'That's got to cheer you up. What else can I do to make your stay a little more pleasant?' He put Sam's phone in his back pocket. 'What about a new computer?'

'You've only been able to make me come here because you threatened my friends, seriously. Do you think I'd ask you for a new computer?' Sam felt his cheeks heat. 'Can I see my friends?'

'Not yet, but I'm happy to give you a tour of the house.'

Sam thought about it. Actually, he did want to see the house. Not to admire it as Woermann would hope, but to see anything of use. Exactly where the shifters were, perhaps, and all points of escape. 'Yeah, all right.'

Woermann's grin widened. 'We're gonna get along beautifully. I can tell.'

The rest of the house was just as impressive. Open-beamed, wood-lined. Woermann showed him the top floor first, making sure Sam counted the bedrooms. He even let Sam lean out of the window overlooking the driveway. The window swung out wide, so Sam could see the road and beyond that the wide-open green areas around Woermann's mansion. If he tried to run, he'd be exposed. Still, Sam found himself more interested in the window. It had no hinge nor latch.

Woermann hustled Sam to the guests' bathroom to show him golden taps and then to the heated indoor pool with a hot spa next to it.

'Look at this,' Woermann said. 'Do you know anyone else that has their own indoor pool?'

Sam didn't like the room, the bleach-stink in the air bit at his nose. His time with the gargoyles also didn't help; rock sank in seconds in water. It wasn't fun for them. Sam had gargoyle hearing and gargoyle eyes, it was likely he would sink too.

'Maybe you could have a swim later,' Woermann suggested.

'Maybe,' Sam replied.

The cold day outside made the huge warm room steamy, and the seats and marble floor looked damp. Michelle liked to look through magazines of houses of rich people, but if she came through something too excessive she'd mutter 'tacky'. Sam saw this scene and muttered it too. He wasn't sure the word was apt (and he wondered why Michelle spent time staring at houses she didn't like) but he didn't like Woermann's excess and the word sounded bitter enough in his mouth to fit his mood.

'People only say that when they can't afford something.' Woermann smiled and Sam suspected it was as phoney as the gold taps. 'I don't know what the queen wants of you, but if you do whatever she asks she'll make you stinking rich. You could have your own pool.'

Sam stopped to look at Woermann. 'I don't really want any of this, I'd much rather have my family back.'

Woermann raised a bushy eyebrow at the last statement. 'I can smell them on you, you know? You stink of them, especially the baby, but the services said you were fostered.'

'Adopted,' Sam said.

'No one smells that much like someone unless the same blood runs through them, or you have some kind of magic. Is that why the queen wants you so much? You make yourself become like those around you? People don't notice it at a conscious level, but it tricks them into bonding with you? No wonder she thinks you're special.' Woermann rubbed his hands together. 'I've watched you too. You can smell any creature, hear like an animal; you could slip into a target's home, a cuckoo. Is that what you are? Are you some kind of special shifter? One that flies with fairies? Can you fly?'

'I'm not a shifter, and I'm not a 'thrope.' Sam studied Woermann. His eyes were golden. 'What kind of 'thrope are you?'

'Why don't you guess?'

'You're getting hairier. Your eyebrows, and I guess you're wearing the coat to cover up how much your body is changing. You're getting bigger, not smaller. A werewolf?'

'You were doing so well until the end.' Woermann chuckled. 'Try again.'

Sam took a deep sniff. The smell of the dogs was on Woermann, but he wasn't a dog. 'You're a cat? But aren't cats small?'

'You don't know much about animals, Sam. Some species of cat are very large. Most don't go in the water. Do you?' He peered at the pool. 'How about a swim? Don't like it myself, but I'm happy to lock you in here. You play ball, and we'll have a nice time.'

Sam stared at Woermann. He wanted to play ball now?

Woermann clapped and grinned as if Sam should get as excited as he. Sam found the grinning Woermann scarier than the scowling one. 'The things she'll give you, if you help her. You could just rake it in.' Woermann gave his speech to the glittering water, gesturing with wide arms to the humid air as if a crowd had gathered, as if he could feel money already gathering before him. Sam thought he couldn't get any crazier. 'Are you sure you're not a cuckoo? Are you in my head, in my nose, making me bond with you? I'm going to have to watch you.' Woermann guffawed.

Sam couldn't imagine Woermann bonding with anyone. The light stink of fear in the house drowning under the heavy stink of fairy dust told him that. Maggie was a monster queen and monsters had no hearts. If Woermann kept company with monsters, he was heartless too.

Woermann walked them back to the first foyer. Sam noticed a solid wooden door in the corridor on the way. It looked as sturdy as a church door and had an old-fashioned lock.

'What's in there?' Sam asked. 'It smells awful.'

'The ballroom,' Woermann replied. 'I use it when I'm not feeling myself. It's my safe room for when I turn. If I went hunting outside, I could get shot.'

Woermann pulled at a bunch of keys on his waist. Sam noted his room key, the brass one with the red ribbon. Woermann opened the door. It was thick and solid and slammed wide.

The room inside may have been beautiful once, but the wooden floor was scratched and dusty and the walls had been grooved with claw marks. Security screens were installed over the inside of the windows. The smell was wretched. Sam turned away.

Woermann locked the room and said nothing, but watched Sam with a smirk. 'Let's see the kitchen, then.'

Woermann opened the door on to a dazzlingly white kitchen, and the stink was pungent and acrid; terror and misery caked the walls and floors. Sam wondered how anyone could eat in this room, maybe someone with a more human nose who had no sense of the meanings of smell.

Woermann marched Sam past tall modern French doors overlooking a threadbare garden outside. The doors were ceiling to floor and, though the cold did not dare breach the thick glass, outside it had stripped away the flowers and the green. Sam noticed the flip locks on the doors. If he didn't need to save his friends, he could just open one of those and be outside in the fresh air. Maybe he could run all the way home.

Sam found himself distracted by the white pantry

door at the other end of the room. From behind that, the muffled noise of dogs rose. No, he had to stay. Woermann's gaze followed Sam's to the door. 'They're all right.'

'They're crying,' Sam said.

'You can hear that? I knew you had a good sense of smell ... but even I can't hear that. Amazing.' Woermann opened the fridge door. 'Chicken or steak?'

CHAPTER 13

Bladder knew he had to get on. The gargoyles had spent half the night trying to figure out how to get to Sam quicker, but walking by night and hiding by day would take too long. At the rate they were going he was still a week away; it was midnight and they'd hardly got past the marina. Sam was ... he couldn't make out the smell, it was confused, but a heavy pong of fairy dust hung over Sam's scent.

'I don't like it,' Wheedle said. 'Does it mean Sam's in danger?'

'Maggie wouldn't dust Sam, it don't work on him,' Bladder said. He was impressed with how rock sure his voice sounded. 'It's Woermann spraying it around, that's all.'

The other two nodded, taking Bladder's words as truth, but his innards churned. Fairy dust meant Maggie was on the loose, and if Sam wasn't at home in the house with the wardings, anything could find him. Bladder felt it in every part of him, solid and hollow: the smell of dust meant Maggie was close to Sam.

And where was that blasted angel? It almost seemed like he was summoned away the moment he could be even half useful.

'Hey! What's that?' a voice called.

'Oh no. Assume positions,' Wheedle said, and the gargoyles froze, Wheedle and Spigot still on the footpath, Bladder further out of the street light, half covered by a hedge.

A group of partygoers raced towards them, giggling and waving their jumpers. Wheedle groaned.

They had to stop while they got decorated in scarves and had cans of drink propped on their heads.

'Not another selfie,' Bladder heard Wheedle mutter before a boy grabbed him around the neck and pointed the camera at himself and the stone bull.

The loud humans fussed over Wheedle and Spigot, so while they weren't looking Bladder sidled further and further away. A young woman pointed at him and lobbed a red woollen scarf around his head while he froze, but then a young man grabbed her and kissed her and she forgot about Bladder and the scarf. Bladder retreated a few more steps.

Bladder stared at Spigot's and Wheedle's solidified faces. They sat like stone ornaments, staring at the road. They were immoveable in the full circle of a street lamp, while Bladder was covered in shadows, and by the time the young woman looked again, he was completely hidden behind the hedge. She stared around, confused, but her boyfriend grabbed her hand and led her back to Wheedle.

Bladder ran to the side road, the human voices fading, and found the dark gap he sought alongside the footpath. His stomach hurt.

Spigot had suggested the quicker way, entrance to entrance, no stopping, although they knew it could mean an almost certain smashing. Also, distances were closer down in The Hole. They could visit Paris if they liked, as long as they found the right drain. Bladder had put the dampeners on Spigot's suggestion, but he'd stewed over it. Spigot and Wheedle sat solid stone behind him, unable to move until the party people left.

He chalked 'DONT FOLOW!' on the pavement.

No chance he would risk Wheedle and Spigot too.

Bladder looked back in their direction. They were on the other side of the hedge. The humans' giggles lessened, getting bored, but they had gained him a little time in which he could lose his pack. He didn't want 'em with him, wouldn't tell 'em his plan. He needed to find Sam quick before the banshee did. He felt it deep in the empty space in his chest that housed his ... housed the empty space in the middle of him. It felt so much emptier now that Sam wasn't where he wanted to be, and Bladder's innards twinged with something other than wind.

Yes, he was willing to risk everything of himself for Sam, but he wasn't going to risk Wheedle and Spigot. They were too young, had never been broken inside or out. It wasn't right to expect it of 'em.

No other human came thumping along the footpath. He scanned the street.

In for a penny, in for a pound, Bladder thought.

The grate at the edge of the road smelt dank and rank, rubbish and rotting leaves collected in its bars, something decomposed between it and the footpath; even the water washing into it smelt like petrol. Under that, under the human stink of it all was a faint, stale monster scent.

Bladder stood at its edge, staring down into the moving darkness below, grey washed into black flowed into shadow.

He heard the crack of moving stone behind him.

'What are you doin'?' Wheedle said. The stone bull scurried across the footpath and stood on the kerb.

Bladder studied the winged bull. 'You're wearing eyeliner and lipstick. I don't think it's your colour.'

Spigot's shriek made them both jump. The eagle scratched a claw at the footpath where Bladder had written his message. Wheedle looked down at it. 'Ho ho, thought you'd go without us, did you?'

'No. You're not coming!' Bladder replied. 'It's dangerous. You remember how much it hurt your leg when that ogre snapped it off on Hatching Day, don't you, Spigot? An' that's when the ogres were in a good mood. Think about what they'll be like now. Every gargoyle what goes there they'll turn to concrete powder.'

Spigot gave a high, strangled chirp.

143

'Imagine that, your whole body, all in pieces. I'm leaving you behind because we shouldn't all risk it.'

Spigot fluffed his brittle feathers and chirruped low in his throat. Wheedle took another step forward. 'But if *she's* got him, and we keep travelling at the rate we're going, we'll all be too late. She could hurt him, or worse ...'

'... make him turn his back on us,' Bladder finished.

'Bladder, he'd never do that.'

'I saw him in The Hole, Wheedle, I saw how she works on him. He wouldn't do it on purpose, but a little bit of his heart, it will always belong to her, even if he don't admit it to himself. Enough for him to do something stupid, and if he crossed a line, he might not be able to forgive himself. Humans run from the very ones that are good for them when that happens.'

Spigot's feathers bristled.

'Where were you going?' Wheedle asked.

Bladder sighed. 'The drain up to the Channel Ferry.'

'Near the boat? I like boats.'

'That's the one. His smell suggests he's not far beyond that. Quick in, quick through, that was my plan.'

They were quiet then, all three, as they stared at the grate.

Bladder didn't say anything as the two other gargoyles walked towards him.

'We're really going to do this, aren't we?' Wheedle said.

'You don't have to,' Bladder replied.

Spigot gave a confident shriek, his eagle demeanour restored.

'Yeah. Yeah, we do,' Wheedle agreed.

They slid into the grate, slipping between Earth and the unearthly place beneath them, using monster magic. Bladder found himself in the sewer, up to his belly in dirty water. A plastic bottle floated by him. Behind, Wheedle and Spigot coughed and spluttered as the gurgling wind in the tunnel blew soggy leaves and chocolate wrappers into their faces. Bladder knew they just had to follow the flow. It would show him to a passageway which would lead on to the Great Cavern.

'Most likely get smashed,' he said, but if they didn't find Sam soon ... A sound like winds in a drain echoed in his belly. What did the great white albatross always hanging around his neck call it? Instinct? That's right. Bladder didn't know where the inside tickle came from, but he had to move fast. He splashed forward.

They came to an opening after fifteen minutes of splashing and *oofing*. It was a dark hole, no more than a boy-sized brownie burrow, but it stank of monsters. Bladder pushed his head into it and dirt collapsed behind him, swirling off with the other rubbish. It was snug all right, but just rough dirt, no rocks. When it became too tight, he dug it out, listening to the others snuffling and raking dirt behind him. It did not take long to reach a conduit full of the smell of ogre paddies and bad breath, but those smells were stale and Bladder put his eyes to an opening; his whole head wouldn't fit, but he could make out a little movement, an imp or two. *Don't get too confident,* he told himself. *Probably the quiet end of the cavern.*

Still, quiet was good. He pushed his head through the dirt. A pixie squealed and took off in the direction of the lights. There didn't seem as many imps around as normal, even for the quiet end. Bladder couldn't see well, a hillock blocked his view. He couldn't remember any end of the Great Cavern having a hillock.

Bladder pushed his shoulders and wings out of the hole. There didn't seem anyone else about. Maybe he'd come out in the wrong place. Did it smell like the Great Cavern? He took a whiff. Nah. The smells were too old. If he was being honest with himself, it was like the Succubi's Cavern, old and forgotten, although there'd been no little hills in that cavern neither. Bladder wondered where they had managed to get themselves. They'd have to find their way to the Great Cavern before they could locate an exit to Sam.

He couldn't even turn his head to talk to the others, so he just pushed through, hoping Spigot and Wheedle knew enough to be quiet.

Bladder stepped into the silence and peered back. Wheedle put out his head and gazed around. Bladder put a single talon to his lips. The bull nodded. A hush of imps moved somewhere to their left as Spigot stepped through. No more than two or three. A tribe of pixies would happily smash gargoyles, but a gargoyle could easily take on half a dozen. Bladder looked up to the ceiling. It was certainly high enough for the Great Cavern, and when he studied the walls, yes, there was the cluster of burrows like the ones gargoyles had once used for their visits downstairs.

Bladder took to the side, climbing deftly. The others followed as soundless as they'd ever been. A wide-eyed bunyip stared at them from a burrow, but it shrieked and ran inside. A bit of a surprise, bunyips were rare, but they were ogre-large. Bladder wouldn't have expected to scare one. What was this place? They loped up a couple of tiers, ran the distance till they came to the constellation of holes the shape of the gargoyle sanctuary and peered into the one that would have been where their pack's old cubby had been. It was dusty, a thin layer of grey covered everything, but when he breathed in, the aromatic echo of Sam's blood filled the place.

Bladder put his paw to his chest, remembering how Sam had put him together. Not just fixing his stone body but his ... you know?

'This is our old place,' Wheedle whispered. He turned and stepped outside again and surveyed the space below, Bladder close behind. 'So, is this the Great Cavern?'

Spigot stared around, his eyes bug big.

If it was the Great Cavern, and Bladder had to agree it was, it was close to empty, and the geography was slightly different. Where Thunderguts would once have had a throne, a large hill stood. It was the largest in the space, but a few smaller mounds encircled it. A thin waspish whine hung over one at the edge and pebbles clattered down on it.

Most of the violence Bladder remembered had taken place in the Ogres' Cavern – the sword Sam broke had released souls and turned ogres to dust – but maybe a few souls had got here and dusted some of the bigger beasts. That huge hill, it could have been a monster of an ogre, or a giant maybe, or some sea monster Bladder hadn't seen before. It was big. Maybe it was a few monsters fallen together.

Thin, scratching sounds filled the space above as nameless, faceless things hid in the walls. Not many though, not armies, not legions.

The quiet gnawed at Bladder, and the few monsters they'd seen were more scared of them than the other way around. Of gargoyles!

'Where is everyone?' Wheedle asked.

'Upstairs, I guess. The sword's no longer keeping them down here – they're free, aren't they? Free to do what they like?'

'Then what are all those piles?'

'You two stay here,' Bladder said. 'I'm gonna look at them. I have an idea what they might be.'

'What happened to "quick in and quick through"?'

'I was expecting the place to be full,' Bladder said. Wheedle opened his mouth to speak, but Bladder used a forepaw to snap it shut. 'I promise, I'll be back in less than a minute.'

Bladder descended the wall and trotted to the centre of the huge space. The silence was breathtaking, eerie, in its way more frightening than the roars, bellows and clamouring of various monster breeds which had sounded when the cavern was full.

His stone feet sent echoes.

He looked back. Two pale gargoyles stared silently down at him.

Bladder drew closer to the little mountain, and on closer inspection could see it wasn't just one huge lump but a collection of smaller lumps. Some the size of boulders, some the size of ...

... eggs.

Bladder sniffed. It smelt like them.

Unhatched monsters, nuggets, beans, pea-sized ones that would hatch a brownie, rock-sized ones that a troll might spring from, ones as big as your paw that'd produce a leprechaun. On Hatching Day each of these would be an explosion of life as they cracked open and filled packs and tribes with new, young monsters. He remembered the day Wheedle had arrived. He'd known he had to claim the little gargoyle. Most gargoyles were hybrids, face of a monkey, back end of a dog, wings of an owl, grotesques, but Bladder was a winged lion, not common, and the grotesques always tended to look at gargoyles who were singular animals with one eye squinted. A winged lion and a winged bull? Oddities. He remembered Wheedle's first word when a pixie tried to drag the baby bull away.

'Moron,' Wheedle had repeated after Bladder.

He was having a reaction to the dirt probably. For some reason his eyeballs felt damp.

Then there was Spigot. Even more singular than Wheedle. A marble eagle. No words out of him, but he was such a sweetie.

There would be no more ogres, which wasn't a bad thing, but there'd be no more Wheedles or Spigots either.

Bladder touched his eye. Sewer water had got inside his pipes, he was leaking. How annoying.

He searched in the darkness, for a nugget the size of a Malteser, a soft-grey colour. A titbit from which a gargoyle would have hatched.

As Bladder circled the hill and Thunderguts's throne came into sight, he could no longer see Wheedle and Spigot. The mound also overshadowed the lamps on the circling pathways, as it sat dark and brooding, a childless lump. The pile of eggs he studied had assembled over the Hatching ground, days and weeks and months of potential monsters building up, unhatched. Dormant.

Bladder squinted, the darkness overwhelmed even his eyes, and he leaned forward to see a tiny grey nugget. He plucked it from the massive hill. A small avalanche of beanies pelted the foot of the stone dais.

Bladder stared at the never-formed gargoyle in his paw.

'Without Thunderguts, the Hatching has stopped,' a dark voice said from the throne.

If Bladder had breath, he would have lost it.

He recognised the voice, old and croaky as it was, but the stale scent of fairy dust floated with it. Bladder saw her. The crone. Maggie.

Maggie? This was it, he was dead. He was broken rock, a tumbled boulder. He turned, stiff and wary. She sat alone on the throne. Bladder glanced around, but she didn't have

Sam with her. Well, that was a relief; at least she hadn't got him yet.

'You're the first creature I've seen here not scampering around in terror. Your kind are braver than I realised,' Maggie said. 'You're a gargoyle. Is that right?'

Bladder was glad his ... you know ... wasn't the kind that beat, or it would have been crashing and thumping against his innards like dance music.

She'd recognised him for a gargoyle. Would she realise he'd been the one who'd thumped into her in Baba Yaga's Cavern? Did he dare speak? He opened his mouth, words wouldn't form.

'Most monsters no longer come here,' she said. 'Except for the few I've ordered down. It's a graveyard to them, they expect ghosts and ghoulies and all kinds of dead things. So many of the great ogres are dead, and more die each day, and with no Thunderguts to breathe on the eggies, there've been no further hatchlings. They'll all just sit here and moulder. The air itself is dying, can you not smell it?'

'Air?' Bladder managed to croak out.

Maggie turned on him, fixing a wild eye on the gargoyle. 'Clever creature! That's right, we need an heir, but Thunderguts died without naming his successor. If only he'd said who would follow him. He could have named me, and I'd be breathing new life into all of this.' She waved her arm at the hills around her. 'Walk with me.'

Bladder eeped. *Please*, he thought at Wheedle and Spigot. *Don't do anything stupid. Don't try to save me.*

Maggie the crone must have seen his face. 'Fear not,

little gargoyle, I'll not harm you. I need to lean on someone when I'm like this. My bones ache and my joints are full of sand.'

Bladder didn't want to throw away his nugget, but he couldn't walk with it in his paw. He dropped it sadly, letting go of the unborn gargoyle.

He sidled closer, hoping her vision was bad when she was a crone, maybe her memory too. Or was she leading him into a trap? She couldn't move fast enough to chase him right now, but if he got close ... WHACK! Hit him with a cane?

He couldn't run though. She'd punish him if he did that.

Bladder gritted his lion teeth and trotted obediently closer, jumping up on to the dais and approaching the stone throne.

Maggie reached a clawed and gnarled hand to him, grabbing his mane. 'Pull me up ... what is your name?'

Bladder gulped. 'Bladder.'

'Ah, yes, the typical insipid name for a gargoyle. Such a shame, you seem a good specimen of your kind. You deserve better.'

Bladder didn't argue. She was being pleasant.

He stepped back, allowing his weight to lever Maggie from the throne. She hoisted a sack up with her, pulling it over her shoulder with a stiff jerk.

'Walk me down to that tunnel there.' Maggie gestured to a cobbled exit across from the throne. 'I need to address the troops in the next hour. There's a lot of hunting needed to get to the next stage. We'll get there, little gargoyle. Don't you worry.'

Bladder listened to the crone's aches and moans as he helped her off the stage, and walked her slowly towards the same opening that led to the drain Bladder wanted to use. Not good.

'In these days, even a brave gargoyle will have a place in my army. Can't be too fussy now there's so few of us left. You'll know, I've lost most of the old ones. They remembered the old days too much, when it was easy to find a victim. Most of them have got themselves killed. The vermin have guns and lights and they fight back. We need to rebuild to be as powerful as we once were. We don't have the numbers any more, so the young ones have become less bloodthirsty.' She looked at Bladder now, really looked at him. The gargoyle shook; his skin shivered. Did she know him? 'They might not come here, but they remember this.' She waved a bent hand towards the egg pile. Bladder could see and hear how much it cost her. Her shoulder cracked as her arm moved.

'At least it's quiet down here. I go up there and I can hear them muttering "How long?" and "What next?" and "When?"' She stopped talking and shuffled more quickly.

What was she planning to do? Bladder thought. *Did it have something to do with Sam? Was that why she was looking for him?*

'So, what is next?' Bladder said aloud. He couldn't believe the words had come out of his own mouth.

The crone slowed, and chuckled at Bladder. 'You are a

brave one. Not a one has had the nerve to ask me directly. Most of the others barely squeak to me. I must admit I do have a short temper. Maybe I should make you my attendant, gargoyle. You are the most courageous and intelligent creature I've seen for months. Things that could smash you in a second are hanging back shaking like milk.'

Bladder struggled to fight the good feeling her admiration gave him.

He peered sideways and up. Wheedle and Spigot stared at him, with open mouths like dark caverns. He looked away, hoping they understood he wasn't asking for help, he didn't need saving.

Maggie the crone continued. 'I believe our only way forward is stolen magic. There's no life magic left in monsterkind now without Thunderguts. Who knows where it went, but it must be handed down. To awaken the hatchlings, we'll steal other magic, and I am determined to save every scrap of fairy dust to this end.' She pushed her arm around so Bladder could see the bag hanging from her shoulder and patted it. The powdered fragrance of fairy dust escaped the sides. She'd managed to collect a lot more than a small tinful, and the burden of carrying it hurt her. 'Fairy dust is the most potent magic in the world and in the right hands, there'll be more ogres, more trolls. Maybe I'll gift you with a little gargoyle or two.' The crone winked at Bladder. He thought of young Wheedle and Spigot, and sewer water dampened his snout. Maggie continued. 'The only time I use it is to ready myself to steal more. I can't afford to waste it. Fairy magic is life magic in the hands of a fairy, and I have a plan to get so much more. That's what we must do first.'

Bladder didn't want to point out that monster plans hadn't always gone too well for them. Thunderguts had wanted the soul sword destroyed to stop the hiding, and this dead place was the result. Hold on, what did she say at the end? 'In the hands of a fairy?' Bladder asked. 'But why would a fairy help you? You're stealing their dust.'

Maggie the crone chuckled at him. Motherly. 'We have our own half-fairy, didn't you know? Half-fairy, half-monster.'

Bladder shook. He knew exactly who she meant.

'My Samuel', she said. 'It's because of him we're free. He released us.'

Bladder looked around the Great Cavern. She was bonkers. Sam destroyed the sword and turned The Hole to a tomb. Still, if she was after him, she might know how to find him. 'So, where is he?' Bladder asked.

'I haven't located him. Not yet. I searched for him, hill and dale, and I wasn't able to feel him for such a long time. Sometimes I can sense him, you know? Maybe it's because I held his soul inside of me so long that we have such a strong connection. For a time, it was almost as if he fell asleep. I knew he wasn't dead, but I couldn't find him, and now it seems as if something has woken him. He's a naughty imp and likes to play, so maybe it's that he wants to come back to us finally, and I must help him find his way home again. As soon as I talk to my troops, I'm going to search for him.'

Bladder trembled at the sudden affection in the banshee's voice. Sam had left the Kavanagh house, which had been covered in Daniel's protective sigils, and now he was vulnerable again. The monsters could track him, if they wanted, and Maggie would kill Sam as soon as hug him.

Bladder had to be careful getting to Sam himself. He couldn't afford the crone or her cronies on his tail.

Hold on! If she hadn't seen Sam, who was the woman in The Lanes?

The softness returned to Maggie's voice. 'Actually, I think I could use you for something else. I hear gargoyles are the best sniffer dogs. Isn't that right? And my Sam's fond of gargoyles.' She turned a hard eye on Bladder, squinting as if she remembered Bladder had been Sam's gargoyle and had attacked her.

Bladder gagged back a little bit of sick.

'No, Sam would have smashed any gargoyle who hurt me. Surely he would. He ...' She tapped at the place where a human would have a heart, although Bladder knew her chest was dry and empty. 'He is fond of his gargoyles, and he feels something for me. We're tied.' Maggie patted the lion on the back. 'See if you can find any news of him for me. As soon as I've seen my troops, I'll be back here. Do you need a couple of pixies with you? They can deliver any information.'

'No, no, I've got a pack. It's fine.'

'More gargoyles? We'll have to treasure you more in future. Who knew the value of you? You find my Sam.

He's off playing somewhere, and he's being a naughty boy, but you talk him into coming home. You're bright, and it's pleasant to have help that'll actually raise its voice.' Maggie clicked her swollen fingers. 'Nasty Nan!' she called, and a shivering she-goblin appeared from a shadow. The goblin didn't even spare a threatening glance at Bladder, she bowed and her long nose trailed in the dirt. 'Are the troops gathered?'

'Been waiting on Your Maj'sty for a little bit.'

'Come on. I know you're all wanting back to the outside world,' Maggie said, and a blight of pixies scurried like cockroaches out of the dark and fled joyously ahead of her, rushing to escape The Hole, and giggling harder the further they ran from the Great Cavern. 'Bring me some news of the boy, gargoyle, and you can pick a bauble and the first hatchling will be yours,' Maggie said, then she leaned on the she-goblin and limped away.

Bladder looked back at the mounds of beans. If she was right and Sam was the key to her hatching them all, then Maggie wouldn't stop searching for him until he was back in The Hole by her side.

Bladder peered up to where Wheedle and Spigot stared at him, mouths open in silent shrieks.

He listened as Maggie and Nasty Nan hobbled away. He sniffed the tunnels, just a sliver of a scent of Sam. Half-fairy, half-monster, mixed too heavily to mistake him. The boy had such a distinct scent. Maggie was closer to Sam than she realised.

Bladder waited until Wheedle and Spigot joined him.

'We've got to get to Sam before some other monster finds him. The fact she thinks I'm that monster may have bought us some time.'

'What do you mean?' Wheedle asked.

'I'll tell you on the way.'

CHAPTER 14

While the gargoyles lingered in the darkness of The Hole, Sam lay in his bed listening as Woermann pressed four buttons somewhere near the front door – *beep, beep, beep, beep* – then wandered upstairs to stand outside Sam's door. Sam pretended to sleep, making soft sounds and breathing gently. The big man padded away and a door – Woermann's bedroom door, Sam guessed – opened and closed on the same floor but on the opposite side of the building.

Sam lay there, quiet and patient, listening to the alarm system bipping every three seconds. Woermann probably set it as much for keeping in Sam as keeping out anyone else. Sam listened. And waited. Then waited some more.

Finally, he heard Woermann purring in happy sleep.

Sam got out of bed fully dressed and stole barefoot to the window he had worked on all day, pulling at its hinge until it had opened to a boy-sized gap.

Everything shone under the gibbous moon, three-quarter-sized and full of spite. Moonlight revealed the side of the house. On the ground floor and even the second floor, little red eyes, part of the alarm system, blinked at Sam, telling him 'We're watching this window, find another'.

Sam climbed sideways towards the corner room and peered in. Yes. It was the guest bedroom with the hingeless window. The window was closed, but it took him no time to get his fingers into the frame. It opened with a sigh, and Sam crawled inside the room, stopping as he did to reassure himself Woermann was still snoring.

The plush olive carpet swallowed the sound of Sam's footsteps. He ran down the upper corridor and took two flights of stairs, sure only a gargoyle could have heard him, and only if it had been actively listening.

The kitchen door opened on smooth-oiled hinges and he stepped into the room. The alarm system on the window blinked at him again, but he wasn't trying to open an outside door, so it didn't pay much attention. The dark ominous shapes transformed into a table and chairs, while the bulky figures across the room turned out to be no more than a fridge and a stove.

He approached the white door at the back of the kitchen. It looked like a pantry from the outside, but Sam's nose picked up the stink of miserable animals and of fairy dust. There weren't only dogs, but cats, rabbits and other creatures' smells he didn't recognise. If he could get them out of that little room, they could all worry about the alarm system afterwards.

He stopped again, listening for the only noise he wanted Woermann making: snores.

The pantry door had no key lock. Sam wondered if it needed some special device to open it, but he pulled down the handle and the door simply released. What appeared to be a pantry door opened on to dark stairs.

So far, so good.

Growling and whining started immediately.

'Shhh,' he hissed down at the noisemakers. 'Be quiet. Don't wake Woermann.'

'Who is that?' a rough, doggy voice called up. 'I've still got all my teeth, you know.'

'I'm Sam.'

The animal sounds stopped and clear voices began arguing. 'Not the cat man', 'Smells worse', 'It's a monster'.

'No, it's Sam. Shut up, everyone. He told you to shut up,' Amira's determined voice called over them all.

Sam inhaled. His ears had to drown out their arguments to listen. Flights away, Woermann muttered.

Sam stepped into the doorway. 'Be quiet or I shut this door again.'

The animal sounds softened into complaints. 'Well, you don't have to be so nasty,' someone said.

Woermann shuffled overhead. The snoring resumed.

'You sure about him?' the doggy voice asked.

'I sure am, Dad. That's my friend Sam. And he understands everything we're saying.'

Sam smiled at the sound of Wilfred's voice.

'Come on,' Sam said. 'This door is heavy.'

'All right then, everyone out,' said the doggy voice, Mr Kintamani, Sam guessed.

Overhead, Woermann murmured happily in his sleep.

Cries of relief and 'Soft, now' came closer and the padding of paws and the clicking of claws sounded on the wooden steps.

Sam stepped back, holding open the door and letting the first wave of animals crawl out of the darkness. A trio of rabbit kittens bounced into the kitchen, followed by two brown rabbits who blinked in the moonlight spilling through the window. The larger of the two stood on its hind legs and sniffed him.

'Oh, yes, I smell it now. Clover. Lovely,' it whispered.

A half dozen shelties piled out behind them and a few more dogs appeared, carrying strange spiky animals in their mouths.

The dogs put the spiky creatures down and grinned in the doggy way, open-mouthed, tongues out.

'Hedgehogs,' a beige dog said to his raised eyebrows. 'So, you're Sam?'

'He sure is,' said the puppy behind them. Hazel. 'Hurrah, Sam!'

'Shhhh,' Sam said. 'Woermann's upstairs.'

'Hurrah, Sam,' Hazel whispered, and jumped up to lean on his knees. He rubbed her ears.

'We can say very honestly, we're very pleased to meet you,' said a lovely beige dog. She licked Hazel's ear.

'Mrs ... Dr Kokoni?' Sam asked.

162

'Well done, young man', said her mate. 'I think after rescuing us, you can call us Andreas and Chryssi.'

Wilfred lolloped around them and slurped all over Sam's hand. 'You're OK, which is brilliant, *and* you just let us out, which is doubly so.' He turned to the saluki pup behind him. 'Now aren't you glad we made friends?'

'Yes, yes', Amira said. 'You're never going to let me live that down, are you?'

'Nope', Wilfred said.

Amira's mum stood behind her daughter. 'Every time I see you, young man, you're letting me out of something. Maybe next time, we'll just have you over for dinner, hey?'

While Hazel, Amira and Wilfred gave his knees grateful puppy kisses, another dozen shifters appeared in the kitchen. Some were dogs, but the rest were cats, rabbits and a couple more hedgehogs, who obviously needed to be carried up steps too big for them to jump. They were followed by the shy, friendly faces of a pair of badgers, and the last two faces belonged to two black and fluffy dogs.

'Is that everyone accounted for?' the larger one asked. He sniffed down the steps to check.

'That's my dad.' Wilfred's fur fluffed up proudly. 'He's a detective inspector.'

Wilfred's parents, two Kintamani dogs, sniffed Sam's face. A cat walked back and forth next to Sam's leg, rubbing itself against him as it did so. She introduced herself: 'Cecile Siamese', she said.

The badgers stared at the kitchen doors. 'Well, next

stage of the escape. We have to get through those. Top of the range alarm system.'

'Just smash 'em and run, I say,' a rabbit suggested.

Sam shook his head. 'Too much noise. Woermann could track you down. We need to get out without setting off the alarm and ...'

'The boy's right, it's a Tutum 520 System. I don't suppose you know the key code?' the bigger badger asked.

Sam shook his head.

'Hmmm, then no idea what we can do to open it,' the badger said. 'I've installed at least twenty of these. He presses six keys then we've got a million combinations to figure out. And we've only got three chances to get this right before we set it off.'

Sam remembered the beeps. 'He pressed four keys.'

The badger sighed. 'That narrows it down to a thousand possible combinations, which increases our chances, I suppose.'

'What if I can sniff the keys?' a bloodhound asked. 'He's a pretty pongy cat.'

'Oi,' Cecile said.

Sam assumed the expression on the badger's face was a wry grin. He'd never met a badger before. 'That narrows it down to twenty-four possible combinations. Twelve and a half per cent chance of getting out. I suppose it's better than three in a million.'

'All right,' said the bloodhound. 'Let's find the alarm pad.'

The thirty or so shifters crept along the corridor

towards the front door. The keypad was easy to find. Right next to the door and, at night, it flickered like the fairy lights in the Pixie Cavern.

'Flip open the cover, then,' the badger said to Sam. 'If we can narrow it down further, we'll get you to press in the code.'

'Me?' Sam asked.

'Opposable thumbs and at least one finger are useful,' the badger replied.

'What if I press the wrong numbers?'

'There's a good chance you will, but even if I could shift back –' the badger shuffled and studied the keypad – 'I haven't got any clothes, and I'm a bit loath to work in the nuddy. Children present an' all.' He waved a claw at the crowd behind.

A rabbit sat up and looked at the stairs. 'I can't hear anything. He's still asleep. Right?'

Sam listened too. The snoring went on.

Sam leaned forward and flipped open the plastic cover of the alarm. The bloodhound jumped up and leaned against the wall. It chuckled. 'Nine.'

'What do you mean, "nine"?' the badger said.

'The only key he presses is nine. He must press it four times. His favourite number. Nine lives and all that. Typical cat.'

'Oi,' said Cecile Siamese.

The bloodhound squinted at Sam. 'Go on then, press them.'

'Are you sure?' a hedgehog asked. 'It seems a little easy.'

'If I'm wrong, then we break the window,' the blood-hound said.

'Which wastes precious seconds,' a rabbit replied.

The bloodhound snuffled over the keys again. 'I'm one hundred per cent certain. You sure it was four buttons, Sam?'

Sam suddenly wondered. Was it four? Or was it five?

'We're burning moonlight,' the cat said. 'No point waiting for it. If we're wrong, at least we gotta better chance than waiting for him to come down the stairs.'

The animals turned their gazes on Sam. His hand shook.

Sam pressed the nine key. Once. Twice. Thrice. Four times.

Nothing happened.

Sam stared at the badger.

'I'm cracking the window. Give me a leg up,' the larger rabbit said, pulling on the bloodhound's ear.

Before the good creature answered, the red lights turned green. But the alarm let out a loud single beep.

Upstairs, Woermann cried out. 'What? What?'

Sam held up his hands and pointed to the ceiling. The little group went as silent as they could, but the marching band tattoo of their hearts beat at Sam. He listened for the footsteps of the man cat upstairs.

Woermann was awake, that was true, but he hadn't climbed out of bed. Yet.

Woermann's pillows flumped as he lay down again. His ears weren't as good as Sam's but if anything bumped, dropped or opened in the foyer, Sam thought the cat man would hear that.

Sam motioned his arm down, and put his palms together under his head. The sign for sleeping.

Sam looked at the window the rabbit wanted opened. The sound of it would ride up the stairs.

He motioned them back to the kitchen.

CHAPTER 15

S am went ahead. Softly, softly, listening all the way until he heard Woermann snoring again. He trembled. *If the cat man woke once, he'd be awake again very soon.*

The shifters followed Sam to the kitchen. They stared at the white door that had been the gate to their cell; a few shuddered, then scooted after Sam as he went to the kitchen doors, the ones that opened out on to the wide brown lawn and round to the driveway. He stopped, listened for snoring and opened the lock near the handle. Sam gestured at the alarm; it was all green lights now.

The door clicked open. Sam stepped outside and felt the clean night air on his face. One ear listened to the outside world, one to the cat above.

The night outside was moonlit and quiet. The fresh air floated into the room, and the animals inhaled as if they had never smelt such air.

'OK, everyone out', Sam whispered.

The rabbits couldn't get out fast enough. They bounced straight across the lawn, towards the hedge, even the babies were as fast as their parents. At the hedge, the adult rabbits guided the little ones underneath, looked back at Sam, waved and they were gone.

The shelties picked up the hedgehogs. Those little ones wouldn't be going anywhere fast unless they got a lift. In a few quiet seconds, the kitchen had almost emptied of animals.

'This way to the road', the bloodhound said, lowering its gruff bark. He raced for the gate and with the help of the shelties dug quick holes, sliding through the slush, their bodies moving underneath and encouraging smaller animals through. A few snouts submerged, Sam heard coughing and spluttering. The rabbits squeezed under the hedge, followed by kittens, puppies and hedgehogs.

Sam stepped outside with the cat.

'Come on then', the badgers said, expecting everyone else to be behind them. Wilfred's, Amira's and Hazel's families remained on the kitchen floor.

'What's going on?' Sam asked.

'There's a thing in the cellar', Wilfred said. 'Right, Dad?'

'A thing in the cellar? What thing?' Sam asked. 'It can't be that important that we stay for it.'

'I don't know why, but I think it is', the detective inspector said as the others nodded at Sam. 'But you lot go on ...'

'And how do you propose to move it?' Amira's mum

169

asked. 'Either we all go now, or we all go and get it, but we have to move fast. No one's leaving you here, Lee.'

'What's going on upstairs, Sam?' Dr Kokoni asked.

Woermann's breath was low and pleasant. Sam said so.

'I wouldn't risk it,' Cecile said. 'Cats are crepuscular and nocturnal animals.'

The bigger badger snorted. 'Crepuscular. Ha!'

Cecile hissed at the badger, then turned to look at Sam. 'It's a creature who likes wandering around at dusk or dawn. But cats are nocturnal too. How long's Woermann been asleep?'

'I don't know, an hour. But he was awake all day.'

'Then he may sleep a bit longer, but instinct is instinct. The closer to the full moon you get, the more that lunatic upstairs will become catlike. Like I said, I wouldn't risk it.'

The adult dogs sat on their haunches. 'You go, we'll catch up.'

The smaller badger gave Sam a snuffly kiss and the badgers raced off. Only Cecile looked back, then bounced straight across the lawn, towards the hedge, where a pair of shelties waited.

Sam watched the shelties guide the badgers under and heard gurgles as they submerged in a puddle, while Cecile, after trying alone, accepted the dogs' assistance.

'I'm almost positive it's why we've all been caught. It's got something to do with that thing,' D.I. Kintamani said. 'Sam, you and the pups need to leave ...'

Dr Kokoni shook her head. 'I still can't change. Not

even a whisker, not even with that door open. I've been trying since Sam let us out. That stuff hasn't cleared my system. We're going to need Sam. Sorry, boy.'

Sam looked at the doggy doctor.

'Your hands', she replied to his stare. 'If we're doing this, we'll need someone to lift it.'

Lift what? Sam thought. He wished they'd tell him.

'On to what?' Amira's mum asked, then she took off, sniffing at drawers and cupboards. 'Sam, heel!' she said, and pointed her nose at the drawer. 'Open!'

Sam did as he was told. All he could see were tea towels and other fabric things.

'The tablecloth', Amira's mum said.

'Brilliant!' D.I. Kintamani replied. 'All right, there's four of us. We take a corner each. Caitlyn, you go with the kids.'

'No', Amira's mum said. 'We're going to need someone to guide us, or we'll go all over the place. I think that should be you. We're going to need the whole pack. Sam puts the ball in the middle, he can take off, and good officer Lee Kintamani leads us out.'

'Agreed', the Kokonis and Mrs Kintamani said.

'It's a plan. We just need to find somewhere to hide it and then we run', D.I. Kintamani said. 'Five, maybe ten minutes at the most. Do we have the time, Sam?'

Woermann's breathing was so low, Sam thought they might have, but he was still confused by what was going on.

'What can we do, Dad?' Wilfred asked, his tail wagging.

'You get out and hide somewhere on the other side of the road. We'll sniff you out.'

'No way,' Amira said. 'You'll need someone up here to stand guard. If it's only ten minutes ...'

Sam's shifter friends dropped their haunches on the tiles. Naughty puppies.

'No time to argue,' Dr Kokoni said. 'Let's just do it, but I will deal with you later, Hazel.'

Hazel lowered her head, but she didn't budge.

Sam heard the other animals leaving, the gravel of the road crunched under bare paws and then they ran on grass. They were putting a lot of distance between themselves and the house. Above them, Woermann growled in his sleep and turned over. He purred again straight away. They had a little time.

Sam and the three dog families stood at the top of the stairs leading to the basement.

The door leered open and the reek of unhappiness, not just dogs but cats and rabbits and hedgehogs and other animals too, punched out. Sam peered into it, and squinted. The first time he'd looked he'd only noticed the dark, but he realised a gentle light glowed up from below: a night light, maybe. Pungent magic wafted towards him, a fresher version of the same dusty scent covering Woermann.

The door had no inside handle. Sam looked around for something to hold the door open and his gaze set on a spatula hanging from a hook. He let go of the door to run for the spatula. The door swung shut like scissors. *Schick.* The dogs jumped.

The spatula wobbled under the door, but it held it open. 'Watch that,' Sam said to the puppies.

Sam followed the dogs down into the cellar.

Unlike the rest of the house, the room had not been renovated; the boards of the floor were rough and unsealed. A mess of mattresses and blankets covered it and lay alongside bowls of dirty water and congealed food. The room was not insulated and an earthy cool seeped into the room. It was the most awful room Sam had ever seen.

Sam heard the distant voices before he got to the base of the steps, and they came from a light on a stand in the middle of the room. The *thing* was a glowing white sphere.

He couldn't hear words exactly, just the tone. The speakers seemed lost, talking to each other, coddling, calming, comforting.

He knew what they were straight away. He also knew why the dogs couldn't go without it. Even though they may not have known what the orb was, soul calls to soul.

Amira's mum spat out the tablecloth. 'Do you think it's more magic? Do you think the urge to take it is so strong because it's an enchantment? What if it's ... evil?'

Sam turned to see Wilfred, Hazel and Amira at the top of the stairs straining to see what their parents were doing.

'No,' Sam replied. 'It's not evil. It's like the Vorpal Sword. It's full of souls.'

'Vorpal what?' D.I. Kintamani asked.

'Sword. Sam found it with the ogres,' Hazel said. The

pup, little more than a silhouette at the top of the stairs, had taken a step into the room.

Sam walked forward and touched the orb.

It had a physical surface, unlike the Vorpal Sword, which had been pure soul. The souls inside the orb hummed under thick, opaque glass which felt cold on Sam's hands. There were hundreds of them inside, much fewer than in the Sword of Souls, but buzzing with power. He sensed rather than heard the souls hitting the inside of the glass. Their hums sounded so far away; he couldn't distinguish their words, and they didn't appear to know he was there.

Sam picked up the orb and flung it at the wall. It hit it with a chink and thudded on the floorboards. The dogs jumped.

'Well, that was useful,' Amira called down.

'Amira, hush,' her mum's voice replied.

'What were you trying to do?' Hazel asked. She was closer than before, almost at the bottom of the steps. Amira stood just above her; only Wilfred remained in the doorway shivering.

'Last time I found something like this, I just broke it, and the souls flew away.'

'Souls?' D.I. Kintamani paced around the orb, sniffing it.

'Whose souls are they?' Amira asked.

Sam didn't know who they belonged to. They were just souls.

'Ours,' the detective inspector said. 'Shifter souls. It all makes sense. Shifters coming back, half crazed with misery, but unable to shift form. Not themselves any more. They really aren't themselves. With only one soul they are no longer shifters.'

The dogs whimpered. D.I. Kintamani took another sniff of the orb.

'Why shifters?' Dr Kokoni asked.

'You take a soul from a single-souled creature, what do you have left?'

'I don't know.'

'You have a dead body,' Dr Kokoni replied. 'But if you take one soul from a twin-souled creature, you might have missing people, but no bodies are going to turn up. There isn't any evidence of a crime.'

'That's horrible,' Amira said.

'But it's very clever,' D.I. Kintamani said. 'We need to do what Sam was trying. We need to break it open, so the souls can return to their bodies.'

Sam picked up the orb. Mr and Mrs Kokoni, Amira's mum and Mrs Kintamani had a corner each and they readied the tablecloth.

D.I. Kintamani stared at Sam. 'Let's get it out of here. I've got a lot of questions for you afterwards.'

Sam heard the creak, and looked up. Wilfred was closest to the exit, but even he had taken two steps down.

'Wilfred!' Sam yelled. 'Get out!'

Wilfred, ever the good pup, turned as if trained, and had managed a step, but the spatula flicked out, flying over the steps and landing on the orb. The door, vicious and quick, snapped shut and smacked Wilfred's nose. They were all stuck in the dark again.

Sam was with them, unable to free them this time.

Bladder, Wheedle and Spigot listened as Maggie the crone limped to the right. They'd followed her, tiptoeing behind her in the dark. As she took every turn they'd intended to use, Spigot's stone feathers bristled more and more. It was only at the last fork she turned left where they meant to turn right.

'Thank goodness,' Wheedle said.

Bladder led Wheedle and Spigot through a passageway. It was raw and rough, and getting rougher all the time.

The tunnel got smaller, until they came upon stones, dirt and tree roots blocking their path.

'Are you sure it's this way?' Wheedle asked.

'Well, I thought it was, maybe it's left more. Let me just remember.'

'What'd she mean about talking to the troops in the next hour? What about, do you think? What's she going to ask them to do?' Wheedle asked.

'Don't know, don't care,' Bladder replied. 'It won't be good, whatever it is. If she's up there somewhere with a few thousand monsters, best we avoid it, don't you think? Oh, yeah, it's definitely left.'

'It must be important if she's gathering them all, and Sam ...'

'Exactly! Sam. The most important things first. Ooh, look. There it is.' Bladder could make out the world above through the small circle of a burrow entrance. He saw the beginnings of a Sussex night overhead and smelt grass and animals close by.

Bladder climbed up and out.

Right between the nesting buttocks of two trolls.

The trolls didn't notice Bladder, but he could see between them, into a valley. Their attention was focused on a large ogre in the centre of a low field, surrounded by thousands and thousands of various-sized monsters seated and looking down on the natural amphitheatre. Bladder backed into the burrow again, but Wheedle and Spigot pushed and *oof*ed at his back end. They forced him all the way out, shoving him into a goblin's elbow. Then the pair fought to see who could get his head out next, making all sorts of noise.

'Get back inside', Bladder yelled at them.

'Hey', a voice said as a hand the size of a small truck picked up Bladder by the tail. 'Looky, I finds me a gumgoyle.'

'Ooh, ooh, ooh.' Goblin, ogre and troll heads turned to look at him. 'Youse is right. Is a gumgoyle. Looky, looky, two more!'

CHAPTER 16

'He's coming,' Sam said.

Woermann slept a couple more hours, despite the cat's warning, and Sam spent the entire time exploring the room trying to find another way out. The dogs flumped on the mattresses, D.I. Kintamani assuring him they had searched everything, but as Sam could climb, he searched the ceiling too. At first, the shifters watched this with their tongues out and eyes hardly blinking. The pups fell asleep.

Woermann came downstairs, his footfalls vibrating in Sam's ears.

Sam clambered next to the door and flattened himself against the rough wood.

'What are you doing?' Wilfred asked.

'Shhh,' hissed Sam.

Woermann came into the kitchen. He gasped and swore. Sam remembered the doors to the outside were wide open. Woermann's heavy tread sped towards the cellar door and he wrenched it hard and moonlight poured into the cellar. Woermann's shadow fell in the doorway. He'd only have to look up an inch and he'd be able to see Sam's face, but the cat man stared at the animals below. The door smacked closed again, and a moment later, Woermann was back. Woermann pushed at the hinge above the door, and Sam heard a mechanism click which jammed the door open. The cat man turned a torch on the dogs, who blinked in the harsh light, and stalked inside the cellar. Woermann's hair skimmed Sam's legs.

D.I. Kintamani barked. The other dogs took his lead and growled and snarled at Woermann. The big man took three more steps down into the cellar. He shone the torch around the room. 'Shut up', he said. 'Stupid dogs.'

The shifters barked louder. D.I. Kintamani yelled, 'Go, go, go', at Sam.

Sam pulled himself out as quietly as he could, and dropped to the floor. He turned to see Woermann's head in the cellar framed by torchlight.

Sam ran for the open lawn, swerved left and lobbed himself up the wall. The moon throbbed painfully above him, lighting up the bedroom windows.

'How could they get out? Oh, no, the boy!' Woermann shouted. Then he swore. Sam heard him drop the torch, and the pantry door slammed shut before Woermann raced to the stairs.

Sam scurried towards the bedroom. Inside the house, Woermann took stairs three and four at a time, up two flights as Sam managed the same on the outside wall. He was still clambering to the open window as Woermann pounded along the corridor outside his room.

He wouldn't make it in time.

Then Sam heard keys jingle and drop, the carpet swallowing the clatter. Woermann swore at having to pick them up and find the right key again. It gave Sam a couple more seconds.

Sam climbed inside. Closed window. Key rattled in lock. Into bed. Head on pillow. Eyes shut.

The door swung open and Woermann leaped to Sam's bedside. He leaned right over and put his face next to Sam's, his hairy cheek brushing the boy's. Sam pretended to sleep.

Woermann breathed slower. Sam felt a cat's unblinking stare burn into his cheek; he wished the man would go away.

Finally, Woermann did. Stepping slowly out of the room, this time making less noise. The keys tinkling all the way downstairs again. Talking to himself all the way, trying to understand how the shifters had got out.

An ogre hung Bladder in front of its big nose, studying him; one eye closed, the other eye bugged out and bloodshot.

Bladder groaned. In the open air, he could smell Sam's scent strong and near. They would never see him again.

The ogre flicked Bladder with a yellowed index finger as long as a man's arm. 'What's iz name?' it asked Bladder.

'My name?' Bladder asked.

'Who else me is ask? Bit fick, this one,' the ogre said to two others, who leaned in to study the gargoyle.

'I'm Bladder.'

'Pleased to meet you, Bladder, I'm Cob.' Cob then put Bladder on his shoulder. He was the size of a decent shed, so his shoulder was a comfortable perch. Bladder looked over his own smaller, less sturdy shoulder and saw two pairs of terrified gargoyle eyes peering at him. A goblin cuddled Wheedle, while a young boggart rubbed its face against Spigot's wing. The stone eagle didn't make a sound.

'An' your pack?' Cob asked.

'My pack? You mean the other gargoyles?'

'At least you cute. Not much for brains, ey, these gumgoyles?' Cob said.

The other monsters laughed. Bladder frowned. It almost sounded kindly.

'I'm Wheedle.' Wheedle's voice shook. 'An' Spigot doesn't talk.'

The goblin hugged Wheedle harder.

'My back, my back,' Wheedle wheezed.

'Sorry,' the goblin said.

'Meetcha, Wheedle. Meetcha, Spigot,' the boggart said. The trolls, ogres and other goblins echoed the greeting.

A dozen manky hands reached for the gargoyles and stroked and tickled their heads. The ogres were a bit rough, like eager toddlers. Bladder thought they might end up breaking something accidentally. He put his ears back so their heavy hands were flat on his head, to stop any rough affection from cracking him.

Affection? Yes, that was what they seemed to be giving. Bladder and Wheedle stared at each other. These monsters were being nice. Maybe because the brutish creatures were young, maybe because they hadn't seen any gargoyles in a long time. Even Cob, as large as he was, had a round and open face. Despite his size, Bladder could see the ogre was little more than a baby.

'Arn' gumgoyles scary?' a boggart asked. 'Din' the little prince have gumgoyles wiv 'im?'

'An' wern it the little prince who got all them ogres kilt?' a little ogre asked.

'He was jus' doin' wot Funderguts axed 'im,' a troll replied. 'Enyways, it ent like ogres ent bin killin' ogres for centuries themselms.'

'An' that's the truth,' the goblin said.

The troll nodded eagerly. 'He jus' done it better an' quicker.'

'Yeah, well we don' wanna be doin' that no more. Ent enough of us. Iz a graveyard down there,' the little ogre said.

All the monsters shuddered.

Standing with his claws on solid muscle, Bladder watched. The smaller monsters leaned against Cob's sides, childlike and nervous.

'What's going on?' Wheedle asked.

'You wanna see? Come up, on my udder shoulder,' Cob said.

Cob put Wheedle on his other shoulder. Spigot squawked but the little boggart didn't seem to want to let go of him. The eagle looked safe enough, so Bladder peered out at his surroundings.

A gathering of bilious, bulbous monsters encircled the largest of all living ogres in the middle of a natural amphitheatre. The audience spread so far back they had filled the meadows behind the one they were in and even further. Bladder could make out movement of monsters ahead, left, right, even behind them that were so far back they could be insects. Bladder realised there was an end to them, a point where he could see fields empty and spaces between the flesh-eating beasts, but the size of the entire population was quite unnerving and there were enough monsters left to cause humans some big problems. There were thousands upon thousands of them. Ogres, small for their species, packed together with young goblins and trolls. There were fewer larger monsters mixed with them. In this field, only a dozen or so of old goblins and ogres of fighting size, but size wasn't everything. Cob would have been large enough, but Bladder peered at the eager face; the young ogre did not have the same menacing expression worn by the older beasts. Most of the crowd were young monsters like boggarts, bogies and baby bunyips, and between them, thousands of pixies, sprites and brownies scurried, their faces all as dim and as harmless as Cob's. Rarer monsters appeared too, a siren in a wine barrel, a three-headed dog, half a dozen giggling tokoloshes wearing AC/DC T-shirts, greeblies, yōkais, bai gu jings, ijiraqs, divs, cucas, and endless monsters Bladder couldn't name. There was even a knab of large toads wearing pink nail polish and Bladder was sure he'd never seen anything like them before.

'Good grief, what is that red thing?' Wheedle asked and then, echoing Bladder's thought, 'Maggie must be desperate. She'll let anyone into this party.'

'Ent a party,' Cob said. 'This is very serious.'

'Sorry,' Wheedle replied.

Bladder almost laughed. 'What's it for?'

'Maggie's got a plan. A plan for us to get more monsters.'

Bladder looked at the crowd. 'More than this?'

'It looks a lot, but back in The Hole, when ebbry-one goes to their own caverns, it's so empty. I'd ravver live in a car park f'rever than go back there.'

'I like car parks,' said Spigot's boggart, its face pressed up to Spigot's. The eagle glared at Bladder as if it were his fault. Bladder supposed it was.

Bladder studied the crowd. It was a frightening storm of monster life, but the greater number really were mid-sized or small. Sam's sword had done a smashing job of ... well, smashing the population, which meant even gargoyles and monsters normally left to stink up the swamp were more than welcome, they were expected to show.

'What's going on? Is that ogre in charge?' Wheedle asked, pointing at the huge ogre in the centre of it all.

'That's Bombottom,' Cob said. 'Her Maggie-stee's general.'

Spigot's boggart said, 'Iz nice to see so many of uz in one place.'

Then Maggie strolled out from behind Bombottom, who put her on his shoulder.

'Does anyone know what she's going to talk to us about?' Bladder asked.

'She got some job for us,' Cob said, and smiled at Bladder.

The crowd hushed, waiting for the banshee to speak, but Maggie wasn't talking yet, she surveyed her army and called down instructions to Nasty Nan. 'Ready the display!'

Bladder leaned closer as Nasty Nan raced through the crowd, speaking in low whispers to the various monsters and imps.

A drumbeat sounded, hollow and otherworldly. The small ogre swung up so he was sitting in Cob's elbow, his face next to Bladder's. 'Iz exciting?'

Bladder thought 'horrifying' was a better word.

He wondered where the humans were. It was well after midnight, that was true. He hoped they were all asleep, because one that wandered into this crowd wouldn't wander out. He took a good sniff of air. Ah, fairy dust hung lightly at the edges of the gathering. It could do anything. He wondered how much Maggie had used to mask this meeting from the human world. She had been so precious about it.

'My people! Thank you for coming. It is so good to see you all,' Maggie called from the shoulders of the ogre.

The crowd cheered. A few pockets burst like thunder in the dry sky. Bladder got it, they were happy to see themselves, to see the monster world wasn't entirely dead. The violence of the eruption suggested this was their first gathering together as a complete community and the size of it would have been reassuring, despite the young and gormless faces.

'My people, we have been beaten back, diminished, left for dead, but that does not mean we cannot rise up and rebuild.'

It wasn't quite as encouraging as the welcome, so the second cheer was half-hearted noise.

Still, Cob raised his arms and Wheedle and Bladder stumbled.

'Sorry,' Cob said.

'Not a problem, not a problem,' Bladder replied, but he and Wheedle decided to leave the tower of Cob's generous arms, as did the little ogre.

On the ground, Bladder couldn't see Maggie between the heads and arms of the other monsters, but he could hear her clearly. She reminded him of Thunderguts before Sam broke the sword, what little Bladder had understood: big ideas and ambition.

'We are smaller in numbers than before, but that does not make us weak or incapable,' she said, and Bladder listened as the crowd cheered again, a little more enthusiastically. He remembered what Maggie had said in the Great Cavern about the lack of courage of these monsters. They were going to be a tough crowd to move.

'To reclaim our place again in this world, the one humans have reigned over too long, we need to frighten them into submission and conquer them again. So we must rebuild our numbers. When we lost Thunderguts, we lost the monsters' life magic. No one was left to breathe on the hatchlings, to bring forth new menace. But I can tell you where there is a great source of life magic: fairy dust.' She strained to lift the sack, her thin arms rising only a little. 'There is enough here to hatch a few more ogres, while those of you already hatched can grow to maturity.'

The ogres cheered.

'But we need much more.'

Bladder wheezed and looked at Wheedle. At least she hadn't said anything about the half-fairy she was looking for to make it all happen.

'We need the right incantation, and one with fairy blood to cast it.'

Oops, spoke too soon, Bladder thought. He turned to Wheedle. 'Probably time to leave.' He backed up, getting behind Cob as he ducked other monsters' large and excited feet.

'But even before all that, we need more dust. Alone, and decrepit as I am, I can do only so much. I caught these fairies by myself. Imagine if each one here did the same. The tonnes of dust we'd collect', Maggie said. 'Nasty Nan, throw them!'

Bladder couldn't see Nasty Nan, but he did see scores of solid chunks of shining green and blue and gold fly over the crowd. One twisted in the air. It wasn't inanimate metal, but a tiny being, glittering and beautiful. A fairy. It fell back to the ground.

'Here's a taster. Bring me as many fairy wings as you can', Maggie yelled. 'And you keep the rest for yourself.'

The beasts cheered, really cheered, and thunderous

laughs lifted the leaves of trees as the crowd stumbled towards the space where the fairies had fallen.

The beasts surged forward, except the gargoyles, who backed away from the mob. The monsters behind Cob leaped and sailed over them, not in the least interested in the gargoyles, who pulled their hoofs, claws and wings over their heads and lay flat on the ground. When the air above them stilled, Bladder looked up. The lowest point of the gentle valley was in throes as it filled with monsters, and he could see it all without a crowd of tall beasts about him. Pixies grabbed at the fairies, ogres plucked at them, goblins smacked flat, fleshy hands down on to them. Bladder wondered why the tiny creatures didn't fly. One raced closer to the gargoyle pack and they saw it, all blurring legs, but wingless. Maggie had already taken the fairy's wings. A boggart snatched it up with hairy fingers. The tiny creature bit at the beast's hand and the boggart squealed and shook off the fairy. The tiny creature pelted away again, heading in Bladder's direction.

'Yum!' yelled an ogre from the other side of the field. 'They taste like sherbet.'

This distracted the monsters nearby, who momentarily forgot the fairy heading towards the gargoyles. They applauded the idea of sherbet-flavoured victims. The fairy itself turned to give a horrified sob, and ran straight into Bladder's mouth.

Bladder snapped his stone jaw down on the creature and sat down, sneering as innocently as he could when the monsters looked behind them, trying to find where the fairy had gone. When they couldn't see it, they lost interest and gazed around to see where other, prettier, brighter prey was darting. Bladder nodded at Wheedle and Spigot and they wandered off as slowly as their panicked legs would allow.

Spigot pushed past Wheedle, shaking boggart kisses from his feathers. The large crowd of dark beasts could not diminish the dazzling bright lights dashing about. Little blurs of light flickered ahead of the crowd. The ferocious party moved further down the field, following fairies as they fled. Several fairies remained on the loose, and the fairy in Bladder's mouth squirmed as much as it could. The squirming didn't bother Bladder, his insides were as stone as his outsides, but its frustrated, frightened screams escaped Bladder's mouth.

A stagnation of pixies reclining against a stark tree stared at him with the first high-pitched squeak, but the thrill of terrified fairies amongst thousands of monsters was enough to distract them too.

Wheedle looked down the field's slope. 'Where's Maggie gone?'

Bladder looked too. She'd set the pack searching for fairies. That was the first part of her plan. The second part was to collect Sam, and they had to get to him before she could.

'We've gotta find Sam,' Wheedle said.

"Ih I ih a oo a ee eh ow oh ih ee,' Bladder said.

'What?'

Spigot squawked.

Wheedle looked at Spigot. 'You understood that? We'll find him as soon as we get out of this field?'

Bladder nodded.

'OK, let's get moving.'

When they came over the rise and found themselves in a smaller bare field, the sound of baying monsters getting more distant, Bladder spat out his passenger.

The fairy sat dazed. A little oxygen deprived, Bladder realised, and winced. He hadn't meant to suffocate the poor thing.

'Are you all right?' Bladder asked.

Wheedle nosed it and it sat up and backed away from them on its hands and feet.

The fairy gazed up to Bladder's concerned face, dropped his pretty face into his pretty hands and sobbed.

'Can you walk?' Bladder asked.

The fairy stood, its tiny legs shaking under it. 'The others?'

'I'm sorry, I don't know. I was lucky to get you out of there. You won't help them going back, you know,' Bladder said when the fairy peered in the direction of the crowd's noise.

'I owe you a boon, my friend. Someday it shall be repaid.' The fairy bowed low. It didn't have wings, but it ran away at a speed that made all three gargoyles' heads crack. With such great speed, Bladder had hope for the others. The little chap went in the same direction they were heading.

'A Boon?' Bladder asked the other two. 'Is that like a Bounty bar?'

Neither Wheedle nor Spigot had any idea.

'Maggie still wants Sam', Bladder said. 'We have to find him before she does.'

'Of course we do. She's probably already set off after him. He's her fairy blood and she won't stop until she's got a cavern full of fairy dust and Sam to waken all those ogres', Bladder said.

Wheedle sniffed the air. 'He's back that way.' The bull pointed his horns back in the direction of the field they had left. A field covered in myriad monsters.

Bladder moaned. 'We'll have to wait till morning then. We can't afford to lead her straight to him.'

CHAPTER 17

It rained in the early hours, barrels and barrels of the stuff, which relieved Sam. The smell of the escaped shifters would be impossible to follow.

When morning came, Woermann remained awake, pacing up and down in the kitchen. Sam couldn't get to the cellar. They'd had one chance and Sam had blown it.

Woermann collected Sam for breakfast, his cat smell ripening. It was stronger than the day before and Woermann had sprouted more hair, so his cheeks and forehead looked fuzzy and black. He took Sam to the kitchen, and the boy ached. His friends were a door and a few steps away.

'You're gold to me,' Woermann said.

Woermann pushed Sam into the bedroom and locked the door behind them. He pulled up a great chair and proceeded to catnap, but whenever Sam moved, the man would jump.

After three forced and miserable conversations, Sam stopped trying to get up. He watched television and looked out the window.

'It'll take forever,' Wheedle said, looking at the ground.

The fields had turned from soft and pliable dirt to complete bogginess. Wheedle and Spigot were up to their bellies in mud, their legs struggling to move forward. A solid yet wet path was half a field-length away. Bladder's wide, flat bottomed paws made it easy for him to find supportive dirt to walk across, but Wheedle's half-hoof, half-toes stabbed into the ground and caused his legs to sink with every step. Spigot was little better; he had only two legs so he was sinking less often, but it took half an hour for them to move out of the shadow of the tree they had settled under the night before.

At least the sun had come out and shone with hot abandon on them. The monsters had gone to ground, avoiding the sunlight, and the horrible hunting sounds had disappeared.

Bladder looked at the path, back at his pack. The smell of Sam had washed away with the night storm. They had been pointing in the direction of the monster field, which looked more mashed and mushy than the one they were in, but that was the direction Sam's scent had come from last night, before they went dormant.

'Just stay in a straight line,' Wheedle said.

'Do you think we're pointed the right way? What if I'm out?' Bladder stared at the fence line.

'The air is drying quickly and you'll pick up on him again. We can't be off by much. His smell was strong last night. He's no more than a mile or two away.'

Spigot raised his head above the mud and shrieked.

'I hope you're right,' Bladder said.

'Well, either way, you can't do anything just sitting here and wondering. You've gotta beat Maggie to the punch, and no point waiting for us. We'll take too long,' Wheedle said. 'Go and find him. We'll catch up. Hopefully, this dries up soon.'

Bladder nodded. It was wet, it was dreary, it was a pain to slurp through mud, but Wheedle and Spigot were safe for the time being, and they knew enough to hide themselves if night came again and the monsters returned. He touched nose to nose, nose to beak, and turned to the path.

'Just tell him we're not far behind, all right?' Wheedle said as Bladder stepped his way across the mushy soil. 'And get to him before Maggie does. And whoever Woermann's working for.'

Woermann's great cat smell filled the space. Sam sat with hands folded in his lap watching some show about robots. Woermann's watch beeped and he lurched out of the chair. His body took up so much space as he moved to the door. He smiled at Sam, and his teeth were large and yellow, every tooth sharp. He seemed to have swollen to twice his previous size like an infected boil.

'Enjoying your stay?' Woermann asked. He leaned over Sam and purred.

Sam's breakfast threatened a hasty return from the bottom of his stomach, and he swallowed a few times to encourage it to stay put.

'I'd rather go home,' Sam said.

Woermann's furry hand slammed the sofa cushion next to Sam and a growl built in the man's throat. 'We have business. Get up!'

Sam shot off the couch and towards the window. The man's humanity was fading. He stared at Woermann. 'What business?'

The great cat grinned.

'We've got company,' he said. His eyes sparkled and his heavy body bounced like a kitten's. He turned to the door. 'She's here.'

Woermann unlocked and opened the door. 'Come on!' he commanded. When Sam didn't obey and backed towards the window, Woermann launched into the room, seized Sam's arm and dragged him into the corridor.

'Don't be afraid, boy, she says you're the key. Although she's a wild thing.' Woermann tittered. 'Can you smell her? She's pure magic.'

Sam didn't know whether he wanted to go, wanted to see Maggie, or if it was just the effect of dust – it was so overpowering, even Sam felt giddy with it.

He wondered how Maggie had managed such huge quantities of dust. It made her unstoppable. What did Maggie want with him? To harm him? Not the Maggie who'd carried his soul like a baby inside her, but the Maggie who wanted a monster-ridden world.

He wanted to run to her. He wanted to run away.

Woermann shoved him down the stairs, then to the front of the house, the fairy dust so thick it called to him, as if it knew he was made of dust.

The cat man giggled, his eyes full of dust and tears. It made his black fur sparkle like a clear night. Woermann pushed open the drawing-room doors and forced Sam into the room ahead of him.

The room was full of creatures, brightly coloured, dancing in the air, reds, yellows, blues, oranges. Squat forms squished on the couches, eating cupcakes and crackers from a buffet table. Others lay on the floor, their faces sticky with sherbet and toffees.

Sam had seen fairies in some of Beatrice's books, and there were some of those delicate, dancing creatures filling the air around him, but others were tall, green and languid as trees, others made of rivulets of water with crowns of dewdrops, while yet more appeared to be stone and metal with sapphires for eyes.

They gave off so much colour, filling the room with a reflection like spilt petrol, reds from almost pink to almost black, blues from ink to off-white.

They all had that beautiful fairy scent. All of them, except for a very short creature in a three-piece suit standing on a stool.

The creatures formed a circle around a woman dressed in velvet black. She stepped towards Sam, her arms out; a fine, golden crown sat atop her red hair. 'Samuel,' she said. She smiled, then spread her wings.

Sam didn't know if he should be relieved it wasn't Maggie.

Woermann had called her a queen. Her orange-and-black wings made her stand out like a dark star against a rainbow.

The little man in the three-piece suit bowed to the queen. He righted himself and announced to Sam, 'Her Majesty, Queen Titania.'

Sam stared.

'Better bow, son,' Three-Piece said.

Sam bowed. The queen smiled.

A group of tiny green fairies flittered into his face. He sneezed and his eyes watered.

'Nature fairies; they make a lot of people do that. If you were the full fairy, it wouldn't, but you're a bit human, intcha?' Three-Piece said. 'Anyone got an antihistamine spell?'

A second sneeze gathered at the back of Sam's nose as another fairy sailed past him. Her wings flittered and covered him with fine blue dust. It smelt of the air high above the ground.

The sneeze dissolved and Sam's eyes stopped itching.

'Your Majesty,' Woermann said. His arms spread wide as he brushed past Sam to bow.

She put out her hand for the man to kiss. He did, with slobbering lips; an attendant passed her a handkerchief. 'What is your will, Woermann?'

Despite this terse response, Woermann giggled, his hands padding at the sparkles in the air around him. He looked at the queen again. 'I got the thing you wanted.'

'What is't?' the queen asked.

Woermann smiled. He had something this fairy wanted. He looked around as if he had forgotten. 'Him.' He pointed at Sam. 'I have delivered as promised, and I believe you promised me something in exchange.'

'Truly?' The queen peered at Sam.

Woermann giggled again and leaned forward. He put his hand to his mouth as if to whisper, but spoke loud enough for everyone in the room to hear him. 'I think he may have let out some of the shifters.'

Shifters! That was right, Sam thought, as the anti-histamine spell began to unmuddle his mind. This was all about shifters. When Sam had thought Maggie was involved in the kidnappings, he knew it couldn't be good, but now he was confused. He studied Woermann's face. He looked as drunk on dust as a human could get, but the queen's face was clear and thoughtful, kind even. Why would the queen of Faery be working with Woermann to kidnap shifters? Why would the queen of Faery want shifters in the first place? He pictured the orb down in the cellar with his friends. What did she want the souls for? Or Sam himself, for that matter?

The queen stared at Woermann. 'Verily? And you know this? How did Sam free the beasts?'

'I'm not really sure,' Woermann replied, his head bobbing from side to side.

'So, you have been careless with your duty and wish to make another wear your failings?'

'Ummm,' Woermann replied. He grinned again and batted at a passing fairy, who squealed as it sailed away too fast. Sam was sure Woermann had forgotten Queen Titania had spoken.

'Well, Samuel is reward enough, so I will still pay you, Woermann.' The queen waved a hand and a group of tiny metallic fairies flew forward. They hummed mechanically, as if clever hands had constructed them down to the whirring cogs in their wings.

They carried golden roses. Countless blooms. Sam couldn't resist reaching towards them. The shiny fairies turned to allow him to touch the flowers, and Woermann snickered. Sam slid his thumb along a petal and its metal edge sliced into the meat of his finger. It was real gold. Woermann's dark eyes stared at Sam's budding blood, and he licked his pasty, dry lips.

'Mine, mine, mine.' Woermann grabbed the roses and grinned, sitting back on the couch and dislodging a group of tiny apricot-coloured fairies as he sniffed the metal blooms.

'Get thee gone, Woermann, before the dust addles you further,' Queen Titania said.

Three-Piece clicked his fingers and four tree-like fairies each took an arm or leg and carried Woermann out of the room. Sam heard the man and his bunch of roses drop to the floor in the foyer.

Three-Piece clicked his finger again and someone carried over a winged chair. The queen slid into it.

'Samuel, set thy heart at rest, thou shalt remain here. None shall harm thee,' the queen said. 'I know Woermann is a rough merchant, but he has his uses.'

Three-Piece jumped off his stool and pointed at it. Sam didn't want to sit. He was wondering if he could make it to the window.

'Don't even think about it,' Three-Piece said.

Sam looked at the short creature. 'What are you? You aren't a fairy?'

'Elf. Christmas elf. Don't like the cold, so I work security for Her Maj. The name's Edgar.'

Edgar motioned for Sam to sit. Sam shook his head and a figure made of blue water shoved him down on to the stool.

'You see us, Samuel, we are multitudinous,' the queen said. 'Nature fairies, small and delicate, working with all the elements.' The metallic fairies giggled as if this were a joke to them. 'There are those of us born of Titans.' She gestured to the loping, beautiful creatures peering at Sam from near the fireplace. 'And our smaller, more human-sized kin.' A lady curtsied to Sam.

'Oh,' was all Sam could think of to say.

'You have caused much mischief for all our kind, Samuel.'

'I have?'

'You have. Tell me true, Samuel, did you free the monsters and the old witch?' The queen stared at Sam. 'You know her as Maggie. 'Twas you, was it not?'

'You let the monsters and that witch Maggie go, didn't you, lad?' Edgar translated.

Sam stared at his feet. It was him all right.

The queen put a pale hand on Sam's knee. He could

smell her, and understood that her dust was of her, fresh and alive. Maggie's dust was the leftovers, beautifully kept, but nothing like this. It was like smelling living blooms after perfume. Perfume was lovely, but after smelling the true thing you would never mistake it again. Queen Titania's magic smelt real and raw.

'Your looks will do as confession,' Queen Titania said. 'Now, you must see what your actions have wrought, my friend. Edgar, summon my Lord Marinell. Let us show what Mistress Maggie has done.'

'You're guilty as sin,' Edgar said to Sam. 'Now, Her Majesty wants you to look at Lord Marinell to see what the witch is doing to fairykind.'

A young man in a doublet and breeches stepped forward, his face flushed at the interest of the other fairies. One of his wings was red-and-gold brocade, but the other was beaten and damaged. Sam could see clear knife lines where someone had cut it and scraped the dust.

"Tis no shame, Lord Marinell, you gave for your people,' Titania said.

Lord Marinell hung his head.

'Maggie did that?' Sam asked.

'She did. Never did you see such a sad sight. The witch has grown in power, and she snatches at our young and fragile. To keep her at bay for a season, Marinell sacrificed his own beautiful wing for the scores of lives she threatened, but with such power she becomes more mighty and steals them anyway. And we must stop her.'

'Lord Marinell gave his wing dust so Maggie wouldn't

nick any of the young ones. She's bally powerful now with all the dust she's collected; Edgar translated.

Lord Marinell stepped back into the crowd.

'Only you can fix it, Samuel; Queen Titania said.

'Me?'

''Twas a bewitched sword kept the monsters at bay?' she asked.

'Yes.'

'And you broke it.'

Sam nodded.

'We forge a similar weapon to replace it.' Titania patted Edgar's head. The small creature grimaced. 'Sorely it grieves us all to do such a thing.'

'We're making a weapon just the same, full of souls and powerful enough to force the monsters back into The Hole; Edgar explained.

Sam knew which weapon they meant. The orb in the cellar, the one full of shifter souls. He paled.

'There, there.' The queen patted his knee. 'Maggie steals our kin and collects their dust. She intends to create hordes of beasts, more than already roam the surface. If she succeeds, then neither fairy nor human will have sanctuary.'

'Sanctuary?' Sam asked Edgar.

'The witch is collecting as much fairy dust as she can, to make more monsters. If she figures out how to turn dust into monsters, then no one's safe, not fairy, not human. You better do as Her Majesty says.'

'Verily, it is so; the queen agreed.

She looked so sad about everything.

'What can I do?' Sam asked.

'When the weapon is completed, you must return it to The Hole. Souls kept them trapped down there for centuries, and so souls must restrain them again.'

'You know you can't just go around stealing people's souls. People die without their souls,' Sam said.

'Not the twin-souled, my sweet. The twin-souled live well enough with one soul, and we have done our best to comfort them. They are sealed inside fairy dust, it makes them happy enough,' she said. 'When the orb calls them in, they cannot leave.' She picked up an oyster and it disappeared between her rosy lips. 'And the twin-souled are not dead. We set them free once a half-soul is taken. We're not murd'rers, Samuel.'

Sam felt sick. He remembered what D.I. Kintamani said: shifters had returned, crazed with misery, ranting, some of them, and no longer really shifters. 'That's not true. They might not physically die, but they aren't ever themselves again.'

The queen sighed and looked so sad, it must hurt her to have to steal the souls. ''Tis costly, no doubt, but you must choose, we all must choose, between all lives or a few souls.'

The fairies and Edgar became quiet. All Sam could hear was Woermann in the corridor giggling to himself and scratching at the walls. It was an eerie sound.

Queen Titania stared at Sam, then picked at a plate. She plucked up a dark mussel between two fingers and slurped it down.

'Do you know the word "meat" was just another word for "food", Samuel?'

'Sorry?'

'A long time ago, I forget exactly when the word was first used.' Titania put her finger into the pâté bowl and scooped a fingerful of pâté into her mouth. Woermann had put out crackers but she left them untouched. 'Humans meant "bread" when they asked for "meat". Hay was meat for horses, slop was meat for pigs.

'A troll visited upon an inn one night and demanded meat. Foul days, dark days those were. The innkeeper offered bread and ale, but the troll would have none. The innkeeper offered the great monster slop and hay too. He offered stew made from one or two chunks of something that had once bled, but what the troll meant by meat was something with a lively juice he could suck out.

'They were foolish, or else they knew exactly what he wanted and tried to satisfy him with lifeless morsels. If they'd given him the horse or the pig, mayhap they would have lived. When the next travellers came by, they found only a boy still alive amongst the bones, no older than your form suggests. It was that boy who taught them what to offer a troll or an ogre when the monster demands *meat*. That is why the word refers to only one type of food now.' She popped the last of the pâté into her mouth and wiped her hands on a napkin Edgar held for her. 'Help us or the world will return to such darkness.'

'You might not like our plans but we're way less evil than monsters,' Edgar translated.

CHAPTER 18

Queen Titania studied him. 'Oh, Sam, you have most wondrous loyalty in you. For the humans and even a little for Maggie – I see it in your looks and I can hear the heavy beat of your heart. What will make that heart mine? What can I do to make you loyal to me?'

Queen Titania rose from her seat and put her hands out to him. She looked so regal and stern, Sam took them. 'Come away with me, Samuel. I'll show you the world you save.'

Queen Titania pulled Sam to his feet and all the other fairies stood. Each sofa, seat and stool erupted into a bush or tree and sprouted leaves. The dishes and cups twisted into flowers and the table melted into the carpet, which turned emerald green as the pile thickened into blades of grass. The sound of Woermann giggling and scratching at the walls was replaced by birdsong and a soft breeze. The fireplace, the walls and the windows faded to the bluest sky Sam had ever seen. Each fairy was exactly where he or she had stood or hovered beforehand, but the world had changed to a sunlit glade. Vibrant green grass matched the leaves of swaying trees, roses as deep as blood, peonies as pink and soft as a child's cheek, daffodils rivalling the sun.

Titania kissed Sam on the forehead. The mark of her lips felt cold. As cold as any of Maggie's kisses. 'This is your place too, Samuel, can you feel it?'

Sam stared out at the beautiful place. It felt like home, like a garden on the doorstep of Heaven. He did feel it, as if he'd been made from the earth itself. He couldn't help smiling.

Sam's feet moved forward before he'd even thought of walking, as if the air pulled him onwards. This was his place. At least part of him belonged.

Queen Titania returned his smile. 'That's right, go and explore. Then you will understand what we must do.'

Sam strolled a path that led him through flower-rich gardens. Fairies of many colours watered flower beds and planted seeds in the dirt, kissing each seed before pushing it into the soil. Under towers of sunflowers, a shimmering bevy of green fairies tended to small animals. A lizard waited patiently as two fairies wound a bandage around its wounded tail. They had some trouble as the tail flicked and flapped of its own will. It settled when they attached the last clasp. A trio of fairies administered a tonic to a brood of ducklings. A fairy in red crooned at a mouse and sewed up a gash along its side. When the fairy finished, he rubbed the mouse's ears, whispered in them and let the little grey ball of fuzz go.

It looked so tender that Sam felt angry at Maggie and the other monsters for threatening it. He thought he understood why Titania was grieving. It was such a sweet place. He felt a tingle inside, his fairy side waking. His back tickled as if wings were deciding whether to grow or not.

He followed the path, which took him down to a white sand shore. The sun glittered off a blueberry-dark ocean, and sea sprites skated across the surface, their silver wings flittering and the scales of their skin catching in the light. They played ball with a pod of dolphins. Sam couldn't understand the scoring system, but the dolphins were winning. The sprites' silver faces twisted with frustration, and the dolphins were cackling and bumping backs in celebration. One broke the water surface, did a dance, its tail flicking water before it dived back head first.

Yes, Sam thought, *if it were my world, I would do anything to save it*. He sighed, realising he was half fairy, so this was his world. He should be looking after it.

He walked with his head down for a few steps. When he looked up, he faced a series of trees, their branches so intertwined his path was blocked.

There didn't seem anywhere else to go in this direction. A sprite waved, he waved back.

Sam turned towards the glade, when a fairy in a yellow-green suit and wings as gauzy as spiderwebs picked him up.

'Would you like to fly, boy?' the beech fairy asked. And

there was air under him and Sam soared through the sky. The beech fairy let him go and Sam readied to fall in alarm, but he continued to glide, moving at a ferocious speed. Underneath him, hay-yellow meadows blurred into jade forests and topaz seas. He rose higher until he trembled with the cold and he could see nothing below him but a mountain range of clouds. It was exhilarating, like flying with Daniel, although a lot colder.

A flock of fairies with pale faces and white and grey attire glided beside him. As Sam had flown before, he was not as in awe of the experience as he otherwise might have been, and he was more interested in the fairies who travelled with him. They changed shape; when they flew faster they stretched. If one slowed it seemed to squish and condense.

'Are you made of clouds?' Sam asked.

'No, clouds are made of us,' one said.

Sam laughed and spread his arms out, the fresh air buoying him up and up as he glided with the cloud fairies.

One of the fairies left dove-grey trails and spun in the air, creating a small cloud. Another fairy flew around it until the cloud grew bigger and softer and turned into a comfortable-looking cumulus cloud. They all flew through it; Sam came out wet.

He shivered, invigorated by the fog against his skin.

'He's cold, Nimbus. Let's toast the little princeling.'

Five or six of the grey fairies grabbed him, laughing and leading him down and down until he could see the ground again. He hooted with them, their cries bursting over red earth rising in ruddy peaks and sinking into dark valleys.

He gasped as they flew him over a volcano. It was magnificent. The air breathed out warm from its red mouth, drying Sam and filling his nose with the smell of molten rubies and diamonds. The fairies let him go and he fell; this time he screamed, sure he would drop inside the glowing gold-swirling mountain. He cried out to the fairies flickering over him, reaching for them, when the up-flow of the warm air righted him and set him down on the outside slope of the volcano.

Sam fell to the hot ground panting so hard he became dizzy. He giggled with relief, his breath so thin he wheezed. The hot, thin air made him giddy. He peered to the clouds. The fairies had gone and left him. He guessed cold grey cloud fairies wouldn't much like the heat of a volcano.

He sat down on the slope and decided he didn't think this volcano was at all like the poster on his Science class wall. It seemed alive, sounded alive, a gurgling ogre turning and moaning.

A copper-coloured face popped right up in front of him. It had bright embers for eyes and its wings were glowing gold. A molten fairy.

'Pan?' it cried, and then, 'No,' in childlike disappointment.

'Boy though,' crackled another.

'Come on, boy. Come on in, come on in. Good for you,' they called, and the words crackled and spluttered like splitting rock.

Molten fairies flew above the mouth of the volcano and gestured him to climb, Sam scrabbled towards them and when he stood on the lip of the volcano he saw the slithering lava turning, eddying and washing in the crater below.

'Closer, boy. Don't slip,' whispered a fairy at his ear. Sam smelt his hair singeing.

He stepped down on to the ledge inside the volcano, and the moving flow of lava stopped. Sam stepped back, gaping as it opened one golden eye. The lava sat up, as golden, bronze and fiery as its skin appeared; when the creature was fully awake and looming over him, oh, how the heat burned from it.

The molten fairies pointed at Sam's open mouth and giggled.

It was a dragon. A running map of melting rock covered its scales and wings, and it spread them out to show Sam how terrifying it was. The very soul of a living mountain.

Sam sweated in its presence and his heart beat so hard that it drowned out the cracking and churning of the volcano itself. It was terrifying; it was magnificent. If Daniel flew him right up to the sun, he didn't think he would ever see anything so amazing.

Sam understood why a dragon's bones could do magic.

It opened its mouth, Sam guessed to spray him with fire or magma, and he put his hand up, in useless defence. The fairies buzzed about it and the dragon cocked its head, doglike, and leaned closer to look at Sam. Its nose moved so near him, Sam burned, his face growing red. It sniffed him and blew a stream of fire into the sky. Then it slid back into its bath of liquid rock and gazed at him a last time out of one eye before closing it.

There was nothing to see but lava.

From his lookout on the rim of the volcano Sam stared, all the way to the sea again, which was so far. The view disappeared only because his eye could see no further. He frowned. Not like looking over Brighton Beach. There the distance dropped away because ... because ...

He remembered ... the Earth was round, it had a horizon.

This was not Earth, nowhere near it, and to not have a horizon meant it was flat and magic. Beyond that Sam didn't know.

He looked out at the not-horizon. The sea was a deeper blue than a few seconds before and the sun was lowering itself down the sky.

He sat and watched the sun. It made a rapid descent into the sea, a glowing golden coin dropped into the water.

It sizzled and Sam saw steam rise off the waves. Around it, tiny silhouettes danced.

The dragon didn't wake up again. It would have been dangerous to climb into its nest to ask it any questions, even if it didn't answer with a mouthful of fire.

He had no idea where he was, and the molten fairies had disappeared.

He also realised he was hungry. It hadn't seemed that

long ago that he'd had breakfast, although he hadn't felt like eating with Woermann growling at him from the other side of the table. Half a piece of toast, Sam remembered. He studied the sizzling sunset again. Even that must have been hours ago.

He stood wondering if something would magically appear to help him fly again, but nothing and no one did. He looked about; the best way down was to climb.

He peered below, into a canopy of trees and saw beneath him, glowing in the doused light, glossy blue balls. He was so far away they looked the size of berries; the trees themselves were twig-sized so he was going to have a climb a long way to get to them. Sam hoped they tasted good. They might be nice to eat.

Sam's heart beat in a happy rhythm and he realised he was smiling. He couldn't help it, as if everything would be all right, as if he'd found a place that sang inside him.

He climbed down the mountain. The volcano top itself was easy enough – it was a cone, after all – and though it was steep, it was at enough of an angle for him to descend in a careful walk. He took off his shoes, though, so his clever gargoyle feet would hold him to the mountain top. He was built for Faeryland.

The smell of fruit carried up sweet and strong from the trees below, making him laugh again, although he couldn't have said why. The fruit shimmered blue at him, nesting in tree boughs, and he had to have them. The smell reminded him of sleep and of sitting in the garden reading a book. He clambered faster.

* * *

He woke on a ledge. He must have fallen asleep, but couldn't remember doing it. The sun waited behind the mountain, casting light over the trees to his right and left. The trees in front lingered in darkness, but he was hungrier than ever.

Sam descended the sheer wall of the mountain. Below him, the base of the forest was darkness. Even with his gargoyle eyes, he could see nothing. He hoped when the sunlight hit he would see ground.

He climbed and did not think about it, putting down one hand, one foot, one hand, one foot until he came to another lip and could rest and have a look around.

He was lucky he had so much gargoyle in him. He had come a long way and the ground seemed much closer. He wondered if that was magic too, if the mountain hadn't shrunk to make his descent easier.

He patted the side of the mountain. 'Thanks', he said.

The mountain shuddered. As much as he appreciated the reply, he didn't think he liked earthquakes.

One tree grew close to the mountain wall, and Sam saw three blue fruits right in front of him, nestled in the V of branches. They were the size of melons, and the smell ... like waking up in the Kavanaghs' house for the first time, like being wrapped in Beatrice's sparkles, like being kissed on the forehead by Michelle. He leaned towards the fruit, and he could have sworn the tree leaned away.

It wasn't that far and he was agile enough, so he

jumped for it, his nose full of kisses and sparkles. The tree lurched and Sam screamed, partly because trees shouldn't move and it was so tall it was a five-storey fall to the ground and many branches for him to hit on the way.

Sam plummeted towards the green earth.

CHAPTER 19

A vine shot out from the tree and held Sam's wrist, catching him, so he didn't drive into the ground. It wrenched his wrist and elbow, and Sam dangled by one sore arm from the tree branch.

Sam wriggled in its tight grip, feeling his hand go cold as the vine cut blood flow. He tried to unravel it with his other hand when another tendril of ivy slid over his face. It shot over, manacled his free wrist and lifted him, so he dangled under the tree.

'Please, put me down,' Sam said.

'It speaks words, my lovelies. What are you?' a voice asked. 'Don't have wings, so you're not a fairy.'

The vines swung him around to show his back to the direction of the voice.

'I'm not a fairy. No.'

'Got no wings, not glowing, not green, not anything we recognise.'

The trees and bushes whispered to Sam. He couldn't understand what they were saying.

'They're right, you know,' the voice said. 'If you had any magic you'd have flown away in a second.'

Sam closed his eyes. He had no magic at all, nothing to protect himself from this moving forest. He wondered what they would do to him.

'You won't harm us, will ye?' the voice asked.

'Me? Harm you?' Sam could hear the voice coming from the bushes, but he couldn't see anyone. Maybe the forest was speaking to him. 'I wouldn't harm you at all. Couldn't harm you.'

'It do look that way. We'll let you go then.'

The vines freed Sam's wrists, and he dropped, bracing himself for a hard fall. He bounced instead into a pile of leaves. It winded him, and he stared up at the blue-fruited tree leaning over him, its leaves shivering.

'So, my 'andsome,' the voice continued. 'Y'arnt a fairy, y'arnt a star, though I saw you fall, and y'arnt a dragon, and here be dragons and all manner of things from the ether. So I suggest, for your own sake, and until you are certain of what you be, a creature like 'ee should avoid fairy food. Fairies come here harvestin', and we're all quiet and shady when they're about, but you don't look to be belongin' here and if'n thou eat fairy food, thou could never leave Faeryland without every day being an agony of ague and aches and coughin's and crackin's.'

'Hello,' said Sam, and sat up. Was it the tree speaking?

'Hello,' the voice replied, and Sam saw movement. The trees swung towards it and waved their branches.

'One-i'-the-Wood,' the voice said.

'Sorry?'

The voice said, 'I. Be. Called. One. In-the-Wood. What's your name?'

'One-i'-the-Wood?'

'Are you sure? I thought that was me.'

The voice sounded friendly enough, but it moved closer and not being able to see who was talking unsettled Sam. He scanned the woods again.

The bushes nearer him shook, and bees scattered. A tumble of sticks fell out of the shrubbery.

'They always want to be hugging an' holding me, they do.' The voice seemed to come from the bundle. Sam saw it move, heard it speak, but it was dead twigs and a few leaves. The top part was woven wood and looked the size of a large melon, although not as round. It was stuck with flowers and bits of fruit.

Sam gulped. He stared harder and blinked. The more he looked, the more the bits seemed to make up a kind of face. A large palm leaf sat atop it, the two raspberries could have been eyes, there was a daisy that might have been a nose, and a leaf for a mouth, the ends lifted in a smile. Then he couldn't see anything but a face.

'Hello?' Sam said.

'Yes, we've done that, but what we've not established is what you're called.'

The twig person lifted its leaf. Its hat, Sam realised. It

put it down on the edge of the moss bed Sam had fallen into and scratched the top of its head.

'Samuel Kavanagh', Sam replied. 'That's my name.' He sighed; he missed the Kavanaghs. He offered his hand, and One-i'-the-Wood looked at it and stuck out its own gnarled dead branch of an arm. Sam took it, feeling the hard twigs in his fingers, and gently shook. He did not want to break One-i'-the-Wood's arm.

'That's a strange custom. Anyway, the trees don't like being climbed; nonetheless, they'll tolerate it if they hafta, but that good tree saw you weren't no fairy thing and done you a great service by not letting you have its fruit. You'd have been addled and lain down directly in this here bed o' moss and stranded here forever. You don't want to be a fairy's plaything, do you?'

'No, I really don't.'

'Well, OK then. End of forest sermon. Are you a-sleepin' or a-gettin' up? I don't mind you havin' my bed for a bit, but I'll want it back soon enough.'

Sam didn't want to sleep and felt he wouldn't want a stranger lobbing into his bed, so he said, 'I need to get back.'

'How did you come to be here, Samuel Kavanagh?'

'I was invited here by Queen Titania.'

'Ooh, my', One-i'-the-Wood spluttered. 'You are a fairy's plaything. The fairy's plaything. You're not wanting to go back to her, surely?'

'Not especially, although your world is very beautiful.' Sam's head cleared. Faeryland was as dangerous as it was lovely and had befuddled him. He'd almost forgotten how he got there.

One-i'-the-Wood waved aside the compliment. 'So, what are you wanting to get back to?'

'I need to get back to my friends, they're in a very bad situation.'

'And I expect they're somewhere else.'

'In another world completely.'

'Well, you're a mighty long way from anywhere where you could start your way to finding them if you really hafta. You need a door.'

'A door?'

'A door between here and there. How did you get here?'

'My world just melted away, and then I was here.'

'Oooh, that takes a lot of magic. The queen must have really wanted to impress 'ee.'

Sam blushed.

'And who are your friends, my 'andsome? An' why do 'ee need to be back with 'em so much?'

'They're shifters. And they're being held by an awful 'thrope. I need to save them. When they're all free, they can go home and I can go home too. I want to see my family and my pack.'

'That sounds like a wonderful collection of wants. How marvellous for you. Well, that definitely means you're no fairy, but if you must find the nearest door, it's right in the middle of Her Majesty's glade an' even that's a long way off. You've completely commenced in the wrong place altogether. Now if you were in the middle-bit near the end of the path that leads to the roundabout, you could begin there. Here's no place to start.'

'But I'm nowhere else, I have to start here.'

'Well, I s'pose we best get you to the middle-bit then.'

'I'm grateful for any help,' Sam said.

'Of course y'are, my 'andsome.' One-i'-the-Wood put on its hat and walked away. Sam struggled to get out of the bed and the twig person was a way off before he caught up. Fortunately, Sam had excellent hearing, and One-i'-the-Wood made cracking noises as it walked and chatted away to him, although Sam was in such a hurry to catch up, he wasn't paying a lot of attention.

Sam fell in beside One-i'-the-Wood, who continued talking. '... Of course, if it's raspberries again I won't mind.' One looked at Sam. 'I'm being most rudely presumptuous here, my dear. You are, well ...' It coughed. 'If you're not, I'm terribly sorry if this is an insult, although I'd be pleased as punch if someone was to ask me, but you are lookin' to be one and, well I'll just say it straight ... are you human, my 'andsome?'

'Mostly,' Sam said.

'Well, isn't that wonderful? An absolute bit of luck. It explains all the wanting. I've got so many questions and ... oh, my manners ... I'm most profoundly delighted to meet you. I am forever your humble servant. I am thrilled. Absolutely thrilled. I have never yet met a human in solid form.' One-i'-the-Wood clapped its twiggy hands and danced as if it'd won some great prize.

Sam loved all his humans, he wished he truly was one, but he was entertained by how much meeting him cheered One-i'-the-Wood. He seemed as nice as the nicest humans Sam had met, but One was surrounded by all this beauty and the fairies too, who could do whatever they wanted. He wondered why One didn't want to be a fairy. He said so.

'Oh, but that's the point; humans be, I hope I'm not being rude here, but humans be a mix-up of a lot of "yes" and "no", an' getting that balance is of great importance to me.'

'A lot of "yes" and a lot of "no"?'

'That's right.' One-i'-the-Wood nodded vigorously. 'You understand me perfectly.'

Sam had no idea what being a lot of 'yes' and 'no' meant at all, but he didn't say so.

'It's all well n' good being all "yes", fairies survive it well enough,' One-I'-the-Wood went on, 'but as you know, it don't suit the magic of the human heart. I've learned that, an' I'm right interested in the ways humans work, as I am making myself into one. As you can see.'

'You're making yourself into a human?'

'I am a self-made man.' One-i'-the-Wood stretched out its arms to show him. 'Obviously, the forest has provided the material: can't make yerself out of nothing, can 'ee? But I did most of the work.'

Sam studied One. Its right side appeared human-shaped, the branch jutting from One-i'-the-Wood's shoulder had a knot and another where an elbow would be, hinged so it bent. The end of the branch had six 'fingers' all poking out straight ahead, one ending with a small yellow leaf. The leg was a sturdy log, also knotted at the knee and finishing with a flattened branch which did for a foot. The other leg was a single unbending stump and shorter than the right, so One-i'-the-Wood leaned. Its left arm was nothing more than a burned stick jutting at a sharp angle from its shoulder. Its body was of the same woven twigs as its head, and something had built a nest inside One's tummy with bits of bark and leaves and patches of fur. One-i'-the-Wood pointed at it. 'Look, I've recently found myself a heart. It's off now, running about collecting nuts, I shouldn't wonder, but at night, I keep it safe and dry, and it sleeps soundly.'

Sam studied the animal nest, it looked messy. 'Doesn't it bounce around inside you?'

'Of course it do, of course it do. But that's what a heart does. It thumps around in yer innards because a heart is a wild animal? It gnaws me, and suffers me something sore, but I bear it all, because a good heart is a tender thing, and when it's hurt and sad I nurse it until it's better and can go roamin' again, because you do that for your heart. I did consider havin' a bird, as they do flutter and I heard hearts do like to go a-flutter sometimes, but I wanted a strong heart, not one so easily broken, and a squirrel seemed a better option. I want a bit of "no", but not so much "no" that I couldn't survive it.'

Sam was sure the trees and flowers were all listening to this. They leaned in as One-i'-the-Wood stumped by them, and swayed back when it passed.

A bird, small and brown, landed on One-i'-the-Wood's head and pecked at the twig that did for its ear, and then its leafy eyebrow.

'I don't understand what you mean by a bit of "no",' Sam said.

'Don't 'ee?' One-i'-the-Wood eyed Sam mildly. 'I suppose 'ee be like a fish then, so much in the water you don't see it. Or maybe cos I got nothin' in my head just yet, an' don't make much sense.' A lily raised itself to be sniffed and One-i'-the-Wood obliged. One turned to Sam and studied the boy's face, blinked its raspberry eyes and screwed up its leaf mouth. 'Thou know fairies be made from a laugh? It's what makes them all "yes" from the beginning. You just hafta look at 'em to see they have so much "yes". They are made beautiful, an' anyone who looks at 'em wants to give 'em things; say "yes" to 'em, as it were. They have magic so they can go everywhere and have everything, and they never want for anything. I feel so sad for the poor blighters. It's a rough existence.'

'Getting everything you want? Isn't that what everyone is aiming for?' Sam said. 'The monsters certainly do.'

'What are monsters, my 'andsome?'

'They're all the creatures born from a last sigh. Right now, Queen Titania wants me to help her fight them. One of them, Maggie, has been stealing the magic from fairy wings.'

'Well, that gives her something marvellous to want,' One-i'-the Wood said.

'Maggie?'

'No, Queen Titania. It must be sheer delight for her.'

'Oh, no, I think she's very upset.'

'Ah, but that's at the surface, all bemoaning her poor

fairies and their unfortunate situation, but underneath it all, she'll have something to want. It reminds her that she cares for things so much she'll fight for them. It will give her something to do, some purpose. Sometimes, when things are easy, a body can forget how much we love. An' the queen's had a lot of time to get too comfortable. She has "yes, yes, yes" till the cows come home and that's why "no" is so good. Although, havin' said that, it's true any creature can be ruthless in war, so I'd stay out of her way, just in case. Her Majesty is powerful n' all.' One-i'-the-Wood picked up a fig that a tree had dropped. It patted the tree's trunk. The tree sighed. 'Now, tell me about these monsters. Are they beautiful?'

Sam shook his head. 'Mostly they're ugly to very ugly, and want to be able to make people's lives miserable, but there aren't enough of them yet. They want to make more monsters very badly.'

'Ah, well, it seems they don't get *anything* they want,' One-i'-the-Wood said.

'No, I don't think they do.'

'Well, there you go. Too much "no" and too much "yes". Both ends make a body miserable. Nothing to want. Everything to want.'

'I think I understand. If you get everything you wish, and if you get nothing you wish, then you'll be unhappy either way, so you need a bit of both.'

'Exactly what I'm saying. Which is why I want to be a human. I want to want – dreams, ambitions, goals. You can't have those without wanting something that you don't have yet.'

'But it's nice when you get it,' Sam said.

'Eventually. But a season of trying and planning and working – it does a body good. Makes life worth living.'

Sam looked at the trees near the path. They veered forward, listening to One-i'-the-Wood. The path was full of more flowers than Sam had ever seen in one place, all vying for One's attention.

'Oh, you silly things. All right,' One said, and scanned all the fabulous colours. It stooped towards a lovely vine of red roses encircling a fine-boned tree.

One-i'-the-Wood bowed to the rose bush, and the rose bush bowed back.

'All right, are 'ee?' One-i'-the-Wood asked.

The roses nodded.

'Now, it came to mind this morning I might be right 'andsome with a bud. Would 'ee mind?' One-i'-the-Wood asked.

The rose bush swayed. Sam guessed that meant no.

'I'm very obliged to 'ee,' One said, and plucked a single red rosebud from the vine. The vine shivered happily.

One-i'-the-Wood pulled off the daisy from the middle of its face and put the rosebud in its place. 'What do ye think?' it asked.

Sam liked it. It did look more nose-like than the daisy.

'I do make myself anew ev'ry day. Come on, Samuel Kavanagh. We have a way to go.'

They walked further along, and One-i'-the-Wood squealed when it came across a green branch on the path. The creature danced and jigged and cried out, 'Look 'ee, look 'ee, Samuel Kavanagh.' Sam was horrified when with its right hand One pulled out its left arm and let it drop on the path and was relieved when the creature pushed the new branch into its place.

'Look at tha', look at tha'.' One flexed its new arm, bending each of the fingers. 'Three straight up and one that do for a thumb.' It reached out and tweaked Sam's nose. 'I couldna done tha' this mornin'. I feel sap running through me now. Thank 'ee, trees', the twig person said, and patted the nearest trunk.

One-i'-the-Wood seemed to bounce a little more. A bramble bush covered in berries swayed into the path.

'Here's for me', One-i'-the-Wood said, and waved its new, green arm over the dancing bramble bush. 'Two for my eyes.'

Sam was not so horrified this time when One-i'-the-Wood plucked out its eyes. 'Oh, that was silly of me. I cannot see. Samuel Kavanagh, would 'ee be ever so kind, and pluck me a coupla right juicy ones?'

Sam found a pair of nice berries. He held them up together making sure they were similar in size and shape and then popped them on One-i'-the-Wood's face. As soon as they stuck, they blinked and lifted in a happy smile.

One-i'-the-Wood bowed to the bush. The bush shivered happily.

Sam studied the berries, they looked so plump and ripe.

One-i'-the-Wood grabbed Sam with its new wooden hand. 'Don' eat nothin' in Faeryland, unless you want to stay forever.' He released Sam. 'Or ye could stay here with us. The woods like 'ee very much, an' ye'd never be short of fairy food.'

Sam looked around at the shaking, swaying, moving plants. 'And I like them all too, but my friends need me, and I miss my family.'

'Oh, such good wantings, such lovely yearnings, a body could fill up with desire like that. An' a family, what a thing to want. I don't have a family.' One frowned and put its twiggy hand on its woody chin and peered at Sam. 'Do I want one? What's good about them?'

'They love you, they look after you, they help you find your dreams.' Sam nodded. He had to remember that: no fairy food would be as wonderful as home.

'Oh my, that do sound lovely. Maybe I should make myself a family,' One said. 'I saw a few willow branches back there. I could weave a sweet little me. Maybe I could become One-of-Two-i'-the-Wood. And we could converse the way I do with 'ee. That'd be very nice. Then we could go and find some dreams together. I'm thinking a pair of finches. I should have more than one dream fluttering around in there.' One poked a twig finger inside its head and bowed. 'I be very happy to have met 'ee, Samuel Kavanagh. I've learned so many things. I learned more about humans than I dared to want, and I discovered monsters.' One looked along the path. 'It's not far now.'

The wood parted, opening to a meadow. A few steps more and Sam was out in a clearing staring at a bright, painted carousel.

It was painted blue and red and gold and gleamed in the beaming sun as it played a lullaby, but there was nothing else around. No swings, no tents. It wasn't a fair. It was a colourful merry-go-round all by itself in the middle of a field.

'The roundabout.' One smiled at Sam and held his hand, leading Sam towards it. 'It's the middle, but if a body travels on it, it'll take you to *her* glade. Now, Samuel Kavanagh, please let me remind you not to eat any fairy food. If you must be with them, be careful. They are dangerous, not because they intend to be cruel, but because others mean little to them.'

'Monsters aren't any better,' Sam said.

One squeezed up its berry eyes and turned its head. In the open space, Sam could see sunlight through it.

The carousel's rides were unicorns and dragons, rainbow-coloured fish and large silver birds. Sam looked at each. A unicorn looked back at him.

Sam climbed on the carousel and moved to the shining, grey unicorn, grabbing its pole. One-i'-the-Wood ran alongside him. The twig person's voice carried back to him. 'I should also warn 'ee, thou probably don' want ...'

The carousel turned, and One-i'-the-Wood was gone.

Sam stood on the grass in the glade again. A flock of fairies filled the space, but Edgar and the queen were nowhere in sight.

CHAPTER 20

A swarm of fairies rushed forward, their little voices pouring over him.

'You came back.'

'Have a nice rest in your bower.'

'Would you like tea?'

'Would you like nectar?'

'Would you like to dance?'

Sam wanted none of those things. He wanted to get back to Wilfred, Hazel, Amira and their families and let them out of the cellar. His mind was clear again and he remembered that Queen Titania had him here to convince him that taking his friends' souls was all right. She wanted him to deliver the orb full of shifter souls to The Hole. He understood Faeryland was worth protecting, but there had to be a better way.

'Well, what *do* you want?' asked a woman-sized fairy in a red velvet dress. 'We can give it to you straight away.'

'I want to go home,' Sam replied. 'I've been told there's a door I can use.'

'No,' crowed the fairies, and created a cloud around him. He was blinded by petals, gauzy clothes and tiny, flapping wings.

'We can't let you use that,' the red-velvet fairy said.

Sam couldn't speak; every time he tried to say something a blossom or a leaf stopped his words and he spat them out to avoid eating anything. Then he realised it was safer to keep his mouth shut. His stomach complained, it was not liking the lack of food.

'Take him to the bower,' said the red-velvet fairy.

Sam was lifted by the throng of tiny creatures and placed into a woven shell high up in a tree branch.

'Now, don't go falling out, will you?' the red-velvet fairy said. 'You can wait for our queen to return, an' she'll have words with you. She won't be so unhappy if you have a slice of cake.'

A creamy fairy floated next to his bower, offering him a delicious slice of something.

'No, thanks,' he said, although his stomach was saying 'Yes, please'. He had to get out before he needed to choose between starving or being bewitched.

The fairies resumed their places. Some danced, some slept, and some made daisy chains and crowned the red-velvet lady.

Sam guessed they had put him in the high tree thinking it was impossible for him to leave, but if he climbed down without them noticing, he could escape and maybe find the door.

Unfortunately, while some fairies slept, others played, and there was no point climbing out while at least one fairy was peering up at the bower. They waved whenever they saw Sam's face.

He lay down, his tummy grumbled, and his often-useful sense of smell was telling him all about the food around him for miles. Sausages to the west, home-baked biscuits to the north; from the east, a medley of fruits like angels would eat (if they ate fruit; Daniel said angels weren't big eaters). To the south, all he could smell was the sea, which was some relief.

Sam was stirred from his thoughts by rustling and the gasps of fairy folk. He peered out of his bower. All of them sat watching a swishing hedge. It swayed left, it swayed right, and threw flowers at them. They laughed at its dance. Those awake roused the sleepers so the dancing hedge had a great audience. Sam took his chance. He stood in the bower, not a fairy looked at him, and he stretched for the tree, intending to climb.

For the second time that day, a tree reached for him. It plucked him in its branches and placed Sam gently behind itself out of the sight of the fairies, then went back to standing straight and still as if it had never moved. It took a lot less time than if Sam had had to climb down.

'Psst,' said a bush.

There'd been plenty of moving plants in One-i'-the-Wood's forest, but none had 'Psst' at him.

One-i'-the-Wood stuck its sticky head out between the leaves. 'Come on, this way.' It grabbed Sam's hand and

231

pulled him through the bush. The bush moved aside a little so Sam didn't get scratched.

'Thank you,' Sam said. The bush bowed.

'I s'pose you told 'em your plan to find the door, did 'ee?'

Sam nodded, feeling silly for having done it. 'I thought they might tell me where it was.'

'If the queen wants 'ee here, they're not likely to let 'ee go easy. Anyway, don' blush, it's my fault, I warned 'ee too late. I came after to see if you were about or if you'd got through, and when I saw your noggin lookin' out over the nest they made for 'ee, I knew ye'd been a bit more mouthy than 'ee should.'

'They're distracted by a dancing hedge. That was you too?'

'Oh, yes, you'd be surprised how much a bush will do for a "Would ye mind?" and a "Please, thank 'ee". Fairies are all for a creature if it's feathered or furred, but if ye grow fruit, they take 'ee for granted.'

'You'll be OK, won't you?' Sam asked. 'If they find out you helped me ...'

'Is this what it means to be a friend?' One asked. 'Fearing for one another? What a wonderful thing. Don' worry about me, Samuel Kavanagh. They don't know much about me, an' I intend keeping it that way. Let's worry about what ye want first. Come on, your door's this way.'

'Hey?' A yellow fairy buzzed up behind them. 'Where are you going?'

'Just for a nice walk,' Sam answered. 'I'll be back soon.'

'OK', said the fairy.

The fairy flitted back to the glade. Sam looked around, next to him sat a bundle of kindling. It jumped up and became One again. 'Best we run, Samuel Kavanagh. They are quite dim, but that one will get to thinking soon and ye'll need to be out when it does.'

One led Sam through the woods as fast as it could. Sam would have loved to have gone faster, but One's stumpy right leg made it hard for it to run, and the twig person felt the need to greet each tree and bush it passed by raising its hat or bowing. The vegetation shivered and shuddered with delight.

'I was thinkin' as ye left', One said. Sam noticed the twig person didn't pant, although it trotted. 'About monsters and fairies, all about the "yes" and "no" – too much of neither is no good. An' I'm wondering, although ye may think it a silly idea, but it do seem to me that a human is a mix of monster and fairy, don' you agree?'

Sam put his arm around One's waist and picked him up as he pondered the idea, but before he had an actual thought, he heard a bewildered scream coming from the glade.

'Oh, I think we might need to move even faster, Samuel Kavanagh', One said. 'The fairies may have discovered yer gone. Put me down, I'll just slow 'ee.' One pulled himself out of Sam's arm and shooed him away.

Sam saw the blur of colour moving to the path, and trotted ahead. He turned to see an angry swarm of fairies, burring red and yellow, orange and green zipping towards them.

'One?' Sam reached back for the twig person's arm.

'Now ye'll move quicker. I've got friends in high places. Give the boy a hand, please.' A tree branch swept Sam further along the path. 'Now, keep going, Sam,' One yelled.

Sam was forced on by tree after tree. As he stumbled backwards, he watched the fairies heading straight for One-i'-the-Wood.

Poor One was not quick, but the trees, bushes and hedges moved over the path. Everything was a mess of wood and leaves. Trees leaned in, blocking the path of the fairies. Hedges reached up and filled many gaps. A few of the smaller fairies whizzed between the obstacles, but most were trapped behind the greenery.

'One-i'-the-Wood!' Sam yelled.

'Don' worry about me,' One yelled back.

Sam couldn't help it. The beech trees along the path and a few hedges pulled at him to keep him moving, forcing distance between him and his friend. He needed to see One was safe. A flight of fairies was on One-i'-the-Wood, and grabbed his arm. An oak tree leaned down and whipped the twig man away. The fairies stared at the dried-up stick in their hands.

'One!' Sam called.

One's voice carried back to him. 'Don' worry, Samuel Kavanagh, it wasn't my good arm. Keep running. Ye be heading in the right direction.'

The trees and hedges closed the path, and Sam could go in only one way. He turned and pelted towards a dark place formed by the shadow. The wood behind him was as kind to him as it had been to One. He heard branches swatting, and the angry 'ouches' of the few fairies still coming after him.

He could tell by the buzzing only two small fairies remained. They wouldn't be able to carry him, but he didn't want to give the others time to catch up.

'Thank you, woods', Sam panted out. 'Thank you, One.'

Then he saw the shadow at the end of the path wasn't caused by trees. It was a space, a darkness that looked nothing like a forest. Sam gathered speed to jump.

'Samuel Kavanagh', One's voice sang out. 'I hope we meet again.'

CHAPTER 21

Sam rolled into a dark room with Queen Titania and Edgar glaring at him.

The cellar.

Titania strode towards Sam, dogs whimpering in the background, and wrenched the boy's head back. She studied his face. 'You are clear-eyed I see. And away such a short time. Was nothing to your taste?'

'I was told not to eat fairy food,' Sam replied.

'Well, the villain that told you, I shall tear limb from limb.'

After what Sam had just seen, he didn't think that would stop One-i'-the-Wood very long.

'You have interrupted our conjuring,' Queen Titania said. 'Watch, Samuel. We preferred you not see this; you have a soft heart, but you will see we are not evil. We take no lives. No lives are lost. Their lives are different, true, but they continue. When you see this, you will take the orb to the monsters' dwelling for us. 'Tis true.'

Titania walked back to Edgar and the orb, their shadows echoing in its light. Eight miserable shapes huddled against the wall, tails limp and tired. Wilfred whimpered.

Hazel followed Sam with her dark eyes and he could smell her desperation. 'She wants to take our souls, Sam.'

The orb churned, as if it anticipated the new arrivals. 'No, please, don't do this.'

Titania's annoyed toes disturbed the thick blanket of fairy dust covering the floor.

Sam stepped between Titania and the shifters. 'If you put their souls in the orb and make me take it to The Hole, I'll be taking these shifters' souls a world away. How will they ever find their way home?'

'Traitor!' Edgar sneered.

'Without a taste of Faeryland, you will never understand,' Titania said. 'Truly, you must love Faery and all her children to know what we lose.'

'It's beautiful, but I can't do this. What you're doing is wrong,' Sam said.

Edgar scowled. 'More wrong than freeing the monsters from The Hole so they can drain all the magic from Faery? You *are* a monster, Samuel.'

'We have to find some other way,' Sam said. 'You can't steal people's souls. You've got to let them go.'

The shifters whined.

'Oh, but you're all right with that witch stealing *our* magic? Monsters killing anyone they like, so long as they are not *your* friends?' Edgar said.

'Can we find another way? Please? There must be another way.'

Titania looked to Edgar, then turned away.

Edgar spoke for her. 'This isn't just about Faery. It's about humans too. Aren't they the ones you like best, Sam? It doesn't seem you're loyal to anyone.'

Sam flinched.

Edgar laughed. 'It shows you just how monstrous you are, doesn't it? Right now, we have a little time when Maggie doesn't know how to build her army and the smaller monsters are too afraid to do too much damage, but read your human newspapers, Samuel, watch your news. Already, several humans have gone missing, some of the bigger beasts are gaining courage. Fairies are being hunted. This is your fault. Your FAULT!'

Titania stared at Sam in disappointment. Edgar patted her arm and her beautiful face was restored. 'Reconsider, princeling. You will set this weapon for us, won't you, Samuel?' she asked. 'Take it to The Hole, renew the safe-hold, bring the monsters to heel? Look to the hounds. They live, they breathe; shall be no different after.'

'Without their souls?' Sam pointed at the orb. 'These belong to people in so much pain.' Sam looked at their faces, Titania's expression was the same, Edgar looked angrier. Sam wept, 'Can't you ask someone else?' He covered his face with his hands. She was right, of course. Once the monsters got bigger so many more people would die. Then he looked at the shifters. Sam could hardly hear his own voice. 'I can't do it,' he said.

'Ah,' was all Queen Titania said.

Edgar touched the queen's hand. 'You should begin the drain, Majesty.'

Titania, beautiful and tall, threw up her arms. The black of her dress and wings deepened. The shifters drew back, whining and whimpering as the words from Titania's throat came out rough and rugged. They were not English, but Sam understood them anyway, understood their intent. They were scrapings of blade against rock, the bubbling of magma seeking the least resistance, seeking a weakness in the soil, ready to explode into black sky. Dark words only darkness understood, simple and untranslatable; foul words.

He knew, regardless of the intention to save Earth and Faery, what Titania did was evil magic.

Her words called for loss, power, death and possession. They weren't fairy words, they came from somewhere even darker than The Hole, even darker than the Hags' Cave, somewhere out of which Sam could never find his way. The weapon maker would have used them when binding the souls inside the Vorpal Sword, but they were older than the weapon maker's time.

D. I. Kintamani, Mrs Kintamani and Wilfred lifted into the air, their doggy bodies held by the swirling magic. They whined as their chests glowed, and howled when the glow shot across the room into the orb. The spell dropped them like rubbish. Wilfred hit the ground hard and scampered under a blanket. D.I. Kintamani looked exhausted, but his deep dog eyes focused on his wife and child, still not understanding what he saw. Mrs Kintamani chased her tail and howled; the other shifters backed away. Sam understood, she'd lost his stronger self and was mad with misery. Then the spell swirled towards the Kokonis. Dr Kokoni backed against the wall, but the venomous green glow of the spell pulled her out and lifted her too.

'No, you have to stop. This is wrong. This is wrong,' Sam yelled, waving his hands to distract the queen.

Titania dropped her arms. ''Tis a necessary evil, Samuel.'

Sam flung himself at the fairy, but Edgar, solid and short, shoved him backwards. Sam fell amongst the other prisoners. Amira's mum softened his fall with her furry back.

Titania turned her attention to Amira and her mum.

'No!' Sam yelled. 'No more!'

Titania regarded him. 'You cannot stop this, Samuel. ''Tis necessary.' She looked at Edgar. 'How might the boy be brought to heel?' Edgar pointed at the orb. Titania bowed her head and moaned. 'Samuel, you are made of sigh and laugh. 'Tis thy soul that disrupts my plan.'

'Yes, yes!' Edgar said. The Christmas elf's face flushed with glee. 'Do it! Do it!'

'Your soul is forfeit, Samuel,' the queen said.

The floor vibrated like in an earthquake. The cellar roof threw down debris, which hit Sam in the face.

The dogs howled.

Titania swept her arm out to include Samuel in the spell.

She repeated the ancient incantation. The words, old

and vile, twisted and powerful, drew Sam from himself. His soul pulled out of his body, the way water sucked out of a straw, heaving from his hands and toes, his ears emptying of himself through the thin hole opening inside his chest, and it hurt like death, and his heart broke to feel it.

Just before she lifted from the ground, caught in Titania's spell, Amira yelled, 'He's single-souled. He'll die.'

Titania's face whitened at the shifter's words. She looked to Edgar. ''Tis true?'

Edgar did not reply. His face was an eager green as he stared into the glow of the spell and the power of the incantation pulled at the queen's arms, forcing her to continue as much as it forced out Sam's soul.

With one last pus-like gush Sam's soul pulled away from his body, and he saw his shape drop to the wooden floor, then he was flying towards the orb as it pulled him in.

CHAPTER 22

Sam's soul slid over the glass of the globe before crashing inside the orb. The world became round and bright and spinning. Sam wanted to open his eyes to see and had no eyes to open. He had no form, he was light inside light and the world made no sense. A single high-pitched note continued in his mind, sounding sad and terrified.

Everything became still.

Sam tried to take a deep breath and had no body with which to breathe. He stopped and tried to make sense of the light.

I'm inside the orb, he thought.

Sam? Sam? a voice called.

Here, he replied. And while he understood a voice had called to him, he had not heard it in his ears but inside himself. The world became a little brighter as a luminescence moved towards him. Although even that was the sense of brightness, not an actual seeing, the way one can feel the change in light behind closed eyelids.

Sam, it's me. Hazel.

Wilfred too. A beam bounced towards him.

Is Amira still out there? Sam asked.

A silent groan moved through the orb, and Sam sensed Amira's entrance. Wilfred and Hazel turned their attention to the newly arrived soul, to comfort her and her mother.

Sam relaxed a little. At least he was with friends.

What in the world is he doing here? He's not a shifter. A body won't survive without at least one soul in it, Amira said. *He's gotta be dead.*

Shush, Hazel said. *He can hear your thoughts.*

But he's ... Amira added.

Shush, I said. There's worse things than being dead.

The souls around him generated misery.

Hazel told him, *I can sense my other self out there. She's so lonely.*

Us too, Amira and Wilfred agreed.

Sam sighed. If he was dead, he would never see Michelle again, or Richard, or Beatrice or Nick. If he'd had eyes he would have cried.

Maybe ... Hazel started, but no cheering words came after.

The environment was soothing. The souls with which he was trapped comforted each other. His worries were drowned out in the voices of the others. Parents humming for children. Children singing for their mothers. Such sad voices, wandering lost. Mates called for each other and cried with each other. Split from themselves, they sounded so helpless. Only Hazel, and the other recent collection of shifters whose souls were on the other side of the glass, felt any compulsion. They moved as close to their bodies as they could, the wall of glass and fairy dust getting in the way.

I *just want to comfort her. Me*, Amira said.

Beneath the pain, Sam felt a raw power. He was still sitting in the heart of a bomb.

Sam had to collect his thoughts. *Collect his thoughts?* Richard used that expression. Sam'd written it into his notepad. He'd say, 'I need to collect my thoughts', then he'd go off and pace in his office. Sam would love to be there now, pacing and pacing and thinking. His feet lifting, setting down again.

He thought of the rhythm, the movement, and then he felt the steady rise and fall of ... legs. Legs! He couldn't see them, but he could feel himself moving.

His 'legs' paced.

It's an illusion, an old voice said. *I've been here a million years and dreamed of throwing a ball and it feels like I have an arm, but the feeling goes away.*

No! Sam sent out his memory of the souls bursting from the Vorpal Sword, the way they'd called to him. He'd seen them too, looking human, the way they remembered themselves in life.

Sam thought about his legs.

I *want to see them.*

He felt a few souls around him brighten. They met his thought with their own. *Things I want to see. Things I saw. Things I'll never see again.* Then, other than his friends, the souls drifted off into memories.

He looked down. Looked. Actually looked. Shapes formed in the light and there they were, his legs, rubbery and see-through, but *his* legs. Everything was a blur in the glow, and brighter than the sun had ever been. It hurt. He didn't have eyes to hurt, so why did it hurt?

He thought about his hands. He'd had hands. He'd climbed walls with those hands. He could throw and unwrap and hold. In the scalding brightness, hands appeared, pulling out of the centre of himself. He was luminescent plasticine.

What are you doing, Sam? Wilfred said. *Do it more! Do it more!*

Sam remembered his body and his arms, his neck and his head. A nose, a mouth, a pair of ears and he gained dimension too. He was sure if he looked in a mirror he would see a body like Samuel Kavanagh's had been. He would look human.

He blinked, driving back the light in the orb around him, and then wished for sunglasses to deal with the over-bright souls. He felt a weight on his incorporeal nose and the light dimmed.

H*a!* he said, moving his ghost mouth.

Hazel, Wilfred and Amira laughed.

Sam looked at him. Around him beads of light were cycling in a living galaxy, orbiting and clustering. Seeing them now, he could not tell them apart. Some zipped past like shooting stars, some hung together in constellations, patches of light so thick they glowed milky white. He closed his eyes, listening to Wilfred, Amira and Hazel communing with their parents. Comforting thoughts. They meant well, but it was an incomplete life. He understood why the souls hadn't minded being bound in the sword. They had only known slavery before; they were whole in the sword.

The souls in the sword could have left any time they liked, Daniel had said.

Sam tried to remember more about Daniel's comment about souls as he walked to the curve of the orb and pushed against the glass with his see-through hands. Fairy magic sealed them in.

None of them could get through the glass. Sam shook his new head. What the fairy queen didn't know about the sword that Sam did is that the souls could move freely. The souls in the sword had been held to it by a different kind of magic – obligation, duty, purpose. They had stayed because they believed they must, and they moved in and out of the sword at will. That had been their power, they slid free, followed the ogres and trolls who hurt humans and demanded justice.

The orb might be intended as a weapon to restrain the ogres in The Hole, but unless the souls could move through the glass surface, it was useless. They were trapped forever and would do no one any good.

He put his eye to the glass surface.

He wanted to see out and found he could. He blinked

a few times. The brightness inside made it hard to make out anything other than the barest movement, so he put his renewed hands on either side of his head and looked harder.

In the light coming from the kitchen above and through the still open door from Faeryland, Sam could see Woermann out there, standing with Titania and Edgar, talking together and staring at the lump of Sam's body lying prone. Dead. Sam put his ear to the glass.

'I'll look after it,' Woermann said to them. The were-cat loomed over them both, having grown bigger in the short time since Sam had seen him.

'Well, at least you have one use. You're not going to be able to sniff out the ones you lost until after the full moon,' Edgar replied. 'We'll be back then.'

Woermann purred. 'You still need my nose though.'

Titania sighed again as she looked at Sam's corpse, then she and Edgar turned to the back of the room, to the Faeryland door. Titania walked through, and Edgar followed. The door swallowed them whole.

Only Woermann remained, leering over the animals. The poor dogs huddled together, the pups pushing their faces under their parents' furry necks. Woermann kicked Sam's lifeless body.

Sam pushed at the glass. The magic had made it solid. He even heard a thunk as his ghost head hit the cold surface.

He slumped down inside the orb. What was he going to do even if he got out? Even if he did make it, he couldn't return to a dead body, so he wasn't much use to the shifters out there in the cellar. Then he thought of the Kavanaghs, of the gargoyles, of Daniel. All but the last would never know what happened to him. He wondered how Woermann would explain his disappearance.

He didn't know how long he had sat there before Amira found him again.

Your unhappiness is going through everything, Amira said.

I'm dead, Sam replied.

I'm sorry, Sam. Amira's bead of light came and bumped against him.

It's all right, I thought I was dead once before. You get used to it.

Time moved like toffee. Sam had no idea how long he sat on the bottom of the sphere. He wondered if the shifters he'd freed had arrived home safely, the rabbits and the badgers. What about the others, the souls of the shifters from the other parts of the country? Where were their physical selves and their second souls?

We don't know, the old man responded to his thought. *We lost connection after they left the place we were locked in. They've moved the orb since then. I don't know what was worse, hearing them outside sounding miserable – some even said their other half had gone mad – or not knowing where they are at all.*

Sam knew he had to help the shifters reunite their souls, even if he never saw the Kavanaghs again.

Anything was better than being trapped in a ball.

Sam stared at the movement through the glass.

I can feel myself out there, Wilfred said. *It's a relief to be close, but he's so lonely and sad without me. It's painful being separated.*

For Bladder, only minutes passed while Sam had been on his adventure. Bladder had just left the paddock and found a solid path leading away from Wheedle and Spigot. He turned to see them struggling forward. Wheedle pushed to dig himself out, and occasionally his face would sink into the boggy field, but it would be up again. Spigot squawked each time his beak appeared above a wave of mud.

Bladder was torn. He smelt a hint of Sam again on a breeze coming from the south, but his pack was sealed in a squirmy fight with the earth.

'Go!' spluttered Wheedle. 'Get to him before *she* does.'

That was enough for Bladder. Even if Wheedle and Spigot were stuck in the field the following night, they could easily hide from any ogres or trolls. Now Maggie had talked to her troops, she would be looking for Sam, not a clutch of dirty gargoyles.

Bladder hit the path, its surface a layer of wetness and slosh, despite that many decades of country walkers had hardened it.

Bladder raced away, his stone feet hardening the dirt more, his claws sending muddy water spraying.

He was so dirty and mucky, even the farmer whose tractor Bladder barrelled past said, 'Odd-looking dog. Awfully dirty.'

At one point, Sam's smell took him across a field and he jumped from post to post, ramming them a little deeper into the earth. The owner of that land would be pleased later in the day when he found his fence not only survived the night storm, but had been strengthened by it. Another time, Bladder fell on his back into soft mud and took at least half an hour righting himself, writhing in the dirt as helpless as an upside-down turtle. The animals in the meadow came to investigate, but when he got back on his feet, Bladder poked his tongue at a confused bull, who mooed in deep offence.

It should have been a short trip, but stodgy fields and limited pathways made it longer than Bladder expected. It was after noon when he clambered over a turnstile and found a path that took him straight into a housed area. He cheered to set down on concrete.

When he reached the hedges of Woermann Manor, Sam's smell was so strong and sad it carried through the air and rested on everything. Sam's sadness at losing the Kavanaghs, his sadness at losing the gargoyles, Daniel, his friends. Such a lot of sadness that if Bladder hadn't already been such a heavy creature, he'd have been weighed down by it.

The smell of fairy dust filled the air too.

Maggie's already been, Bladder thought, and drops of sewer water filled his stone eyes. He forced his way through the hedges, breaking twigs and squashing leaves. *Mustn't give up hope yet.*

He sniffed through the front gate and followed the smell till where it was strongest, near the kitchen doors.

Sam was in the garden, standing in the rain-freshened sunlight staring up at the sun like a gargoyle.

Bladder cheered. He had to get Sam away from this

place, right after he hugged him until his ribs hurt. Bladder didn't know what he felt strongest, panic or pleasure. He looked around to make sure there was no one else in the garden and rushed forward. 'Sam, Sam, Sam! Hurrah, I found you. Oh, Sam, it's so good to see you.'

Sam turned. He moved oddly, loping, then stepped through the kitchen doors, long-armed, long-legged and languid.

'Sam?' Bladder rushed into the kitchen, getting grubby, muddy paw prints on the floor. Inside, Bladder smelt misery, animal and raw. 'What's going on? We've got to go! Are you sick? Is she here already?'

He sniffed the air; there was a hint of fairy dust, but not enough to turn Sam odd. Bladder trotted towards Sam and considered his blank and stupid face. What was wrong with him?

Woermann appeared behind Sam. 'Get it!' he said.

Bladder laughed. 'Would you listen to him, Sam! As if you'd do anything he says. Pack looks after pack.'

Woermann laughed too.

Bladder didn't like the sound and peered as the cat man lunged forward. His arms seemed longer. His hair was growing from all sorts of places. Maybe he had done something to Sam, they moved in a similar way.

Sam grabbed Bladder around the waist.

'OK, I got it, time to leave', Bladder wheezed. 'You got strong, Sam.'

But Sam didn't take Bladder back outside; he carried him towards a white door.

'Sam, what are you doing? No, no, no. You mustn't. Sam, this isn't you. You've been bewitched.'

Woermann turned the key and the door clicked open. Bladder struggled but Sam held him in sinewy, strong arms.

'Don't need you. Happy here.' Sam's voice came out bland and bored, he didn't sound like Sam at all. 'Woermann's rich. Going to look after me.'

'But your pack? The Kavanaghs?' Bladder shrieked as he stared into the dark cellar.

'I don't need any of you!' Sam screeched just as loudly.

The shock of Sam grabbing him knocked his fight for a second, and he couldn't, just couldn't hurt Sam, but he struggled to free himself as Sam carried him through the dark doorway and threw him. The boy was as strong as an ogre.

Woermann chuckled.

When the door at the top of the stairs slammed open and outside light poured on to the animals in the cellar, Amira's mum comforted Dr Kokoni as Wilfred and Amira howled. Sam heard it from inside the orb and woke, and pressed an eye against the globe's surface to see. From the doorway came a flurry of swear words and insults that filled the room with life and intensity. The dogs seemed invigorated and encouraged by it. Then a shape flew down and yelled in pain as it hit steps. Swear, insult, swear, insult as it rolled to the cellar floor. Woermann waited at the top of the stairs, his silhouette stood hands on hips.

'Best you stay here out of the way', Woermann said. 'Don't want you running off with the queen's toys.'

The door slammed, the light disappeared; and the shifters calmed, their barking fading. When the shape tumbled on to the floorboards it did not cease its noise, its rolling left its mouth free half the time. Swear, muffle, swear, muffle. A few rock-solid cracks resounded and the swearing sounded pained. It came to a stop between the tribe of shifters against the back wall and the orb itself. As soon as it did, the figure righted itself, sat up and looked around.

The voice groaned, and rushed back up the stairs and screamed at the door, pounding on the wood. 'You idiot! You idiot! You absolute waste of space! Completely human, that's what you've become! I came all this way because I thought you were worth it. I wanted to help you! But you? You? You get one sniff of money and you give up your friends, your family! And your pack! You low life!'

Sam cheered the courageous, abusive figure.

Then the creature roared out a disappointed song.

Sam could hardly see the bulky shape; it sat too far from the orb to be clear. Its fur stuck out at all angles, but it was a decent size. A Labrador, maybe. It sure was matted.

'It's no good', D.I. Kintamani called. 'The door's sound-proof. He won't be able to hear you.'

'Yes, he will', the shape said. 'Stupid, selfish, ungrateful ...' It must have had a terrible cold. It sneezed and its voice sounded husky and full of snot.

'Come down, let's wrap you in a blanket,' Dr Kokoni called. 'You sound sick.' She patted Mr Kokoni, who lay on the floor, head between his front paws, crying and saying 'so lost' every now and then.

'Don't feel the cold,' the shape said, then howled at the door. It rammed it a few times, making the animals in the cellar whine in response. When the door didn't budge, it trotted down the steps. Once at the bottom again, it fell in a heap and sniffled.

Sam watched with interest through the glass, his hands still cupped around his eyes. Something about the lumpy shape was familiar. Maybe it was a relative of Hazel's.

The creature turned its face to the orb, and despite its lumpy body and ratty fur, Sam recognised the face. Sam shrieked with joy! He knew exactly who it was. Maybe, maybe there was hope for them.

Bladder! he called.

'I came all this way for nothing,' Bladder said to the animals outside the orb, but few seemed to be listening.

Many edged back; he was a large stone lion after all.

'Can you believe it? Before he threw me down here, Sam told me he was happy; told them he didn't want to see his family or his pack any more.' Bladder wailed. Sam had never heard him make that sound before.

Sam wished Bladder could hear him. Sam had had conversations with the sword souls, so it was possible. He could hear Bladder, which meant his ears worked.

He should be able to make Bladder hear him too.

Hey! he called. *Can you hear me?*

Yes, we can hear you, the orb souls called back.

Not you, I want someone out there to hear me.

The thoughts weren't directed at Sam, but he heard them anyway. *Poor boy's gone daffy. Crazy. What is he going on about? We can't hear them. Why would they hear us?*

Sam could see his legs; he could see the souls around him. He could see and hear out of the orb, so surely he could make a noise.

Bladder! he called.

Bladder? Mrs Kokoni's soul replied. *Poor boy's gone doolally.*

Sam, stop, what are you trying to do? Amira's soul asked. He could hear Hazel and Wilfred's worry directed at him too. He flinched, their voices echoed now he could hear inside and out. Wilfred, Hazel and Amira's outside selves wept intensely; three soul voices in his head, three jumbling in his ears.

He blocked it all. Getting them out was all that mattered, and Bladder could help.

'Bladder?' This time he heard himself, in his own ears. A whisper of a voice. A touch of volume.

Sam put his eye to the glass. Nothing. The dogs and Bladder were still talking.

'Bladder!' Sam called as loud as he could. The noise in his ears was a library whisper, but louder than before. 'Bladder! Bladder! Bladder!'

Bladder tilted his head and closed one eye. 'What was that?'

In the cellar, Mrs Kintamani wailed. It sounded half crazed.

'She all right?' Bladder asked, distracted again.

'She lost a soul', D.I. Kintamani said.

You can help her if you listen to me, you silly gargoyle. Sam smacked his glowing hands on the glass. 'Bladder, Bladder, Bladder.' He could hear himself getting louder.

A pup stopped sobbing, and staggered forward. Hazel. 'I heard it too. A voice said "Bladder".'

'That's me, I'm Bladder.'

Sam screamed it out.

Hazel sat up, her ears pointed and alert. 'That's Sam's voice.'

'Sam's voice?' Bladder said and peered around the room. 'You're hearing things.'

'No, she just put Sam in the orb', Hazel said.

'*She* who? *She* what? Sam's out there.' Bladder gestured to the door.

'Queen Titania sucked us into that thing.'

Bladder peered at the orb.

'Yes! Yes! Look!' Sam yelled. 'I'm in here, Bladder!'

'What are you talking about? Sam just kicked me down the stairs. He couldn't be in there. It's not big enough. He'd hurt his back.'

'Not his physical form. His soul.'

'His soul?' Bladder limped towards the orb. 'His soul? How'd it get in there?' The stone lion put his forepaws on to the orb. He slid off and hit the ground. Sam heard the crack and following sizzle as Bladder replaced whatever had broken.

The gargoyle stretched up so his nose touched the lower curve of the orb. Sam looked down at him.

Last time Sam had seen him, Bladder had been a beautiful clean grey. The creature in front of him was dirty and muddy and wet.

'Sam?' He looked back at puppy Hazel. 'You telling me his soul's in there?'

Wilfred, Amira and D.I. Kintamani outside confirmed it was so. Their souls had been taken too. Sam could feel those very souls hovering about him.

'Well, Sam, I have to tell you I just saw your body upstairs and you're a complete jerk without a soul.'

'He didn't die,' Dr Kokoni asked. 'Single-souled creatures can't live without a soul, but he got up like a zombie. It's made my fur stand on end.'

Sam hit his head against the glass. His body got up? He would have seen that happen if he hadn't been sitting down feeling sorry for himself.

Bladder laughed. 'Sam's body's not human, he was made the monster way! We just gotta get his soul back inside it.' The gargoyle turned to the orb. 'That's a relief. I must say, your other half's a rotter, Sammy. Thank goodness it's not all you.' Bladder tried to lick the orb, but it flicked his tongue away. 'So, how do we get you back inside your body? Cos if we don't, I am gonna have to kill you. It,' he corrected himself.

'How long have I been away?' Sam yelled.

'Say again? I can't quite hear you.' Bladder put his ear on the orb.

Sam repeated himself, as loud as he could.

'Two days since you left the Kavanaghs' house. Two of the most difficult days of my life', Bladder replied. Sam had to listen hard, the gargoyle's voice distorted so often.

'Daniel', Sam said. 'You have to get everyone out of here and find him. He'll know what to do.'

'Like that well-fed duck will be any use. Last time I saw him, he couldn't even walk into the house without knocking his head. He's supposed to go through stuff. He's useless now. And he's off in Heaven somewhere. Not exactly a place I can get to. Have you got another plan?'

Woermann returned to the cellar an hour later.

The visit confirmed Bladder's statement to Sam. Behind Woermann, a writhing imp of a boy lumbered in. He did not move the way a human might, but with apish limbs and a four-legged gait that made Sam think that if his soul hadn't been put in at the beginning, boggarts might have claimed him.

The imp sneered at Bladder.

'I know what you are now. Should have realised my Sam doesn't have such an idiotic face', Bladder said.

Sam studied the stupid and cruel expression on the imp's face, so unlike the face he recognised in the mirror. He wondered how Bladder had not seen it wasn't him in the first place. The imp cowered as Woermann patted it.

'Hai ya!' Bladder charged at the cat man. Sam knew how much the gargoyle weighed and Woermann flinched too, but the man had grown, become hairier, and his teeth looked more pointed.

Woermann, though gargoyle-shy, didn't seem as nervous as when he'd been in The Lanes. His irises were golden slits and he walked with an elegant stoop, his hands needing to touch the floor, to take the weight of his staggering bulk. Even hunched as he was, his widening head scraped the cellar ceiling and his hair coursed down his back in raven glossiness.

'Stop him,' Woermann growled as Bladder leaped forward.

The imp jumped between them and with skinny arms. He surprised them all by tossing the gargoyle to the ground. Bladder howled as his back leg broke off and rolled towards the shifters. The imp ran towards it, grabbing the leg.

'Can't walk, can't walk!' The imp laughed as it waved Bladder's leg in the gargoyle's face.

Bladder lay in pain.

It terrified the shifters even more, and they howled.

Full moon'll be out tonight and I need to hunt,' Woermann said, and leered at the little group.

D.I. Kintamani growled and huddled the little pack against the orb, trying to stay out of the way of Woermann's cattle prod and crying when the prod struck his leg.

Woermann laughed as he jabbed at the dogs.

'No!' Bladder cried out. 'Leave them alone.'

The animals threw themselves out of Woermann's way. Wilfred, Amira and Hazel ran for the dark corner. The grown-up shifters may have been subdued by the loss of their souls, but they showed as much courage as they could, growling and barking. Even Mr Kokoni stopped sobbing. He growled and got a prod between his eyes for his efforts.

'Ooh, you three still have fight in you, don't you?'

Woermann thudded towards the shivering pups.

'Run! Wilfred! Amira! Hazel! Run!' Sam yelled.

The Wilfred, Amira and Hazel inside the orb screamed too. 'What's happening?' Amira's soul cried out.

Outside, Woermann asked, 'Who wants to be my dinner?' He reached down, grabbing at Hazel, who shrank from Woermann's huge claw. Bladder, three-legged and wailing, shook himself out of his pained groans and hobbled forward, sinking his stone teeth into Woermann's arm.

Woermann yowled and dropped both his cattle prod and Hazel, then stretched around and yanked at Bladder. The gargoyle stuck. The wildcat's blood flowed between the gargoyle's teeth.

The imp reached out and snapped off Bladder's right forepaw. Bladder screamed at the crunch. His bite loosened. Woermann's face was pain and fear, but he shook Bladder away. The gargoyle's stone body fell to the floor. His scream rang true, so deep from inside, that the souls in the orb heard it too and wailed as loudly as the shifters outside.

Hazel's soul sobbed. *She's so frightened, Sam.* Sam knew she meant her physical self.

Wilfred and Amira sobbed with her.

Woermann pointed at Bladder and the imp picked up the gargoyle.

'Sam! No! No!' Bladder yelled, but Sam wasn't out there filling the imp's body, he was in the orb watching everything, ramming his helpless fists against the glass.

The imp dropped Bladder at the perfect angle and

the gargoyle's head snapped off and rolled towards his dismembered body. The shifters and souls sobbed in unison.

'The rest of you, into the truck. The pet shop will get a pretty penny for you purebreds', Woermann slurred as he picked up the cattle prod, poked it at the animals and herded them to the top of the stairs. Then Woermann leaned over, scooped up the pup and handed it to the imp. 'For later', Woermann said. The imp nodded and carried Hazel up the steps.

'Please, no', both Hazel the pup and Hazel's soul cried out.

Woermann herded the other animals, leaving the door open. Except for the grey stone carcass lying in pieces on the cellar floor, there was no one who might escape. The cellar fell silent.

CHAPTER 23

Souls buffeted the orb's surface, hitting themselves again and again and bouncing back like glowing rubber balls. They may not have seen the awful events outside, but they had felt them and seen them through Sam's thoughts.

Sam had to save Hazel.

Think, think. Pace, pace.

He strode up and back, sure that he knew something. A memory of Daniel. Something Daniel said, and his own memories. He strained to remember the Ogres' Cavern, the broken blade.

The souls from the sword had appeared to him, they had separated out from the weapon itself and spoken to him. They hadn't been locked in, but although they had been tied to the sword, they moved freely.

'What did Daniel say? Daniel said something about that. Someone help me think.'

Daniel had been so uncoordinated. He'd lost all the graceful and divine ability he'd had when Sam had first met him. He couldn't get through walls any more. For all Sam knew he could be outside the house now, knowing exactly where Sam was but unable to get through the solid bricks.

Then Sam remembered what it was that Daniel had said.

'Angels are creatures of pure spirit. There is no reason for pure spirit to be contained by anything physical. The physical part can be contained, jailed, manacled, but if the soul chooses not to be bound, nothing can hold it.'

So, nothing should hold us all in here either. Not a glass orb, not magic.

'A soul is a free thing wherever it is, if it wants to be,' Daniel had said. 'Many souls are bound simply because they think they are.'

They could fly free if they'd wanted. Nothing could hold them.

Sam also remembered that even Daniel – who knew this so well – had struggled with cumbersome wings and heavy limbs after weeks of work; how could Sam, who'd never trained at this, be any better?

Because he had to. Sam needed to get out, so he needed to be better.

Better than an angel?

Yes.

He pushed at the glass. It was solid, but it wasn't

the glass that kept him in, it was dust magic. Was magic stronger than spirit?

'No. Nothing is. Daniel says nothing could keep a soul restrained if it doesn't want to be.' Sam pushed again. His hand slid through the glass but hit the magic on the other side. His fingers tingled and when he pulled them back, they smelt of rancid dust and reminded him of Maggie.

For a third time, he put his arm through and this time Sam felt the magic bend until it broke. His arm glowed through the outside of the orb like a ghost. He guessed that maybe that's what a ghost was; a soul who remembered what it looked like. The way the souls in the sword had.

He pushed again and found his chest moving through the glass. Not his head yet, as if his head didn't want to leave. His body bent back the way you do when reaching through a small window as far as your arm will stretch.

Sam heard Woermann upstairs, yelling at someone to wake up. Was it the imp? Something about driving. Sam knew Woermann couldn't drive the truck, it would be almost impossible in the shape he was in, and the imp couldn't because Sam had never learned. It must be the poor man from the pet shop, the one Titania had so dazed with dust he'd do whatever he was told. He was as much a prisoner as the shifters. Why was Woermann yelling at him?

Sam looked around. The souls in the orb were still spots of bright light, huddling together.

He had to get them out before they became complacent again. He had to use their misery to help them.

Bladder was broken, but right outside, and Sam knew

he was fixable. His greatest, immediate fear was for Hazel. Woermann was becoming a monster.

He had to convince the shifter souls to leave.

How close to moonrise were they? How much time did he have to save Hazel?

Finally, time became important again.

'A soul can't be bound by anything,' Sam repeated for the third time.

Well, we have been, haven't we? Mr Kokoni said.

'Only because we've somehow agreed to it.'

But it's magic. You can feel it as soon as you get to the side of the orb.

Sam sighed; this was going to be hard.

Don't give up, Dad, Hazel said.

'No, don't.' Sam sent his voice into every head. 'A soul is not a body. A soul can imagine itself free, and break through anything.'

Then why are we in here? Amira's mum asked.

He told you: because we've somehow agreed to it, Amira said.

But the magic ...

Blow the magic, let the boy finish, for goodness sake, D.I. Kintamani said. *Something about what he says makes sense. Go on, lad. We must at least try.*

Yeah, Wilfred cheered him on.

Finally, the prattling and arguments died away and the low hush of interest washed over him.

'We have to be able to picture our way out, I think,

imagine it, and for that reason we have to reshape. See ourselves physically, so we have eyes to see out of the orb,' Sam said.

How we gonna do that? Dr Kokoni asked.

It didn't start well. At first only half a dozen souls grew eyes. Hazel, Amira and Wilfred, D.I. Kintamani, Dr Kokoni and an old man with a jolly laugh. The slow arrival of bulging globes sticking out of the sides of glowing souls was a bit of a shock.

When those souls said it worked, more joined in. Some struggled.

Can't do it, a woman's voice cried.

'What do you miss most?' Sam asked.

Not eyes. I want arms, to comfort my little one.

Sam felt what she felt then, the misery of the toddler soul cuddled near her.

'Imagine arms, want them desperately.'

She did. A sudden explosion of streaks of white light burst out of the side of the soul and sprays of fingers grew from the ends.

I can feel them! I can feel them! she cried out.

It looks like some strange fungal growth, Sam thought.

We can hear your thoughts, young man, D.I. Kintamani said, but he chuckled too, his swollen eyes wobbling as he laughed.

Soul after soul changed shape. Some of the souls managed it after someone they trusted changed and vouched for Sam's declaration that his soul was in the shape of a boy.

Arms, legs, heads, fingers, noses, mouths and eyes all grew from the glowing spots. Those who could see the others laughed at the sight, and realised they too were as strangely bulbous as anyone else in the orb.

The souls' confidence built; if eyes and legs could grow then so could torsos and heads, and soon hundreds of souls huddled in front of him. As tiny stars they took up little room, in human shape the area was cramped. All eyes were on him, and he needed eyes, because if they could see what he could do, they would believe him.

Sam turned and pushed his arm through the wall of the orb, his hand stretching into the air of the cellar outside, but he smiled. He felt the cold. He wondered if that was his imagination too.

The souls gasped. The souls at the periphery of the group, those against the walls of the orbs, copied him and pushed arms through. Some thudded against the magic, but some younger ones found their arms slipped through. They laughed.

'Sam, you're brilliant!' Hazel said.

If he'd had blood in his form, Sam would have blushed.

Young souls found the idea that they could imagine their way out an easy concept to grasp. Their parents and grandparents, seeing the evidence of their newly popped-out eyes as young arms and legs broke through the orb, were not slow to follow. Families dived out of the globe.

The other souls let the Kokonis, Kintamanis and

Salukis push to the front. 'We need to get out, reunite our souls,' D.I. Kintamani said to Sam, 'then we'll be back for you and Hazel.'

A wave of terror flew from Dr Kokoni and her husband as they pulled Hazel's soul through the crowd to the glass. 'Hazel, find your body, get out and make for the road. We'll come back for you,' Mr Kokoni said, then turned to Sam. 'If you can, save my girl.'

Wilfred waited for a space to jump out. 'We've gotta get to that truck. Let's go, let's go, everyone.'

Hazel rushed back and kissed Sam on the face. It felt warm, like sunshine, but Sam could feel her thoughts. *Where was her body? What if it was somewhere more horrible than the cellar?*

Sam thought back at her, I *will find you.*

Then she and Wilfred were gone, diving through the glass.

The speed of departure increased. The more souls got through, the quicker the next lot left. The power of belief improved by others' success.

'Amira!' her mother called. 'Us now. Hurry, hurry.'

Sam looked through the glass and saw the cellar exploding in a fireworks display, the room filled with beautifully coloured light, the joy of freedom causing the souls to glow red with courage and blue with confidence, a happy orange, freedom green. Most had reverted to the tiny dot, as if believing that they would move quicker in that shape. He could feel their thoughts, rather than hear words.

Sam had never been so satisfied to be alone in his whole life.

If Bladder hadn't been lying on the floor in pieces, it would have been perfect.

He dived through the glass and magic membrane. The fairy dust let him go with a resigned 'pfft'.

CHAPTER 24

Sam watched ghosts whirl around the kitchen, and it would have been joyous to see souls zip out over the grass outside, creating erupting, stirring constellations heading in every direction, if the last blush of pink hadn't been settling in the direction of the city. Sunset. It was getting darker, and Sam couldn't see a moon, but he guessed a full one would arrive soon. Woermann's bristling body hair gave that away. Outside, the truck sat waiting to leave. Next to it, the shopkeeper from Collars and Crufts slept against a tyre; he didn't even cower although Woermann yelled at him. Sam smelt the air, someone had been too generous with fairy dust.

Sam watched a cluster of souls fly into the side of the truck. Only Hazel hung inside the kitchen.

Sam looked around. 'You're still here?'

'The pull of my other soul is so strong, Sam, I can feel it.'

'Can you tell which room?'

'Just this way.' Hazel moved towards the kitchen wall. 'Sam, I've gotta go to her. I can't hold on any more.' She slipped through the bricking.

Sam didn't have another soul. He stilled himself, listening to the sounds of the house. Nothing. He was going to have to search for his body.

No, wait, Sam thought, *I should find Hazel first. It's no use getting back to my body if I don't know where Hazel is being kept.* Where would Woermann have taken her?

Sam zipped through the French doors into the night air, skirting the perimeter of the manor. He pushed his ghostly arms through a wall and floated back into the house. He checked the bedrooms. Messy, but empty. No Hazel in any of them. No imp boy either. He had an awful thought: what if he couldn't return to his body anyway? *No, don't think that.* He needed it, and it had a variety of useful talents: it could be seen by humans, it could fight and it could carry a small dog to safety.

The shifters barked inside the truck, locked in and frustrated. As soon as he'd sorted Hazel, Sam would let them out. The pet shopkeeper grunted and Woermann staggered away from the vehicle.

Sam floated back downstairs and looked in the rooms along the corridor: a library, an office, a guest bathroom. No Hazel.

Sam shot up the corridor towards the drawing room, diving between open doors and searching the corners. A huge fire twisted and illuminated the room with its dancing shadow; the thick power of fairy dust filled the air. Even as a soul he could sense it.

Woermann sat in the chair Titania had used as a throne. His hands clutched the wings and his wild head turned and turned. Woermann's eyes shone old gold, his irises narrowed to feline half-moons.

He hardly looked like the Woermann Sam had met in the cafe.

The cat eyes looked up, directly at Sam. Woermann growled. Sam floated up and away, then out of the drawing room.

So, not there. Where would Woermann have hidden Hazel?

The ballroom! Where Woermann went to protect himself when he turned. The scratched walls, the security screens on the windows. Sam's nose had told him what else the cat man did in there, but he had not wanted to think about it at the time.

Hazel would be there.

An angry barking came from the truck. The truck's lights had turned on, but the driver moved sluggishly in the driver's seat as he stared at a hedge. He fell forward on the steering wheel into another dusty nap.

Sam sailed around to the side of the house to where he'd seen the ballroom door and popped through the wall, the graininess slipped away from him. He wondered what had held Daniel back. The bricking tickled, but it didn't put up resistance.

The ballroom was huge. Twice the length of the school

basketball court and twice as wide. It was a good place for a cat to play with its food.

Sam listened.

The dog's breathing was soft and low.

Sam looked out of the window.

There, low in the sky, a grey settle of clouds glowed with the moon sitting behind them.

'Hazel,' he whispered.

'Sam.' Hazel's voice came from the corner of the room.

Hazel's soul clung to a solid security screen. 'I want to go back in, I really do, but I'm so scared,' she said. 'She's so frightened too. What if I get back in there and he eats me? What do I do?'

Hazel and Sam studied the dog on the floor. Hazel-pup stared straight at the Hazel next to Sam and whined.

'She knows you're here,' Sam said.

'Of course she does, we belong together,' Hazel said.

Outside, heavy footsteps started up the corridor.

Hazel-pup huddled in the corner, making herself small and quiet as Woermann stalked up and down, swearing to himself. Growling, purring, arguing against an unseen foe.

'I'm here, Hazel. I'm going to help you,' Sam said. 'Now I know where you are, I'll be back with my body.'

Hazel's soul reached out and held Sam's hand. 'She needs me,' she said. 'Oh, Sam, I'm so scared.'

Sam felt scared too.

Hazel's soul zipped across the room, she no longer looked like a ghostly version of herself, but had transformed to a pretty orange light. Hazel-pup ran towards the glow, it knew where the soul was and gave a yap of joy, the fear forgotten in the run.

The orange light zipped closer and the pup lifted off the floor, floating, then the soul and pup collided in an explosion of light. For a few seconds, they spun in the air together, and the small creature glowed with a glorious blinding light. A sound rang in Sam's ear, two souls singing together in a chorus of greeting and gladness. *Welcome, welcome, welcome*, they said to each other. Then gently the pup floated down and returned to the floor.

Hazel, twin-souled again, looked around, her eyes glowed, and then she remembered where she was. She dashed back to the corner.

'Help me, Sam,' she yapped.

Sam knew where Hazel was; now he had to find the imp.

Don't rush, he told himself. *Think*. His body was all monster, all imp, with enough fairy to confuse everything. But this past day had taught him that fairies, while not precisely bad, were inclined to look after fairies. It would be looking after its own skin.

He flew over Woermann, who paced the corridor, pushing doors open. From the back, the great cat's hair had thickened and sprouted. He was shirtless now, black fur rippling and shining in the swinging hall light. Woermann was turning into one healthy cat. His ears stretched to inky points, his hands swung at his sides, each great finger ending in a sharp talon. Every time his right arm swung, it brushed over the clutch of keys hanging from his belt.

They jangled. He stank of fairy dust.

Woermann seemed less in control than ever.

His ability to speak was disappearing. 'Imp?' he called. 'Moon. Here. Now.'

Sam guessed his meaning. The moon was coming and Woermann needed the imp to help him with something. He was a huge brute and terrifying; the imp was staying out his way. If Woermann had been searching for Sam, he would have avoided him too.

Where hadn't he looked? The imp wasn't in the kitchen, not in the bedrooms, not in the drawing room.

He drifted ghostlike through the door and watched Woermann, more were-cat than man, sniffing the air. 'Imp! Imp!' the 'thrope called, and then roared. He was using all his animal senses to find Sam's body, and surely with such strong scenting abilities it could find one stinky monster.

How do you hide smell?

Sam grinned; he knew where the imp was hiding.

He zipped into the pool room and hovered over the water. He'd guessed right, his body had sunk like a stone gargoyle, and like a gargoyle, the imp had no problem with the lack of air. You can't drown a gargoyle. The little beast sat at the bottom of the pool, legs spread and head hunched, hiding from Woermann as the cat man roared about the house. Sam had seen boggarts and brownies cringe in the same way when Thunderguts had commanded them, and he was their king. The imp didn't have the same duty to Woermann. It stared around the water, looked at its fingers, counted its toes and blew the occasional bubble.

It looked up at Sam. Its face was so lost and miserable, Sam might have felt sorry for it, if he hadn't remembered what it had done to Bladder and Hazel.

Outside, Woermann screamed, high and hysterical. 'Help!'

Sam ploughed head first through the water and into the imp's body. He had a moment of confusion, floating upside down. He could see through eyes, feel his soul inside himself. His fingers tingled, his toes twitched. A barrage of horrible noises hit his sensitive imp ears, despite being water-muffled.

Woermann's screams were far worse on his gargoyle ears.

Sam slipped and slid as he moved towards the side of the pool. His limbs were heavy and uncoordinated. A body was a weighty thing. He pushed himself up to grab the ladder, hitting his knuckles on the metal. Pain! Real pain shot up his arm. He hoped he didn't take long to get used to his body again. When he finally burst free of the surface, his ears filled with the great cat's roar, and the baying blood barks from a pack of hounds beating against the insides of the truck. He flopped on the edge of the pool, sopping and lumpish.

He needed help. He could let the shifters out, but Woermann was searching for the imp, and likely to stop Sam if he saw him. This was a two-person task. One to release the dogs, one to help Hazel. He needed Bladder.

Sam heard the great beast lope back into the drawing room and collapse on to a sofa. 'Imp!' he called.

Sam breathed in. He only had a little time before Woermann's final transformation.

He raced towards the kitchen, the cellar door a black throat down which he fled.

He fell down the stairs and found Bladder still in four pieces. The break at the neck revealed his dark, hollow stomach.

Empty.

For a moment, Sam worried that Woermann had stolen his friend's heart, but it glowed next to a blanket. He picked it up in his hand, feeling its comfortable weight. One crack had completely healed, and it warmed his palm.

Heart in, and then pushing. Bladder's body weighed half a tonne and the winged lion's head was big. He'd moved Bladder's head before, and he'd been in a much weaker condition. Also, he'd seen what the imp had done with his muscles. He was stronger than he knew. Still, the lion's bottom was heavier than his head.

Sam shoved the two pieces together.

Fizz.

'You treacherous half-born son of a ...'

'Not now, Bladder, listen to me, I need your help to let the shifters out.'

'Sam? You sound like you. Is that you all in one piece?' The gargoyle's face grimaced, then he decided to listen. 'OK, what can I do?'

'Let me put your legs on first.'

Shizzle. Hiss.

The gargoyle stretched each limb.

Sam said, 'Woermann's turning. You've got to let the shifters out of the truck outside and tell them Hazel's in the ballroom.'

'The pup? That beast will tear her to pieces. Let me do it, you go get the dogs.'

'Woermann's calling for me and he'll pick up my scent soon. I might be able to use the fact he doesn't know my soul's back in my body. And you know I won't break as easily as you.' Sam tapped Bladder's leg.

The lion's face pulled down in a grimace. 'Then let me come with you.'

'We'll do better if there's more of us. D.I. Kintamani knows about 'thropes, and he knows 'Thrope Controllers. He may know what we need to do to stop Woermann.'

'I don't like this.'

'No more talking, Bladder. We're running out of time. He's getting stronger and stronger. I've got no idea how long we've got, and the front door won't hold him when he changes. Let the shifters out, maybe together you can come up with a plan.'

Bladder raced up the steps, his stone mane skimming both sides of the doorway. 'What are you going to do?'

Sam dashed up behind him. 'I've gotta get Woermann inside the ballroom, so he can't hurt anyone, and get Hazel out.'

'That doesn't sound easy. I'd rather do it for you.'

Woermann's bellow resumed, he was moving towards the kitchen. 'Imp. Need help.'

Sam shuddered.

'Imp!' Woermann screamed.

Sam raced into the kitchen as Woermann stared into the yard, distracted by the smells from outside. The were-cat peered out the open door and yowled. 'Imp!'

The truck sat in the yard. The dogs inside had ceased barking.

Woermann inhaled the smell of living animals floating in on the cold air.

'I'll get him out of the kitchen,' Sam whispered to Bladder, then rushed up the stairs. 'Here I am!'

Woermann, huge and wobbling on his hind legs, turned from the delightful scents coming in the door.

Woermann snarled. 'Look. For you.' He panted. 'Need help.'

'How can I help?' Sam said. 'Don't you normally do this for yourself?'

'Hands changed too fast. Fairy dust maybe. Can't use keys. Get me in room,' Woermann panted.

Sam rushed forward. Woermann lifted his arms, letting Sam unclip the keys from his belt.

That part was easy, Woermann wanted to give him the keys.

The cat purred.

'Soon. Must.' Woermann stopped, sniffed deep, finding the scent coming in the open kitchen door fascinating.

Woermann breathed in the outside world and purred.

It was going to be easy to get Woermann into the room, but he also had to free Hazel. Maybe if the cat was distracted.

Sam looked back at the cellar. Bladder's grey eyes peered at him from the dark. Sam raced towards the ballroom.

Woermann roared into the dark cool evening.

'Hazel,' Sam whispered through the ballroom door, 'come for the door and turn left immediately.'

Hazel whined from inside, but he heard her pad towards the door.

The first key didn't fit the lock, nor the second. Sam listened as the dogs rattled inside the truck, baying at the cat's roar. Woermann, the little bit that was still human, chuckled at the reply.

Third, fourth, fifth key. There were twenty keys on the ring. Which one was it? Sam shook as the sixth key slid inside the lock. It turned.

He gave a silent cheer and opened the door.

Sam looked at Hazel. She peered left and put one paw out into the corridor, then stopped, staring behind Sam. Sam turned to see Woermann filling the corridor and glaring at him.

'OK, maybe not out. In, Hazel!' Sam yelled.

Hazel darted back into the ballroom, and Sam stepped inside too, as the cat man hurled four-legged down the corridor towards them.

Sam turned and swung the door.

Woermann's roar shook the frame. Only the barest patch of skin on his chin suggested any leftover humanity.

Sam pushed the door to a close, but before he heard

the lock click, the titanic weight of the cat man bundled into the wood, slammed the door open again then rolled on to the floor.

Sam skidded backwards across the rough wood.

Woermann trained his gaze on Sam and licked the back of his paw, extending his red tongue along to the end of his talons. He caught himself, and growled at Sam. 'Close door,' he said, his human voice almost gone.

Sam rushed for Hazel, who cowered in the dark. He had one chance to get her out. The door stood wide open. Before he reached the pup, Woermann leaped between them, swung a lithe paw and Sam flew backwards.

With still enough human in him, Woermann padded towards the door and smashed it shut.

'Sam?' Hazel said.

Sam got up, sidling past the cat. It stared at him with hungry golden eyes and sprang into him. The cat's head collided with Sam and he thumped into the wall, which showered him with plaster.

Sam knew if he'd been truly human or a shifter, he'd have broken his back or his ribs. A gargoyle would have been shattered.

The were-cat padded up to him and pushed its enormous face up to Sam's. Its sandpaper tongue flicked out and licked his cheek. It stepped back, nose lifting in a sneer. It didn't like the taste of him. It turned its gaze to Hazel. The pup whimpered.

'No!' Sam said.

* * *

As soon as Woermann left the kitchen, Bladder raced for the open door, straight towards the truck.

The shifters barked from the back. Bladder jumped as the headlights went on, the truck driver peered around straight at Bladder sitting on the grass. The man didn't flinch at all, as if he were used to seeing gargoyles running around. The engine purred awake.

Then Bladder heard a better noise, stone feet pelting along the gravel driveway. Wheedle and Spigot!

'Hey!' he yelled.

Wheedle and Spigot came flying at him. 'You're safe.' Wheedle screwed up his eyes and beamed at Bladder.

'We've got to stop that truck and open the back doors.'

'If you like,' Wheedle said. The truck reversed jerkily towards the driveway and the gargoyles ducked to avoid flying gravel. 'Better move quick,' Wheedle said.

Bladder launched himself at the bonnet and landed with an explosive thud. The shifters inside barked louder. The van continued reversing, but the driver's mouth hung open. Bladder thought he could fit his whole paw inside it if he tried. Still, the van didn't slow. 'Stop, you dusted idiot,' Bladder yelled.

The driver moved slowly, driving a few more feet before moving his hands to the gears.

The truck stopped.

'Now, get out,' Bladder instructed.

The nasty scrape of stone against metal came from the rear of the truck as Wheedle and Spigot undid the doors.

The barks rang out clear through open doors. 'Bladder?' someone asked.

'Wheedle,' Wheedle replied. Bladder harrumphed. They didn't look anything alike.

'Out you come,' Wheedle said.

Padded paws hit the ground. 'Everyone OK? Thanks. Thanks.' Their voices collided with each other.

Bladder looked at the driver. 'You can go now.' He jumped off the truck and ran to the back of the truck. 'Which of you is D.I. Kintamani?'

Sam jumped and climbed the wall as the werecat padded over, interested but calm. It had grown into a huge and glossy blank panther. As Sam clambered higher, it purred and turned its head.

Sam heard Hazel's sharp gasp from the opposite corner of the room. The panther's black head lifted, leered at Sam and showed sharp teeth. Drool dripped from its grin and the cat padded towards the noise.

Sam scrambled across the wallpaper. The panther glanced at him a couple of times, but its true focus remained on the exciting noise coming from the corner.

Hazel's heart banged. She watched Sam scamper across the wallpaper. 'Help!'

'Coming!'

Sam jumped between Hazel and Woermann. The cat bared its teeth. It had a lot of teeth. Sam backed towards Hazel.

'Run to the door, Hazel.'

Her eyes remained wide, fixed on the cat. She hadn't heard him. The cat pushed back into its haunches and readied itself to spring at Sam. Sam backed against the wall and shifted over, giving Hazel a small corridor to run through. The cat looked at Hazel, licked its lips, but turned to Sam and purred deep in its throat. It was enjoying the game: kill the boy, eat the girl.

It leaped forward and Sam leaped too, grabbing on to the wall. The cat's head slammed into the plaster where Sam had just been.

That should keep it down, Sam thought.

Sam lowered his foot, and the cat sprang up and purred up at Sam. He was making the hunt too much fun.

Sam raced four-limbed along the longest wall towards the empty fireplace nestled at the end of the room, leaping ahead of the cat's casual tread.

Hazel dashed along the other wall, towards the door, and the panther swung around, and with one paw hit her like a ping-pong ball across the room.

She huddled for a moment, dazed, but the cat seemed to have decided he wanted to play with the pup again. Her quietness, low breath and shrinking into the shadows gave her no cover. He strolled to where Hazel sat.

'Come on, Hazel,' Sam called.

The pup found her legs and skidded past the great cat. Sam expected Woermann to take off after her, but instead he turned with slippery, slow ease, purred again, and padded in the direction Hazel had taken.

Outside the door, dog barks resounded. Hazel barked

back, running for the door, knowing there was no point in trying to camouflage herself any more. 'Help! Help!'

'Hazel, get to the door,' Sam called.

'I'm trying,' she yapped back.

Hazel turned from the door, towards Sam, with Woermann between them.

Sam dropped to the floor right next to the fireplace. He grabbed a handful of soot.

The cat peered at Sam, took a deep, satisfied sniff of him before stepping towards the Kokoni pup.

Hazel took off.

The hunt continued. Although Hazel ran with her haunches rolled forward and her tail between her legs, the great cat trotted after, following her darting with predatory ease. It batted her with a velvety paw, playing, and she rolled into the middle of the room.

The pup sat on the floor dazed for a second before registering the cat padding towards her.

'Hazel, to me,' Sam said.

She darted head first, the panther loping behind her, both racing in Sam's direction. Woermann focused on the juicy pup tearing towards the fireplace. Hazel scooted by Sam.

Woermann ignored him, his large eyes following the pup's path. His panther feet rumbled the floorboards as he sped up, enjoying a real hunt.

Sam waited, three steps away, two steps, one, and threw the soot as straight as he could. The black muck hit Woermann in the eyes.

The cat roared.

Sam turned to see Hazel inside the fireplace. A good spot if she only had to worry about Woermann's head. The cat would never get its huge noggin in the little space, but the panther had deft paws as well, and would be able to flick her out like a juicy nut.

Sam grabbed the pup and tried to run for the door.

The panther continued roaring, his sight gone for a short while but its hearing and smell still good. He backed to the door, putting his large body against the wood. Until he moved, no one was getting out of there.

The door handle jiggled. Someone outside was trying to get in. The panther roared when it heard D.I. Kintamani's voice. 'I *have* turned the key, it won't open.'

'Windows,' yelled Bladder.

Sam wasn't sure if he could climb one-armed, but he was about to find out.

The shifters' barks came from outside the house now, as the panther used a paw to rub at its eyes.

Hazel shook in his arms. Her ears pricked, alert, questioning.

Woermann's frustrated roars vibrated in Sam's ears.

Sam used his feet to push himself as far up the wall as possible, limping up the wallpaper like a wounded spider.

Halfway up, he allowed himself time to look over his shoulder. Woermann blinked. There was still soot in its eyes, but Sam had no doubt the great cat could see enough. Woermann padded towards them, sniffing the air.

Sam climbed a few more paces. Next to his hand four deep claw marks wounded the plaster. Sam scaled higher.

'It's running,' Hazel said.

'Hush,' Sam replied.

The dog stared over his shoulder. 'Scoop my poop, ya mangy moggy.'

'Hazel, didn't I just say hush?' Sam asked as the cat growled low. 'Bad dog.'

The half-blinded cat hurled itself against the walls and windows. Glass broke, and Sam heard a security screen rattle near his head. Metal ached against metal as someone forced something into the security screens. Sam ignored it, his hands reaching higher. Hazel flinched.

Sam climbed, a limping, jerking ascent, but he progressed. He peered down at Woermann again; the cat had retreated to the other side of the room. *What was he up to?*

When Sam heard the running paws, he knew the answer and scrambled higher as the cat roared and leaped.

Hazel screamed and Sam felt a solid paw hit his back near Hazel's head. His grip on the pup weakened.

'Don't drop me, Sam,' she cried.

The world around them darkened a little, but Sam shucked Hazel higher on his shoulder. The muscles in his back ached. The cat had hit him with more force than he'd ever felt before. His vision cleared and he saw the clean ceiling, no claw marks. If he could get his feet up that high ...

Woermann's paw tread retreated to the opposite end of

the ballroom again, building energy, purring low at his meal. Sam clambered on to the ceiling and with Hazel resting on his chest, looked over his good shoulder. Woermann gained speed, racing across the floor. The padding stopped as the panther left the floor and punched low on Sam's back. The pain was explosive. Sam shuddered and felt his arms weaken. If his hands didn't stick by themselves, he would have fallen.

'Hold on, Sam', Hazel said.

The dogs outside barked, human voices mixed with them, and the security screen rattled and fell.

Hazel whined. Sam peered down to see what Hazel was whining about. His gaze was distracted by an outline outside the window. He swore he could see the moon but it was blotted by misshapen blackness. Hazel barked at it. Glass scraped and crunched. The heavy tread of something retreated, someone running away.

Goodness knows how heavy Woermann was, he was angry and determined to dislodge Sam. The panther ran. Sam closed his eyes as the heavy feet gathered speed. The sound echoed against the walls, the shifters' barking chorus sang to its heavy drum. He heard the power in Woermann's legs and knew the panther could jump high enough to dislodge him and Hazel. A little more was all it would take. The cat's heart pumped and Sam smelt the acrid scent of adrenalin as it pushed off the floor.

Sam's teeth clenched closed; he could not help but hear every sound as the beast left the ground and flew towards them.

Boom! Something exploded through the window,

and Woermann *oof*ed as a projectile collided with the cat's heavy body. Woermann's talons, a cat's whisker from Sam's face, missed him completely, flying sideways as the cat's trajectory changed.

Sam saw the cat's head hit the wall. Its roar snapped off as it was knocked out. Then a second thud sounded as the heavy fur bomb hit the ground and shook the room.

Another heavier clunk came as the unknown projectile fell to the floorboards and cracked like stone. Sam lost his grip on his weakened side, and his arm and leg dropped. Hazel slid off his chest and he flailed, unable to catch her.

'Sam!' she screamed.

A dozen voices yelled.

After that, all Sam heard was heavy breathing and a pack of dogs racing around outside barking like their lives depended on it.

CHAPTER 25

Sam's shoulder ached and the room was quiet.

'Sam!' Hazel called.

He let his wounded arm swing out so he could look at the room. Hazel sat in the arms of a large stone bull.

'Wheedle?' Sam watched the floor weave and wave like the sea.

Someone shrieked.

'Spigot?'

Sam climbed down, three-limbed again. His heart beat fast, but he felt sleepy. He got most of the way down the wall and jumped the last bit, sliding to the floor.

Sam sat down. That was enough for one day.

'Where's Bladder?' Sam asked.

'He's over there, your friends are putting his head back on. He just flew across the room and tackled the cat. You should have seen it. His face was like this.'

Wheedle bared all his teeth and tried to look fierce. It didn't work.

Sam wished he had seen Bladder.

The cat lay near the door, its body curled near the skirting board.

He sniffed the cat; it was still alive.

'Rope. We need rope,' D.I. Kintamani said. Sam peered across the room and saw the shifters in human form wearing various makeshift outfits: towels, tablecloths, curtains. 'We won't be able to move him.'

Wilfred ran into the room wearing a sweater so long, it looked like a dress. 'Will silk scarves do?'

'Perfect!' D.I. Kintamani said, and Wilfred reddened at his father's praise.

'Geneve, help me tie up this big cat,' D.I. Kintamani said.

Mrs Kintamani grumbled. 'Put the gargoyle together, round up the children. Now it's tie up the cat! I can barely keep my towel up.'

'Leave the gargoyle to me,' Wheedle said. He put Hazel on the ground and she ran to Mrs Kintamani.

Sam heard the sizzle.

'Sam! Sam!' Bladder yelled. 'Is he OK?'

Sam smiled at Bladder and collapsed on the floor. 'How did you stop him?' Sam asked. Bladder looked blurry.

'Force and velocity,' the gargoyle replied. 'Makes being hit by half a tonne of handsome stone feel a whole lot worse.'

Sam felt a wet tongue on his cheek and everything went dark.

He woke up belly down on a bed inside a rattling house. His friends, in pup form, lay snuggled up to him. He opened one eye; Dr Kokoni had her hand on his neck.

The gargoyles, in an interesting tableau, had lined up one after the other along the side of the bed, all staring at him. They looked so dirty. If he hadn't known them he would have found it creepy. Actually, he did find it creepy.

He moved his head, and everyone else moved too. The puppies bounced to their feet and the gargoyles blinked awake.

'Easy, easy, Sam,' Dr Kokoni said. 'We're getting you to a shifter surgery, you've had some nasty knocks. Don't move.'

Sam struggled under her hand, rolled over and sat up. 'I feel fine.'

Dr Kokoni squinted at him. 'You're kidding me. I was worried about internal bleeding. You were so bruised. I didn't think you'd walk for ages.'

Wheedle pulled up Sam's sweater and stared at his back, rubbing hard hoofs over the skin. 'It's gone yellow. Is yellow OK?'

'It's great,' Dr Kokoni said, peering around too. 'It was black an hour ago.'

'Told ya,' Bladder said. 'He's a gargoyle, knock him about and a few minutes later he'll get right back up again.'

Sam felt around to his back. 'It really did hurt when Woermann hit me.'

Bladder sniggered. 'Try having your head knocked off. What is it? Four? Five times now? I'd very much like to mention that I never once lost my head before I met you.'

Sam squirmed.

'And he's worth every single one, right?' Wheedle asked.

Bladder muttered something.

'Speak up,' Wheedle said.

'Every single one, but it doesn't mean I have to like them.' Bladder put his face up to Sam's and gave him a hard kiss on the forehead.

Spigot put his head on Sam's lap.

Sam looked around. Mr Kokoni and Amira's mum were sitting at a table sticking out of the wall, and Mrs Kintamani and D.I. Kintamani sat in seats in front of a big window. He would swear Mrs Kintamani was holding on to a steering wheel, and he could see the world outside the windows rushing by, house after house, as the moon sat low and light on the horizon. It was nearly morning.

Maybe he was hallucinating.

'What is this place?' he asked.

'It's a mobile home, Sam. We found it in Woermann's shed. He probably used it on his hunting trips,' D.I. Kintamani said.

Sam sat bolt upright. 'Woermann?'

'Safely stored in the truck. Still howling. He built that thing so nothing, including himself, could get out the back.

He was roaring when we left. I left a message on 'Thrope Control's answering machine. I'll ring again in the morning.

'I would have called an ambulance,' Dr Kokoni said, 'but having a panther howling and, well, you're not entirely human, so ...'

'Yeah, we didn't think a normal hospital would cope,' Amira said.

Wheedle nosed him, sniffed him. All the gargoyles did. As if this seemed to be the thing to do, the pups joined in. It hurt when he laughed.

The puppies dived on to the floor, rolling into small piles of clothes before changing into humans. They'd obviously developed a talent for shifting and dressing simultaneously.

'That looks really weird,' Wheedle said.

'This from a talking rock,' Hazel said.

'So, I'm not speeding on a life-saving mission any more?' Mrs Kintamani asked. 'In which case, does anyone want breakfast?'

Mrs Kintamani pulled the bus into a service station car park. Despite her husband's protests that they needed to get back and report on the incident, in the end he gave in to the Kokonis, Ms Saluki, three gargoyles and four hungry children. The stare his wife gave him may have also helped.

Sam was glad they took the food back to the bus and ate it while on the move.

The quicker they left, the quicker he could get home.

CHAPTER 26

Mrs Kintamani drove fast and smoothly, even with three gargoyles in the back seat, and turned down a side street near Sam's house and parked. He could see home across the way. The three gargoyles jumped out, their paws cracking the asphalt.

'Can we come too?' Hazel asked.

'I think Mr and Mrs Kavanagh will have enough to think about with Sam home, let alone three pups hyped up on sugary breakfast drinks.'

D.I. Kintamani winked at Wilfred, who tried his best to settle on the bedcovers, but despite looking human, he still bounced like a pup. Sam, his pack and D.I. Kintamani got out of the mobile home.

Bladder winced.

'Bladder? You OK?' Wheedle asked.

'Think I ate too much eggy bread, I keep getting heartburn.'

'Yes, heartburn,' Wheedle agreed, and grinned at Sam.

Wheedle rubbed his face against Sam's. 'We love you, Sam,' he said.

Bladder looked at the roof. 'Up we get.'

Spigot screeched in Sam's face. Sam stroked his beak.

'And Bladder loves you more than anything in this world,' Wheedle whispered to Sam. 'You ignore his noises.'

'We'll talk about it as soon as we ...' Bladder waved a paw at the detective. 'Stop wasting your time with smooching, you saps,' Bladder called. 'We gotta get on the roof before a crowd shows up.'

Sam walked up the steps of his home. It wasn't a mansion like Woermann Manor, nor did it have all the expensive furniture and fittings, but the Kavanagh house was far more beautiful. He rang the bell.

The door opened and Nick stood there, still in his dressing gown, looking miserable and sleepy. Sam remembered a similar time only a few months before when Nick had looked the same, only he'd been waiting for Beatrice. Instead of yelling his name, though, Nick grabbed Sam, pulled him into a hug and the house. He looked over Sam's shoulder and studied Wilfred's dad. He was still wearing one of Woermann's sweaters, which was far too big for him.

'Detective Inspector Kintamani,' Wilfred's dad said to Nick. 'I would show you ID, but I've left it in my other suit.'

Nick loosened his grip on Sam and stared at him. 'You're back for a visit, right?'

'I've come home.'

Nick grinned and yelled back into the house. 'Dad, put the kettle on! Mum's gonna need a cup of tea.'

'Who's that?' Michelle trotted from the top of the stairs, a baby in her arms. Beatrice laughed and a burst of sparkles exploded across the room right in Sam's face. Happy stars. Michelle pulled her dressing gown around her as she saw D.I. Kintamani's serious face. Then she forgot it and grabbed Sam for a kiss. He caved into her arms.

Michelle smiled at the detective. 'I'm Michelle Kavanagh, Sam Kavanagh's ...' Michelle stopped. 'I mean Sam Woermann's ... I don't know.'

Richard's hoot sounded from the kitchen.

They put out an extra cup for the detective, but he shook his head. 'I can't stay long, I need to get everyone home and put in a statement, but I will be back.'

Michelle nodded at the detective, then she put her arm around Sam's shoulder. 'You were just going to call us yesterday and when you didn't ... I didn't think we'd see you at all. We've been putting in papers to see if we are allowed some access.'

Sam felt so happy to see them, he cried. He couldn't have been happier but his eyes wouldn't stop leaking.

Michelle's eyes weren't half as wet as his. 'Have you been all right?'

'I'm not going back there,' Sam said.

Nick whooped.

Richard and Michelle looked at each other. 'You always have a home here, you know that,' Richard said. 'But your ...

father may have a thing or two to say about you staying here.'

D.I. Kintamani frowned. 'Woermann was never Sam's father. It's going to take some time to explain, and first I could do with a change of clothes.' He lifted his arms and the jumper swam around him. 'It's a very odd situation, but I expect you're used to that with Sam, so bear with us. When I've put a statement in, I'll come back and tell you everything. Let me allow you to get reacquainted, OK? Call me if you need me, Sam.'

'Where's your phone?' Nick asked.

CHAPTER 27

Sam spent the rest of the day with the Kavanaghs, talking to the Kavanaghs, eating with the Kavanaghs, just being with them. He tried to explain what had happened at Woermann Manor, but he was so tired it didn't even make sense to him. He felt worn out all day.

Michelle shooed him up to his room and came in to give him one more kiss. When she left, he went to the roof to say goodnight to his pack.

He checked the street before scaling the wall past those lovely protective sigils to the roof. Above him, the moon shone, although not as full and sour as it had been the previous night.

'Hey, Sammy', Bladder said when he saw him. Wheedle sucked on a sugar mouse, while Yonah nestled yet again on Spigot's back; the eagle looked pleased with himself.

'Yonah! So good to see you', Sam said.

Yonah leaned into Sam's face, rubbing his cheek with her soft white head. Her peace ran through him. Sam stroked her snowy back and she leaned harder, her hot head warming his skin.

'Where's Daniel?'

Yonah cooed, Spigot shrieked and Wheedle interpreted. 'Yonah says he'll be here any second.'

'Fantastic,' Bladder said. 'Just the person I wanted to see.'

Daniel soared from the clear sky and landed solidly on the roof. He looked better than he had before he went away: his wings were smooth, his hair was glossy, he had a healthy glow, and he put his hand on Sam's head straight away. Sam felt great.

'Hello,' Daniel said. 'Look at you all staring at me. Is there something you want me to do?'

'Seriously?' Bladder said. 'Now? Your timing is rubbish.'

Wheedle chuckled. 'I gotta agree with him.'

'That big bird is the most useless waste of space in the world. Right?' Bladder shook his head.

Sam was happy to see his friend. 'Daniel. You're finished.'

Daniel grinned. 'Yes, Taki called me a fully qualified archangel. The whole process was exhausting.'

Bladder rolled his eyes.

'I think we better tell him what happened when he was away,' Wheedle said.

The angel sat down as Sam and the gargoyles told him

about Woermann – now not so much of a problem – but they did need to discuss Titania and Maggie's plans urgently. Wheedle described how The Hole had changed.

Daniel studied his beautiful hands. He frowned and didn't say much.

'I want to see,' Sam said.

'No, most definitely not,' Bladder replied.

'It's where I was born,' Sam said. 'No more ogres is one thing, but no more gargoyles?'

'I said no, Sam,' Bladder said.

Wheedle shook his head. 'You know that won't help – he'll go when you're not looking. Haven't you noticed him, Bladder? He ain't a scared little imp any more.'

Bladder sighed and squinted at Daniel. 'Can you put a thingy on his body now, big bird? One that stops other monsters seeing him?'

'Yes, but it won't last long,' Daniel replied. 'Half an hour, maybe.'

'Well then, we better be quick. Go on, do it.'

Daniel pressed a thumb into Sam's forehead. The swirling angel fingerprint brightened his face.

'Come on, then,' Bladder said.

'Angels can't go into The Hole,' Sam said.

'Because of all the despair and grief running loose, no hope and all that guff?' Bladder asked. 'Too many monsters to take?'

'That's right.'

'Horsefeathers will be fine then. I told you, it's nothing like it used to be. Come on.'

Sam listened to the house. The Kavanaghs were organising an outing, a celebration, for after Sam woke up. They didn't see Bladder's leonine rump disappear into the grate. Nor did they see Spigot, Wheedle and a white dove drop.

'Yonah!' Daniel yelled after her.

Sam stepped towards the gutter.

'All right.' Daniel exhaled. 'If she can do it ...'

Sam jumped into The Hole. A sharp spot of divine bird-shaped light moved ahead. Then the whole place filled with Daniel's light.

The few dark things ahead raced away, frightened by the sunlight that had come downstairs.

The gargoyles set the pace, running through corridors and tunnels until they came to a rough hole in a wall. 'In there,' Bladder said.

'Let me,' Daniel said, moving with elegance through the dirt wall. His head popped back through. 'All clear.'

The group stepped one at a time through the entrance.

Sam felt the dankness of The Hole, but something didn't seem right. It was a graveyard.

Sam stared about. The emptiness made it appear bigger. Only quiet met them.

'Told ya, nobody down here now,' Wheedle said. 'The few remaining ogres and trolls and the rest of impkind are roaming free upstairs.'

Daniel shuddered. 'All that despair, all that darkness and grief, running around above.' He put a hand on Sam's shoulder. Sam guessed it was as much to gain hope from Sam as it was to encourage him.

'Yes, but ...' Bladder said. 'Look at these things.'

The group moved to the centre of the cavern. Some of the mounds had collapsed, so they walked over as many as they stared up at. Daniel's wings lit a silver glow over the thousands, perhaps millions of little sighs spreading everywhere. It turned them to long, terrifying shadows.

Wheedle leaned forward and picked up a tiny one. In the angel glow it looked slightly different, not so dark, the sigher's grief not so deep. A regret, not a despair. 'No more ogres and boggarts,' Wheedle said, 'but you're right, Sam, no more gargoyles neither. Wonder what this little guy would have looked like. You know, that's the wonderful thing about a gargoyle's hatching, every one is a surprise.'

Bladder clutched at his chest. 'Blasted indigestion.'

Daniel frowned. 'You're getting this a lot?'

The gargoyle burped. 'Yep.'

Daniel placed his hand on Bladder's chest and the lion sighed. 'Ahhh, better.'

Daniel's frown did not leave.

'Come on, better get you back up to your house, Sam,' Daniel said. 'The Kavanaghs are wanting to enjoy your return.'

The troupe returned to the human world, feelings mixed and swirled between them all. A little hope, a little relief, a little sadness.

They pulled themselves up through the grate and back to the roof.

Wheedle looked at the grey nugget in his hoof and

sighed a few times. Sam leaned in and sympathised with the sad bull-faced statue.

'What'd you do, angel? That's the best I've felt for ages.' Bladder tossed his mane. Fairy dust flew from his stony fur and tickled Sam's nose.

Sam sneezed all over Wheedle's hand. 'Sorry.'

'S'all right', Wheedle said, and wiped the snotty bead down the front of Sam's T-shirt.

The nugget wiggled.

'It moved.' Wheedle dropped the bead, which jumped around on the floor, click-clicking on the bricking.

A tiny claw shunted out the side of the bead, and another from the other side. One back leg, then two. The half-formed thing sat up. The top end of the sigh flipped off, revealing a tiny grey face, somewhere between a monkey and dog.

'Sam, you didn't just sneeze that awake?' Wheedle asked.

The newborn gargoyle stared around at its new family.

Yonah cooed.

'Sam, did you just do that?' Bladder asked. 'Oh boy, oh boy, ooooh boy.'

T.C. SHELLEY studied Creative Writing and Literature at university. She has been teaching English for over twenty years and her first school was classified as the most remote in Australia. She loves an audience and long before she took up teaching was writing and performing her poetry and short stories. She began writing novels to entertain her daughter, who wisely suggested that she try to get them published. Shelley lives with her husband, her daughter and two dogs in Perth, Western Australia.

Sam's story is far from over ...

Discover his third adventure

COMING 2021

The future of monsterkind is in Sam's hands